FACTORY

Factory

Tricia Yost

Radial Books

Also by Tricia Yost
First Things
Votives: Entries from the Daybooks of Gertrude Tate, 1898-1952

Special thanks to Chris Bolton, Ben Kostival, Jill Osier, and Frank Soos for their close reads, feedback, and support throughout the many versions of this story.

This book is a work of fiction. Any references to historical events, real locations, or real people are used fictitiously.

Published by Radial Books
radialbooks.com

Factory / Tricia Yost, 1st ed.

ISBN: 978-0-9984146-0-7

Cover Art: *Factory by the Railroad*, Jon deMartin, 2008.

Typesetting services by BOOKOW.COM

1

My throat warmed and I got a fuzzy feeling in my head as I drove over to Courtney's house. I was looking forward to seeing her, but a little nervous too. I hadn't seen her since a drunken night over Christmas break. Because we had chosen different colleges, we hadn't talked much since the previous summer. Only a few phone calls and a night of drinking, toasting and singing along to three-weeks dead Roy Orbison, whose warbling baritone and tough life Courtney had grown fond of since we'd split Toledo. That drunken night turned into a long day of hangover. Tequila. My head pounded for hours. I was sure the worm had elongated and was squirming through my cortex, destroying what little gray matter I had left. Because we hadn't kept in touch, I felt far away. Used to be we knew each other's thoughts and didn't bother to finish sentences. I had an ally in everything. We were two girls against the world. We went from seeing each other six to seven days a week to not at all. And from this abrupt shift, a solid block of tension had stamped out its territory between us.

I hadn't been able to tell Courtney how bizarre I felt not talking to her or seeing her daily. I hadn't told her about the sharp smell of seaweed and kelp that emanated from my Korean dorm mate's care packages. I hadn't told Courtney about a weird crush on my Philosophy for Beginners instructor, Meg O'Connor, and O'Connor's deadpan, ironic lectures, flip-flops, and pink toenails or the even weirder flirtation with the hippie prof of my English class who showed up a little too frequently at the beaten-down retro theatre I ended up working at. I hadn't spoken about one of my classmates killing herself in the common bathroom and the cloak of unease that fell over the freshman residence. I hadn't told Courtney anything. Or anyone else. And I certainly hadn't told her about flunking three classes first semester. For that matter, I never directly told my parents, either. The school did the honors, sending a letter home before I got there. Marietta keeps parents informed when they're footing the bill. That's what I got for going to a small-town liberal arts school, a policy that ruined me. The reason I did so poorly, beyond my heart and head not being in it, was that I flaked. No other reason. Pure and simple backing down from the challenges of college life. At least that's what I told myself at the time. There was something else gnawing at my guts, though, if I really thought the situation through. Some sort of fear. Some reluctance to put myself out there. Something else.

A mere four miles from where I squatted, Courtney lived on the south side of Central Avenue in the land of three-story houses. Sculptured hedges and fairway lawns surrounded the dwellings, providing space between neighbors. Conversations couldn't readily be overheard. No one really knew what went on behind the large, clear windows and heavy oak doors. Enormous trees flanked the sides of the wide road, and few cars were parked there, the driveways being long as they were. The Chambers' house, perched on the divide between Old Orchard and Ottawa Hills, had five bedrooms, three baths, and several other rooms. More space than a family of four needed, what with one child dead and the other away at school most of the year.

"What took you so long?" Flaring cigarette in hand, wearing baggy pants with patches, an orange shirt, and leather sandals, some reggae granola punk chick matrix happening in her appearance, Courtney sprinted from the wrap-around porch and tackled me against the car.

"Henry Bauer."

"Doesn't he realize you're a grown woman and can take care of yourself?"

"I don't think he's completely convinced. He probably wants to dump me at the nearest convent, but can't because…"

Poking at the long cherried tip of her cigarette, Courtney wasn't listening. Such a conversation might have continued in my head: 'but can't because we're not Catholic and the nuns already know about me. I'm marked as a bad seed in the little white holy books of the Sisters of The Catholic Girls Academy. Convents can't be too awful. You get a bed, a room, endless free time. The bride of Christ thing might get in the way, though. But after watching Dad's behavior as a husband, Christ seems like a saint. Sure, nuns might have to get on their knees for him, but they keep their clothes on and their mouths closed and they don't have to cook dinner.' But the conversation didn't continue because I was spellbound by the stranger in front of me, and not in a good way. Courtney used to be the girl next door in khakis and a wrinkled blouse with a bit of a wild side to her. Now the wild was all there was. Her hair was matted and tangled like a wooly mammoth's.

She looked up, grinning, having successfully ashed the cigarette with a fingernail. I stared at the dirty mop on her head.

"Cool, huh? Dreads are the rage at OU."

"Are *you* a grown woman?"

"What's that mean?"

"Nothing." She looked like Medusa. Her haircut was *intentional*. She *boasted* about the look.

She craned her neck into the cigarette and clamped her lips tightly on the filter, inhaling deeply. "So what do you want to do?" she asked.

"I don't know." I never did. Constantly making decisions was exhausting.

"Town's the same." She exhaled tobacco and tofu into my face.

3

Toledo never had anything to offer teenagers or college kids. Out of high school, unmarried, without pensions or stable work, and unable to drink, they were the lost generation redone. In Toledo, we sought dark woods and abandoned alleys in which to get stoned or screwed, then faced the endless problem of what to do after burning the joint or buttoning the pants. Prospects were bleak for the unimaginative.

Courtney dropped her cigarette. "There's a band playing in BG."

From behind the screened porch came a holler, "No butts in my bushes! I saw that Courtney Marie Nicole!" Pudgy, deeply tanned, Margaret Chambers, Courtney's mother emerged from the porch door. Her round coppery face, wrinkled from sadness and too much time in the fake sun, peered through the screen. Since her son died, she'd been managing a small chain of tanning salons. She hadn't worked a day in her life before then. A friend had hooked her up with the job to help keep her mind off the sad, reversed chronology of a child dying before the parents.

"Hi, Mrs. Chambers."

"Lee, darling. How are you?"

"Don't answer. Don't answer. We'll be here all night," Courtney pleaded, hands on my shoulders, shaking me.

"Fine. You? Mrs. Chambers?"

Among our friends and even the kids at college, Courtney's parents and my parents probably had the only marriages that lasted. Fact is, ideal relationships don't really exist, and for the Chambers, with both of them working round the clock, avoiding everything was merely an exercise in endurance.

"I'm good, dear. Busy at work. Inventory is such a bear. Every year more things go missing. Soon there'll be nothing left. You try to hire good people and what do they do? Skim off the top and bottom any chance they get. A bottle of lotion here. Sunglasses there. Free light when no one's looking. I won't be surprised if one of these days someone walks out with a whole bed, extra lights and all. Pick those up, Courtney," she said, referring to the cigarettes on the lawn. "It's bad enough you brought home that nasty habit. I don't want my yard looking like the city dump. You'll kill the flowers."

Courtney scanned the neatly groomed lawn. "What flowers?"

"They haven't sprouted yet."

"Bloom, Mom, flowers bloom." She plucked the butts from the tall grass and deposited them in a pile on the porch. "I'll get those later."

Annoyed, Mrs. Chambers bent down and scooped them up, her face contorting when the stale tobacco tickled her nose. "How was school, Lee?"

"It had its ups and downs." I wasn't about to start discussing how annoyed I was to see Tom Cruise in two hit movies within months of one another. The guy has weird teeth.

"We missed having our Court around, and you, of course."

"Thanks."

"At least you didn't come home with wild hair or piercings all over."

That Courtney might be pierced in places I'd only seen in the shadowy adult theatre in Marietta stirred and frightened me. I looked at this girl who used to be a jock, who used to frown when other girls neglected to shave their legs. "The trend hasn't hit the hills of Marietta. Maybe next year," I told Mrs. Chambers, though I wouldn't be there to witness it.

"Heavens no, you've got such pretty hair. Take care of it. Don't let it get nappy and for god's sake don't shave it. We met two of Courtney's girlfriends down there on parents' weekend. They were both bald. Girls shouldn't do that to themselves."

"It's a statement, Mom, about standards of beauty. And besides, it *does* accentuate their faces." Courtney's previously sweet demeanor had turned to snobbishness.

"I don't want to hear any more of your theories. I can't believe the things they teach these days. Go have fun. Do whatever you're going to do. Lee, talk some sense into that one." She wagged a leathery finger at Courtney before disappearing through the darkened doorway.

Cinching me in a headlock, Courtney dragged me to the car. "I told you not to get her started."

"She means well." From the bent, passive position, I unlocked the passenger door. Feeling chained, I waited patiently for Courtney to free me.

"You don't have to listen to those complaints for hours and hours." She ducked into the passenger seat of the Escort.

Appearance was an easy enough thing to change or change back. Courtney didn't have her dad barking down her neck about money and school and what to do with her life.

"Where are we going?"

Head cocked in consideration, she looked at me as if she'd never seen me before. "You're not you somehow."

"What?" I snapped, shocked. I was wearing the same jeans and T-shirt from a year ago. I considered my body. I hadn't gained or lost weight, hadn't changed my hair. "It's me. Two arms, two legs."

Courtney studied me, perhaps expecting to find some major oddity. A growth I hadn't noticed. A new mole with spindly black hairs darting forth. A third nipple or tenth orifice. Maybe I was the changed one, but I was still in my own skin, which had never felt right anyway. A body is a strange thing to wear.

The engine's roar consumed us.

"No, I mean, yeah, you look like you, but something's off."

We used to know exactly what the other was thinking. We called each other soul mates and thought we had a kind of clairvoyant, separated-souls-in-another-lifetime thing. Even after I switched high schools, we were of one mind despite the distance. I went to her basketball games and she tramped the woods with me. We were close. We had even kissed. But right then, in the beaten interior of the Escort, I couldn't find my way in, especially with the hair jutting dangerously from her scalp.

"Let me know when you decide what it is," I said, feeling tension above my brows and my cheeks approaching a scowl. I wasn't the one who wasn't me somehow. I wasn't off.

Winding the concrete lanes of the interstate, I drove us south toward Bowling Green. As we crossed the brown waters of the Maumee River, I grinned hard at Courtney.

"What?"

The memory slipped by her.

"The river. Remember the day we cut tenth period and I picked you up and we hiked along the banks in the mud?"

"Sort of. Yeah, I guess. Yeah, I do! I got two detentions for skipping and couldn't make up the assignments."

She remembered the consequences, not the thrill of cold water cuffing our shins and the sun warming our backs, not talking about going to Florida for spring break senior year or going to the same school for college so we could be together. A wave of annoyance swept through me and I tried to push it away and bring myself back to the present, but I couldn't pound down the feeling that we were distant cousins at an obligatory reunion.

"School was so great, you know?" she said. "I had so much fun. Everyone down there is so open and I tried so many things. There were parties every weekend and people doing crazy stuff. Trips to Kentucky for races and moonshine. Just wild." She drummed her hands on the dash. "This one weekend I took two tabs of X and had the wildest sex with this thirty-year old grad student. It was so trippy."

"Trippy?"

"Straight from the trippy 60s. Classes were fine, you know, but everything else blew my mind. Total killer. I loved it. We had fun in high school, you know? But that was kid stuff. Nothing like college. I was free."

She didn't ask how my year went so I turned up the radio, hoping the bass would beat back my need for her to see me. Courtney shook her snaked hair to the music, staring out the window. She was air and I was granite. There was no mixing us. She felt unconstrained and I felt tied and alone. I wondered if she was free of me.

"My year was a little bizarre."

"How come?"

"A girl in my dorm killed herself," I said, treading dangerous territory. Usually, I let Courtney bring up death. "I went to a movie with her once. That's not true. We ended up being at the same movie and recognized each other from school. The movie was art film called *Camille Claudel* about two sculptors. The female one gets put away in an insane asylum by her family and left there. It was awful, not the movie, the whole thing with my classmate. She was an art major. Kind of a loner, but you never really can tell with people anyway."

Courtney was still. Her face paling. The memory of her brother in mind. I suddenly felt stupid and mean and wanted to re-shoot the last five minutes.

"How?" she asked off-handedly and gazed out the window past me. "How'd she do it?" At what, I wasn't sure, possibly at her brother, possibly at regret.

"She took a handful of pills and slit her wrists in the shower."

"Did you find her?"

"Her roommate did. She went home. I'm not sure if she came back. You know how those things go. People walk around on tiptoes for a while and then one day everything's back to normal, though it's really not."

She blinked at me and kind of nodded.

"What do you think about Nick these days?" I asked, carefully, trying to pull us back to a significance we shared.

"Nothing really. I've got other things going on." Subdued momentarily, she rolled her shoulders then whipped her head side to side, cracking her neck. I waited for her to say more. She used to talk about Nick all the time—what she thought when she found him, what death was like, why he killed himself—telling me everything that passed through her head. She relied on me. I missed that. Being away for nine months made me think about all kinds of things, especially what living at home was like. Unless she was holding out, Courtney had responded in an opposite manner. She left home where it was, three hundred miles away.

"Can't live in the past and all that," she said.

Towering over the town and against the hanging sun, the university stadium stood empty and superfluous, echoing what I was beginning to feel. I tried to fill the emptiness or mask it. I tried to push it away. I needed to hear something real from Courtney, to feel like we still knew each other.

"So, what do you have going on then? Like, for the summer?" I asked.

"Haven't decided just yet."

"Work?"

"Maybe. Mom says I can work at a salon if I fix my hair. Like that's going to happen."

"Really, you like the dreads?"

I pulled the car into a parking lot and turned the key. The engine quieted.

"They're not just Rasta, you know? Indian holy people and some Tibetan Buddhists have them. And then there's this whole culture of crust punks in England. You should've come to OU. Your whole world would have been blown."

I imagined just how much worse off I would've been had I gone to OU for school or on weekends. OU was a known party school. I would have fried even more brain cells with pot and booze and pills. I would have passed even fewer classes and probably be pregnant or saddled with an STD or two.

"We were only an hour away from each other, if that," I told Courtney. I was still seething on some level about the fact that we hadn't kept in touch. I called her several times first semester and sent emails. She was piss-poor about replying. "We could've seen each other. You had a car."

"Yeah, I guess, but you know how those things go when you're in a new place with new people. I'm sure you were just as busy with classes and new friends."

I wasn't, but I also wasn't about to throw a surprise pity-party right then and there. I could feel annoyance oozing from Courtney's pores and wondered if I'd turned into a needy little bitch. I didn't want to be that person. I wanted the two of us together again against the world.

"I had sex with a girl," I said, maybe to blow her world.

"Who hasn't?" she said. "Let's go in."

"I'm serious."

"Fuck off," she looked me over carefully. "Really?"

I nodded.

"At school? Who was she?"

"No, before that," I said.

"In high school? No fucking way."

"Yes way."

"Who?"

"Hailey Berger."

Her face porcelain, Courtney didn't register recognition of any sort.

"The one who was always dying her hair different colors and got busted for the graffiti."

"Seriously? Her? Really? You're fucking with me."

"Yeah," I swallowed hard and shifted uncomfortably in my seat.

"She was such a head case."

I didn't reply. I could see why she thought that. Hailey was an outcast, part self-imposed, but certainly she was teased and ridiculed. No one understood her or tried to, but she didn't care. She kept on dying her red hair, spiking it or shaving it. She kept on wearing loads of rubber bracelets and dark eyeliner. She kept on questioning teachers and trying to start insane discussions about whether the Bible was good literature or pulp fiction or just why those who believe in a supernatural creator weren't marked by shrinks as delusional. We were in a Catholic school, after all.

"You're fucking with me, aren't you? You're not? What was it like?"

"Good, I guess. She was fun." I remembered the heat and thrill of sneaking around with Hailey. And just as quickly the thrill turned to a fist in the head. "Until she wasn't."

"You're a carpet bagger? Is that what this weirdness is about? A coming out moment?"

Suddenly I couldn't swallow. My gut hollowed out. I was on the spot, a place I didn't intend to be. I'd kept the Hailey thing to myself because even to me the relationship didn't seem real, and trying to talk about it always felt awkward and wrong. "I don't know," I said. "I don't think so." I didn't. It was just a thing that happened between two teenagers.

"How can you not know? You either like the penis or you don't like the penis."

"It's a little more complicated than that."

"I doubt it. *I* like the penis. Seems simple. Why are you telling me this now? We've been friends for three years and you never said a word."

"Seemed as good a time as any. You're telling me about punk crusts and I'm telling you about Hailey."

"Crust punks," she corrected. "Dirty English anarchists right out of *Mad Max 2*. Anyway, I don't know what to do with that information. What am I supposed to do with that information?"

"Same thing I'm supposed to do with your story about taking ecstasy and fucking a thirty year-old."

"Older guys know their stuff. Especially if they're dorks. They try so much harder. That's your lesson. That's what *you're* supposed to do with that information. I don't know what to do with the image of two girls with sticky fingers. Especially hers. She was such a douche. Can we go in now?" Courtney shot out of the car like a sprinter off the blocks. She paid the cover and found the dance floor while I drifted toward an empty spot against a side wall where I could watch her and the door and the bar and everyone else, where I could hang out with my jealousy, ire, regret, confusion. I shouldn't have told her about Hailey. Telling her was as good as telling a wall. Worse, because she was judging me. A wall wouldn't judge me. A wall would hold me up and take my punches.

Grateful Dead covers rang dreamily from the six-member band. Courtney, in her baggy pants and scraggly hair, melted into the crowd of torsos and arms, losing herself in the cacophony. Her body vacillated in a two-foot perimeter. Her hair moved of its own accord, springing like a slinky. Eyes closed and unconscious of people or objects, she was untroubled in that space, in that moment. Free. The wall kept me and a strange crowd kept her. We weren't who we were a year ago. That's what distance does. Splits two people in ways neither is aware. Watching Courtney only a few feet off, I felt sadness push at me and try to knock me over, but the wall held me up.

I thought of us, not two years back, hiking along the highway, behind the dividing fence, past private property lines, into the backside of Wildwood Metropark, a forbidden zone. Tall trees and hulking bushes knotted the area in darkness. I hated walking in the woods after dark, especially with a head full of acid, which made the trees people and the grass water and everything ominous, but I walked in the dark because I felt safe enough alongside Courtney, who was invincible. We were out of our heads that night, throwing lit matches at each other because a cool trail snaked behind them and we wanted to prove we weren't wimps. Courtney had learned the game from her brother before he killed himself. He and his friends used to play with firecrackers until Jimmy Delgado blew off his pinky finger. A match missed Courtney and hadn't gone out before hitting the ground. And poof, dry, dead grass burns fast. But not faster than two sixteen-year-olds can run when the thought of being caught rushes straight through them. We cleared the woods before the flames overtook us, and luckily, before the fire engines arrived. From the hood of Courtney's car we watched the field burn bright against the morning sun.

Several Dead songs later a guy startled me out of the melodic reverie the band and my memories had spun around me. He was a good four inches taller than me and thick with muscle.

"Dance?" he asked.

"Not particularly."

A strand of his dusty blond hair fell over his eyes. "Wanna get high, then?" He peered sheepishly from behind the strand.

"Yes."

"I'm Derrick." He thrust a Herculean hand out for a shake.

"Lee."

He led me across the crowded floor, down a narrow hallway coated in bad graffiti, and out a door into a fenced area at the back where a nasty waft of garbage forced its fingers up my nose. A trash-bin was overflowing with bottles and rotten food. To the bin's left was a stew of urine and vomit.

"Yeah, sorry about that," Derrick said. "This place doesn't attract good drunks."

We passed his pipe back and forth until I was sufficiently stoned, confirmed by my dry, squinting eyes and a general sense of well being settling in my chest. I'd forgotten how lovely the effects of marijuana could be.

"You know," Derrick began, "Jake thinks THC is a massage for the central nervous system, but I say that's shit. If anything's a massage for the CNS, yoga is. Yoga is calm in a fucking electrical storm. You can pretty much bet on how you'll feel during and after yoga. But THC, shit, especially if you don't know where it's from, weed could have any number of effects. You know, there's the analgesic effect, which in itself isn't fully understood. There's relaxation, euphoria, space-time fuck-ups, and any number of sensory alterations. Then there's anxiety, malaise, though that's usually after the shit wears off, and appetite overdrive resulting from stimulation of the hypothalamus, which triggers hunger centers, and a cascade of hormone releases. To top it off, there's the crazy anti-emetic characteristics that can decrease aggression in some people. Just think, if more hard-ass violent criminals were susceptible to *that* and smoked a lot, well, shit, prisons might not be so overcrowded."

An hour later, Derrick's topic of conversation, which had taken the horrors-of-prison-life track, plus the weed and a few white pills Courtney had given me, I was seized by major paranoia. Five pseudoepinephrine tablets had hit my heart, turning the red organ into a speed-metal drum, and my mind spun and whizzed, desperately trying to free itself of the body. Courtney and I were following Derrick, who I'd come to learn was an ardent pot-smoking, pill-popping, body-building honor student working on a master's degree, and his wiry, silent friend, Jake, to a party, first stopping at a green BP for "goodies."

"I probably shouldn't have told you," I said to Courtney.

"It's totally cool. You know, there were lots of random hook-ups down at school. You wouldn't believe the stories. It's no big deal if you're trying to figure something out. I'm cool with whatever. I'm not one to judge," she said, then skipped ahead and started walking next to Jake.

Derrick, his muscular bulk overwhelming us, his straight jaw loose with a smile, started to explain, "Goodies are *good* for you, relatively speaking. We are not here to load up on empty calories. Beer, alcohol of any sort, is the exception. Think of beer as liquid bread." The four of us wandered the brightly lit aisles, our eyes slits, keeping out the light. "Reasonable carbohydrate intake is acceptable. Reasonable amounts can be easily worked off." He dropped to the dirty tile floor and served up twenty push-ups.

A phone was glued to the clerk's face. He was talking low. Surely, calling the cops for the simple reason that I felt guilty of something and was now sufficiently fearful of prison and equally certain I was going to wind up there by the end of the night. We ditched the place and walked another block to a liquor store. More bright lights. Precarious wine displays waited for the odd elbow to send them crashing.

Two cases of beer propped on Derrick's shoulders, Jake toting a bottle of Canadian whiskey, we lumbered down fraternity row to an old, beaten-up house, nestled in a cul-de-sac. Judging by the peeling wallpaper, tacky floors, and cracked windows, the house had been in students' care for years. With school being out for the summer, few bodies filled the rooms. Music played low and small stands of people were drinking or smoking or smoking and drinking. They nodded at Derrick as he passed.

After dumping most of the beer in the fridge, Derrick and I slumped into a ratty, musty couch on the back porch. "You're kidding. Really? School's easy. You find your subject and pour all your time into that," he said, after I'd told him about flunking almost everything. "Learn that shit inside and out. For me it's biology. Two hours a night minimum. For a Shakespeare course, rent the movie version and read along with the actors. I'm not certain whether I'll go the doctoring, teaching, or research route. All I know is, I get a woody when I look at parasitology and cell division. As for the other classes, you have options. You can download papers off the web. You can pay your classmates. Risky, though, and probably not worth the trouble. Best just to grind through."

"I'm not an idiot. I just wasn't into it."

"Why'd you even bother, then?"

"Going to school was expected of me. What else was I going to do?"

"Anything. Everything. I mean, shit, the kids in Beijing were camped out in Tiananmen Square for weeks in support of economic and political reform, and what are we doing? Drinking and drugging and fucking and passing time anyway we can. American kids are assholes."

Brain scattered, heart slam dancing in my chest, this was not a topic I wanted to volley around. Political reform? Doing grandiose things with our small lives? I'd come off sounding like a moron. "Let's find Jake and Courtney."

"That's all you've got?"

"I don't know what to say. We live in a very different place than China."

"Okay." He jumped up from the couch's permanently sagged cushions.

Sliding into detective roles, we snuck around the drafty house, peering around corners, and covering one or the other as we broke for the next safe nook. I wasn't sure who was the good cop and who the bad. We quietly opened doors and stole glances. One room mimicked an opium den. Ratty tapestries were draped crookedly over the windows and bodies were sprawled over the floor and over one bare mattress in the corner. Unmoving. Lifeless. Stale smoke twined toward the ceiling where it hung limply. A solitary candle burned close to its base.

"That takes drug use too far," Derrick whispered, gently closing the door on the view. "Heroin's nasty shit."

"You ever done it?"

"No. You?"

"No, but I understand the draw."

"What draw?"

"To lie down and let life pass."

"You're not a suicide chick, are you? All dark and creepy an' shit? 'Cause that's fucked. You 'understand the draw.' What the hell is that? You wouldn't be here if you did."

"Fuck you. Don't jump down my fucking throat. You understand it. Otherwise you wouldn't be popping pills and downing six packs."

He stared at me for a long moment.

"Just don't off yourself on my watch, all right?"

"All right."

The next door was locked. Derrick smiled wickedly, the conversation wiped. He pulled something silver from his pocket and jimmied the handle open. He was taller so I moved in front of him for a better look. There was Jake, standing with his back to the wall, delight spread over his face, his pants bunched below his knobby knees. In front of him, on her knees, was Courtney, her hands gripping Jake's bony backside, holding on for dear life. Her head corncobbing furiously. She did say she liked the penis.

Dislodging itself from my ribcage, my heart pounded against my throat. Derrick rested his hard jaw on my head and I leaned back into his solid frame as we watched Courtney's head shift to and fro and side to side, her mangled dreads darting. We watched Jake's face contort and go loose and contort again. Unable to look away, we watched for a few minutes, then without speaking we went back to the ratty, musty couch. A man with a gray ponytail, old enough to be any of our fathers, was draped over the dirty cushions, snoring loudly. He was missing a shoe and his sock was caked with mud. We descended the steps into the thicket of weeds in the backyard. Overhead, stars flamed in the dark sky. The air around us was moist and warm. My heart finally slowed to a waltzing pace. I moved closer and put my hand on Derrick's abs, looked up, and kissed him. My heart wound up again and let loose a flurry of beats. I had cottonmouth, but his kiss was wet enough for the both of us.

"That girl has mad skills," he said.

"And she's a good kisser."

"How would you know?"

"A best friend knows. How old are you, anyway?"

"Twenty-four. Why?"

"No reason."

2

Six in the morning, tired and coming down from the late night, I eased the Escort down our street, careful not to tap any of the cars parked bumper to bumper on either side. The muffler dragged against a mislaid concrete slab of the shared driveway. My parents' yellow house looked small and fragile under the bluing sky. The left side of the roof sagged. Paint was chipping away and the lawn was overgrown. I didn't remember the house being in such bad shape. From the porch I could see into the neighbor's living room. Much like ours it had a recliner and a lumpy, stained sofa arched around the room's focus, an enormous television. If the TV had been on, I could have seen clearly whatever was being broadcast.

"Where the hell have you been?" Dad asked, waiting at the door.

"Out with Courtney."

"Your high school girlfriend?" he barked.

I stared at him dumbly. For a second I couldn't breathe or move. "Yeah, Courtney. Brunette. Basketball star. My age. A little taller."

"You were supposed to be home hours ago."

"She looks weird these days. Her hair's all over the place and she's jumpy or something."

"Hours," he said again, more unkindly.

"I'm here now."

Wet rings had already formed in the pits of his blue buttoned-down postman's shirt. "The deal is, you live under this roof and you don't keep the car out all night."

"You're gonna be late for work," I said, trying to weasel by him.

He cut me off, blocking admittance to the hallway with his protruding gut. "I don't give a rat's ass. I haven't been late in thirty-two years. But you wouldn't understand anything like that. You had a whole school year to fuck around. A whole life. Don't think I'm about to let you keep it up while you live under my roof."

The only thing I wanted to get away with was being horizontal in my bed.

"You reek. Where you been?"

"None of your damn business."

"You been drinking? You been drinking and driving my car? Is that what you spent the school year doing? Drinking the time away?"

"And smoking and sniffing coke and shooting heroin and screwing all my professors. That's really why they flunked me. I was terrible in the sack, especially with the lady teachers." I slid past him and into the kitchen where I filled a glass with water and drank.

"Is that it? Problems with sexuality? Womanhood? The root of it all is that you're a damn *girl* who doesn't know how to be a *woman*? Because I'll tell you, it's no prize being a guy. Life's a bitch for everyone at some point, doesn't matter, girl, boy, white, black, Jew."

"No," I nearly shrieked, choking on the water.

"Then what is your damn deal?" he said, looming closer, intimidating, his face reddening. I felt nervous, like a cornered animal, and wanted to get away, but I didn't move. He was scrambling close to something that made me feel like I was on the edge and about to fall thousands of feet. I didn't move. I couldn't. "I'm desperate here, Lee. We didn't spend three grand on that rehab for you to throw your life into the gutter. What's it gonna take? High school rebellion's one thing, but you're technically a damn adult now. Should we change the locks? Kick your ass to the street? Is that what it's gonna take? Or a second go at rehab? Or worse, the county jail?"

If a grizzly comes at you, you're supposed to lie still like a lump of dirt. The bear may sniff at you and paw you a couple of times, but if you don't move, he'll lose interest and wander off. "No," I said, calm and quiet as I could.

"Well?" He rubbed his forehead, distraught, his shoulders dropping with the weight of his fury. "Talk, then. To me or your mother. Doesn't matter. We want what's best for you. You get that?"

I couldn't muster a grunt. I knew they wanted the best for me, good things. I couldn't get there, though. I couldn't get past myself.

"Your mother didn't go to college. I didn't. You were the first, kid. Of us. Of any of the grandkids. It's tough, but you step up to those things. You don't hide away like a scared cat in the closet. We've forgiven a lot, if you ask me," he said in a sort of sigh as he looked toward the small overgrown weedy rectangle of a back yard, a yard which was so unlike the well-groomed lawns of the luminous institutions tucked away in small academic towns. We had visited several of those colleges not two years ago. My parents took time off work to do this. I could feel their expectation and discomfort as we followed along with the other parents and their lofty college hopes. I don't know what it was about Marietta that sealed my decision. The distance from home? The proximity to OU? Certainly not the academic standing. I didn't care much about that. Marietta was one of the schools that let students and parents sit in on classes. I sat two rows behind my parents and off to the left in an introductory physics class. They tried to be attentive as the instructor chatted on about the impossibility of knowing an object's velocity and exact location.

"I didn't understand a word of that," Mom whispered as we exited the lecture hall.

"It's Heisenberg's uncertainty principle," I said sharply. "It's impossible to measure the present position and determine the future motion of something, a particle, at the same time."

"You'll do just fine here," Dad had said with a blend of pride and bewilderment.

After that we walked around the town with its brick buildings and sleepy charm and took a ride on the Valley Gem Sternwheeler through the muddy water. It was a nice day.

"Seriously, kid," he said, more quietly this time, as if to himself. "You had some fuckups, but you're smart. You did that Lincoln essay thing in seventh grade and then had the advanced math thing. Your test scores. You have a goddamn brain. Why aren't you using it?"

Some small, strange part of me longed for those quiet idyllic Marietta streets, if for no other reason than to be there and not here. I didn't have an informed answer that would explain my motives to his satisfaction. Not in the least. I had some ideas, though, ones I didn't want to let myself think about. My parents had forgiven and overlooked a lot. They were none too pleased when they found me alone in the attic of the garage doing bong hits with an empty two-liter plastic soda bottle, minus the bottom third. I was also using the blue bucket that my dad had bitched about not being able to find. Without that bucket, he couldn't wash the car. Without that bucket, I couldn't quickly inhale copious amounts of THC. That was the least of the fuck-ups, though. I was not a well-adjusted teenager.

"Anyway," he gave up, "Happy Housekeepers called last night. Lady said job was yours if you wanted it." Still fuming, a tangle of anger and concern, he paused, perhaps unsure of what to say or do. "How the hell can you go in after being out all night and expect a fair shake? You're on thin ice, kid, and the ice is cracking."

Arms crossed in front of me, shoulders hunched, my face burning, my stomach on fire, I had no white flags to offer. I didn't want to hear another of his tirades. Once he got going, not even three singing fat ladies could suffocate him. I tried to think happy thoughts, tried to beat back his disappointment and expectation and worldly advice, but his words came at me, bulls in the streets of Pamplona.

"You've got to sell yourself some if you want to get anywhere. Just knock this shit off, already."

I dangled the car keys from my index finger. "You're gonna be late."

He snatched them and left.

In the shower, warm water drizzling on my face, my body was so tired I felt it sinking toward the drain. My head, though, was hot and angry. I considered calling Derrick and spending the day getting stoned, lazing near Lake Erie in the sun. I could show him swan dives off the high board at Pecona Beach. I could listen to him talk about complex carbohydrates and communism in China if I had to. That's what I should have done, lived for the moment, for pleasure. Isn't that what it means to be alive in the world? Following a whim to sit in the sun with a nicely chiseled boy? Instead, anger and guilt fueled me into yanking on clothes for an interview. Dad's words floated through my head: The position was mine if I wanted it. Paid six dollars an hour, which was more than minimum wage and more than I'd ever made considering I'd never held a job, a legit one, anyway. The delivery job in Marietta didn't count. I was paid cash, which was handed over in illicit paper sacks.

Happy Housekeepers headquarters, a small suite in an upper scale strip mall, was a nightmare of bright colors. Flowers cramped the front entrance and Thomas Kinkade prints stared from the walls. The desks and file cabinets were a nonstandard, hideous blue. Amidst the happy pinks and yellows, I was in shabby sneakers and a torn, paint-splotched shirt.

A lady in a polyester suit with a pink ruffled blouse gazed at me. Her mascara-laden lashes blinking slowly. "You don't match her description," she said brightly.

"Description?"

"You went to school with my daughter, Molly. Molly Carlisle. At The Catholic Girls Academy. She would have been a year behind you."

"Oh," I mumbled.

"I guess there's not too much mixing of the classes. She remembers you, though. Said you kept the teachers on their toes." She smiled. "I see from your application that you went to CGA and had a year of college at a private institution."

I silently dared her to ask me how that year went. I could tell her all about the ugly embarrassment of flunking out. I could tell her all about my parent's ire and concern and their brilliant idea of restitution, my paying back eight grand of the tuition funds they'd forked over.

She pulled something from a drawer behind the counter. "Never mind. Here, we're backed up today. We have clients in Sylvania, Ottawa Hills, and Perrysburg. Very important people." She scratched at the corner of her lips with a long pinky nail. "Two have important dinner parties tonight. Put these on and we'll get going. Most of my staff is working already." She held out nylons, a black skirt, and a pink shirt with the Happy Housekeepers logo ironed on the right titty pocket.

I stared at her mouth where she scraped more dried lipstick away.

"You are Lee Bauer, correct?"

"Yeah." I wished I wasn't.

"You'll have to wear better shoes tomorrow."

"We'll be cleaning houses, right? Using chemicals."

"Yes?" She didn't understand.

Eight grand loomed like a Damoclean sword. "Nothing."

"And you're Henry's daughter?" she asked, again, brightly, still holding out the clothes. "He works with my husband, the branch manager. Always says good things about your dad. What a hard worker he is, never gives him any grief. That's why we don't have to go through the usual questions. If you're anything like your father, you'll do just fine."

I nodded and smiled as brightly as I could. Inside I was sinking and souring. Toledo was too small. I was fucked. My dad would get daily updates about my performance. I couldn't be late. I couldn't call out fake-sick. I took a breath. I tried to be positive. I'd have a job, after all. It'd be quieter around the house. I took the clothes and followed the direction her crooked finger indicated. The noxious scent of bleach, ammonia, and musty mops greeted me in the back room. Sliding out of my jeans, I considered the reptilian nylons. I hadn't worn any since seventh grade Confirmation. We weren't allowed to wear them with the plaid, pleated skirts at CGA, only knee-socks, always pulled up to the knee. I stepped into the left leg, stretched the netting up my shin and thigh, stepped into the right one, tugging the thin mesh up my leg, causing a run from toe to mid-shin. I groaned internally. I put my jeans back on.

"Um, Sally," I'd noticed her name tag, "I mean, Mrs. Carlisle, I've snagged these." I held them out like a broken toy for her to fix. "I'm sorry," I said, because I had to.

"You'll have to pay for those out of your first check. Don't worry. Here." She placed her tube of lipstick on the desk, reached into a drawer and handed me a new pair. "Do be more careful this time."

I shuffled back to the closet like a scolded child. The pink shirt was smaller than I was used to. My breasts nudged themselves into prominence, forthright and assertive at last. I laddered the nylons up my legs, careful not to run them. I imagined wearing the itchy things five days a week, the chafing thighs, the catcalls, the sweat. I buttoned the skirt, ready to greet the day. I couldn't move. I felt like a hooker. I stood for a second, dreaming up street names: *Trixie, Stardust, Eugenide Uvula,* and a version of my own name, *Sara Lee. I'll pound your cake.* But I couldn't make myself laugh because there I was in the storage room, feeling absurd and out of my element, like my mom must have felt when she was a waitress, dressed in the brown jumper and orange striped shirt, a pained smile cemented on her face. Six dollars an hour was not worth the black skirt and pink shirt and every pair of nylons I would tear. Six dollars was not worth happy Sally telling me to get down on all fours and scrub. Six dollars was not worth my dad getting daily reports from Sally's husband on how terrible I was at cleaning toilets. I slid back into the jeans again.

"Do you have a different uniform?"

Her pupils grew large as beetles. Her lashes blinked, dusting the air with tiny flakes of mascara. "What do you mean?"

"Slacks, maybe?"

"Pants are a part of our men's uniforms."

"Can I wear those?"

"You're a woman," she whispered, as if revealing a secret.

I already knew the secret. "I've only been a woman since the operation last year, so technically, I should get to wear pants."

Her thick lashes cursed me. "Excuse me?"

"That was a joke. A little joke. Look, I can't scrub toilets in tights."

"They're not tights." She should have been teaching semiology. "They're nylons. Our customers wouldn't like you in pants. We have a reputation to maintain. You should understand. Your father always looks sharp in his blues, or so I'm told."

"I'm not my father."

"Pardon?"

"What about the comfort of your employees?"

"Skirts are very comfortable, and they look nice."

"What about the women's lib movement?"

Again, her lashes cursed me.

"Another joke. Kind of."

"You know. I don't think you're going to do very well here with that attitude."

Too exhausted to deal with Sally anymore, I walked back to the closet, flung off the shirt, and replaced it with my ripped one. I had nothing against skirts or feminine appearance or even pink, but I wasn't about to scuff my knees or play Barbie and wear banana clips eight hours a day. I dropped the uniform on the desk.

"You still have to pay for those nylons," Sally called after me as I walked out. "Hey! Hey!" The words fell at my heels.

A city bus opened its doors to me and I climbed aboard. I thought of my dad at work, his shoulders aching from the weight of letters, his feet blistering because he needed new shoes. Though he was at work, his voice would still be in the house. I couldn't go home. I wasn't cut out for the Happy Housekeepers world, for a nine-to-five job, for nylons and painted nails, for cleaning rich people's houses. The streets of Toledo blurred as the bus wound through the city, stopping and starting, nabbing riders, letting others off. Some in suits, others in tattered clothes, but all in their own worlds. Their eyes were glazed over, their expressions resigned or pleased. Resilience all around me, people maintaining their clothes and tastes, their relationships and jobs, living their lives without much effort. I couldn't fathom what was in their heads. Absent gazes suggested nothing. Surely something was there, some sense of purpose had to be pushing them through each day. I wanted to believe that anyway.

The bus trundled up the narrow lanes of Secor Avenue past university dormitories into the Ottawa Hills area. The brick houses gained stature and familiarity as we rode along the edge of Courtney's neighborhood. The sun illuminated its many trees. Thin and thick trunks and the odd shapes of leaves made me wish I knew their names.

"You busy?" I asked when Courtney answered the door.

"I'm expecting someone." Rising to her toes, she looked toward the street. "Jake. You know, the guy from last night."

The back of Courtney's bobbing head flashed before my eyes. "You had a good time, then?"

"I don't know. The night was pretty average." Her dreaded hair was clumped around her bony face. Her eyes were glassy and sunken. She looked worn, tired. I wondered what was happening to her. "We'll see what he's like in the light of day."

"I had this interview today. It was ridiculous."

"I thought your parents were against all that."

During high school my parents refused to let me get a job. Mom's reasoning was that the early years should be enjoyed because I'd spend the rest of my life working. "Not anymore," I said, thinking of my dad's latest commentary on the issue: "You'll shovel shit around a nuthouse if you have to."

She studied something in the stone on the porch. I didn't know how to make my face more interesting. "Jake says he's got this three foot bong. I'd ask you to come, but I'm pretty sure we'll be naked most of the time."

"I don't really want to work," I said, "but I sort of screwed up."

The phone rang. "That's probably him. I'll call you tomorrow."

"Okay." I half waved. Her snarled hair turned away from me. I backed off the porch and was soon on the smooth sidewalks of neighboring streets where the dense leaves of rutty tree branches blocked clean views of the sky. Without direction in the humid air, I managed to find my way home, like always.

Central air on full force, the house was cold. Dad, Mom, and Michelle sat at the kitchen table, prettified with chipped plates and paper napkins. Dad had pulled Illinois Angus from the basement freezer and had grilled up shoulder clods for the three of them. He'd bought steer in bulk around the time I left for school. A meat and potatoes man, like any Midwesterner, years of consumption had settled around his waist. Mouth tireless as ever, he said "You get the job?" before shoveling a bloody cube into his mouth. My stomach turned, and I turned, walking straight to my room.

3

When I was in sixth grade, my mom handed me a pamphlet called "The Beauty of a Woman's Menstrual Cycle." The pamphlet explained in full detail, complete with pencil sketches, the egg's fourteen-day ripening in the ovaries, the egg's "journey" out of the ovary and into the fallopian tube. In one drawing, big bad progesterone was lining the uterus with blood and tissue, "cushioning" and "decorating" the home for the eventually fertilized egg. But, if the ripe egg didn't become fertilized with a sperm after traveling the fallopian highway, it sadly disintegrated and began to fall apart. The uterine wall dismantled and flowed out the cute little cervix and flowery vagina in the form of blood. The cycle was described as a very happy, natural, and beautiful process. I thought it was ugly, not beautiful. Rhinoceroses in the gut. Underwear spotted with red, clumpy surprises. Bleeding through thin shorts at inopportune times. Fists forming in the head at the slightest provocation.

Giving me the pamphlet already taxed her comfort level. There was no talking about that or its obvious counterpart: sex, which I had to learn about on my own. Spying on my cousin, Samantha, was the easiest way. She secretly snuck away from holiday gatherings, and I secretly followed. She'd usually end up behind our garage with the neighbor boy, his hand buried to the forearm down the front of her Jordache jeans. She flipped when she saw me, begged me not to tell on her. I never did, under the condition that I could watch.

She frowned but agreed so long as Neighbor Boy couldn't know his prowess was under scrutiny. The next time she visited she sought me out before she knocked next door for Adam. I didn't think much of it and went and watched them from behind the branches of a nearby bush.

Samantha was a porn star that day. With Adam's hand down her pants, or him riding her, her face contorted in pained delight. She rotated her hips and fell limp against the garage wall, then melted into the ground beneath her. She gave head like it was the only thing she'd ever wanted to do, took Adam's adolescent penis in her mouth like a pro. I was mildly amused each time I saw his pants at his knees, his hips slightly thrusting forward and back like he was trying to knock Samantha's uvula from her throat. What they were doing didn't look like much fun. I didn't have the word for it then, but now I would call the activity desperate. They never looked at each other and they never talked. But Adam always walked off like a skinny peacock displaying his feathers, and Samantha smugly wiped the dirt from her clothes and smoothed her hair like she'd gotten up from falling down. Little did I know I'd be mimicking her in three years, going through similar movements yet with a different level of commitment altogether.

Hailey Berger was polyamorous and the only one in our peer group who knew what that word meant. She streaked her red hair with metallic blue dye and stomped around in army boots and long skirts. The girl liked to stand out, and yes, she was a bit of a head case. A year younger and alphabetically, Berger to my Bauer, Hailey sat directly in front of me in three of our six classes freshman year. She used to flap the teacher's handouts at me behind her head, never turning around. That we became inseparable for five months sophomore year is still a mystery to me and something I don't think too closely about. One minute she was the ridiculous girl with the crazy hair and crazy outfits who sat in front of me, speaking out in class and speaking out of turn, the next minute she was the crazy girl who wrote on school walls and made the mall fun, and finally she was still the girl in front of me, and the girl drawing tattoos on store mannequins, but also she had become the girl who got naked and crushed her naked body into mine. She was all of these people and more, a total Sybil.

Lying on my stomach in my bedroom, memories of Hailey jumped through my head, strong and sour memories. And memories of my cousin's sexual escapades. I'd seen burlesques and low-budget pornos, thanks to an indifferent theatre owner's willingness to let a young co-ed walk through the wrong door on Tuesday afternoons. Starting with Hailey, I'd had a fair amount of sex for my age, but my fantasy life wasn't very potent. I tried to vitalize it by stripping Derrick of his clothes piece by piece, his muscles taut from the flow of blood. He looked good and moved with agonizing slowness, teasing me. While he teased I went for the *ménage a toi* and put my mouth on another woman's nipple. Just once. Just to try it. So when I was forty I could look back and say, yeah, I had some liaisons with women. I experimented. The thought of a porn star's long fingernails thrusting around inside me sent a wicked shiver up my spine. I felt silly thinking these things. Still, I went back to the nipple. I went back to Hailey. To kissing Courtney, her putting her damp lips against mine. But with Courtney it wasn't sexual. The scene wasn't pornstar, where you see open mouths and dueling tongues. It was much better, though I couldn't decide exactly how.

The phone chirped.

My folks, unacknowledged Luddites, didn't own an answering machine. The phone chirped and chirped. My mother slept all day and woke cranky if disturbed, so I had to answer, sticky fingers and all.

"Hello?" Almost out of breath.

"Hi. May I speak to Lee Bauer?"

"You got her." I was on the edge of the bed, shirt no underwear.

"This is Kelly Brown from Icy Bites. We've reviewed your application and would like to hire you on for the summer season."

"Icy Bites?"

"The ice cream factory."

"Oh. Right. Yeah." My shoulders broke at the thought of work.

"You'll need to take a preliminary health screen. Do you have a pen?"

"Yeah." I grabbed a pen, a book off my sister's desk.

"You can set up an appointment with Toledo Health Services." She gave me the number. "Explain who you are and for what company. There's no charge for the testing. The sooner you do this the sooner you can start work."

"Okay."

"Give us a call the day after you visit the center and we'll get you set up, make you part of the ice cream team. Have a good day."

Ice cream team? I hung up the phone. Health screen? Fuck. That meant piss test. I'd smoked only two nights ago. The requisite twenty-one days had not passed. All I needed was my parents finding out I hadn't been sober since the spell in rehab. I couldn't add more fodder to my father's outrage. He already suspected the worst. With confirmation, he would have blown a valve, and though we didn't like each other, at nineteen I didn't want to deal with his death. I dialed the number.

"We can fit you in at four today." A pleasant voice said, ready to accommodate.

"Today's no good," for lots of reasons. "What about tomorrow?"

"Morning or afternoon?"

"Afternoon."

"Four o'clock again."

"Yeah, that's good," barring a tsunami, which Lake Erie wouldn't gift me with, but I was counting on nonetheless. I hung up the phone and called Derrick, hoping he had a detoxifying supplement, a magic remedy. He wasn't home. Growing anxious, I pulled on my jeans and made a break for the 7-ELEVEN. Nineteen-year-olds didn't deserve such stress.

Under fluorescent bulbs' dull hum, I grabbed a twelve pack of Mountain Dew, two gallons of cranberry juice, and a gallon of spring water. No piss test was going to get the best of me.

"Looks like you got some serious drinking to do." The clerk thought he was funny.

I smiled snarkily and paid the comedian. He'd worked there forever and I wondered if he remembered me spilling Slurpee all over the floor on his shift two summers back.

Plopping down in front of the TV, I cracked the first Dew. Cold and refreshing. By the third one, a sugary film had coated my teeth and I'd developed two cavities. I pushed on. I had to cleanse my system somehow.

Mom woke. To avoid any squinty-eyed inquisition, I slid the evidence under the end table next to the couch.

"Hi, dear."

"Morning."

Her eyes in a fog, the bags beneath them gray and puffy, my mother passed into the kitchen. "What's all this cranberry juice in here?" she asked.

"Health kick."

"Oh, honey, you don't need to diet. You're just big-boned."

I sucked down the fourth can of Mountain Dew and crushed it in my hand. I hated when she called me big-boned. She should've been happy that I wasn't anorexic or bulimic, that I wasn't trying to look like the models in her *Cosmo* or *Working Woman*. I'd learned early the impossibility of those standards. The gaunt aesthetic. Skin and bone wasn't pretty. Three peas and a can of tuna a day wasn't all I wanted to eat. I didn't care much about what I wore and I didn't care to moisturize and smother my face with blush and liner and shadow. My mother cares about these things. Despite having to mop floors and direct high school dropouts to set tables, she's quite the lady. Outside the restaurant, she wears floral dresses and open-toed shoes. She wants men to hold doors for her. With her 50s brand of feminism, it's a wonder Michelle and I were low-maintenance: no make-up, no monthly hair-do, no tanning bed.

"Don't worry, the kick won't last," I said. "Hey, do you remember that pamphlet you gave me on the menstrual cycle? That cheesy seventies thing?"

She frowned, thinking. "I didn't give you any pamphlet. We sat at the kitchen table and I drew pictures."

"You didn't say a word. You gave me a pamphlet. *It* had pictures."

"What about it?"

"Just wondered if you still have it."

"If I gave it to you, you should still have it. Anyway, I'm going back to bed. Tell Dad there's a plate of food for him in the fridge and he should heat it up in the microwave on high for four minutes."

"Okay," I said, my eyes twitched rapidly. I thought the uncontrollable flutter might be pamphlet PTSD or the way Mom catered to Dad. Then I looked at my feet and saw the empty vessels of caffeine and sugar.

4

Despite dust on Pete Rose's ugly mug on the cover of *Time* and the sticky covers of kids' books, the waiting room at the clinic had a scent of sterility. The small room held five chairs and one table bursting with months-old magazines. I sat in my manic Dew state with an itchy crotch and a full and fully irritated bladder. My knee was jumping ninety beats a minute and I was paranoid I'd be busted for drugs once again and told I wasn't good enough, clean enough, for factory work. The chair next to me held a tattered copy of yesterday's *Toledo Blade*. The cover story was on local tourism. For the life of me, I couldn't imagine people planning trips to this town. Settled shortly after the War of 1812, Toledo was named for a Spanish village of the same name. Now Toledo, Ohio, means Jamie Farr, Tony Packo's, The Mud Hens. A small town getting big, the 49th largest city in the United States. A good place to raise a family. A union town. Glass. Autos. Tools. Ice cream. Low crime. Good schools. A city like any city, but with less happening. Toledo wasn't New York or Chicago or Detroit, but I wasn't one to complain since I'd never been to those cities and had no desire to see them. Courtney had always wanted to go, and I would have gone had she planned a trip. But to me, other cities were just bigger versions of small cities. They had bigger buildings and bigger crowds and bigger sports teams and more crime and bigger versions of nothing to do but live out each day just like the day before.

A woman, dressed in deep rouge hospital scrubs, called my name. She explained the procedures then put me in a booth to test my hearing.

"Trouble sleeping lately?"

"What does that have to do with my ears?"

"Nothing. You've got excellent hearing. Must not have been to too many rock concerts."

"Seen my fair share," I said, defensively, for no good reason. I didn't care about concerts much. They'd lost their allure after watching Billy Idol mock fuck a blow-up doll on stage. The faux sex was spectacle more than art or anything else.

We moved to the scale. Height: five-seven.

"You weigh that much?" She'd been conferring with my mom.

"Guess so."

Handing me a cool plastic cup, she said, "You hide it well. Can you pee in this for me?"

"Absolutely." Provided my bladder hadn't shriveled or disintegrated. I been up half the night and on the toilet through half of that. I still felt waterlogged and wrong, though. I pissed like a champ. The cup overflowed and would have made a good hand warmer in winter. I'd go into business yet, show my parents I could be somebody. I considered dumping some yellow and adding some water, but I knew that would trigger sensors or some kind of alert.

"We didn't need *that* much," the lady said, taking the cup from me.

I shrugged. No one had offered to hold the cup and tell me when to stop.

"Have you taken any drugs in the last thirty-six hours?"

My heart thumped hard. "Just a few speed balls, I think."

"Prescription or over-the-counter?" She grabbed my arm, slapped at my veins. Clearly in no mood for tomfoolery.

"No," I said, wondering if a lie detector test came next.

She jammed the needle into my arm, immune to patient discomfort. This was *her* job. She did this all day. Slapped people. Stuck people. The sadist. She deposited the vial of blood in a stainless steel contraption and pressed a button. The thing spun like the wind of a Kansas tornado. My drug-infested blood in there. I watched the dark red go round.

"You can have a seat in the waiting room."

On a worn cushion, I was motionless, frozen, wondering if I could be arrested for testing positive. I stared back and forth at the two doors waiting for the nurse to barge through, pointing me out to the cops. After blowing the Happy Housekeepers job, all I needed was to blow the factory job on account of drug use. I couldn't imagine explaining that to my dad and watching his face crease from anger to disappointment to utter resignation at his fuck-up daughter. I wasn't pleased with him, either, but I didn't want to fight with him much more. I preferred we ignore each other like we used to. The prospect of flunking the test made me want to bolt out the door before the nurse smugly cast me aside. The prospect of having to explain my smoking habits over the course of the past year, or why I wasn't good enough for factory work made me wish desperately for the tests to reveal some deadly disease. At least then I would have gained some sympathy.

I admit that I wasn't the most vibrant of people. I didn't have passions that drew others to me. I hadn't let myself latch onto anything. That was no fault of mine. I was a GenX baby and wasn't supposed to get too excited about anything. This behavior had come early, so early, in fact that my parents sent me off to summer camp "to be a part of things, to find something to love, a hobby."

I was in fourth grade and had barely been out of the backyard.

"The camp is in the beautiful rolling hills of Western Michigan. You can horseback ride, learn to water ski, do crafts. There's archery." Brochure in hand and fake smile on her face, Mom pitched it to me.

"I don't want to go."

"You'll have fun."

"Why can't I stay with Grandma like I always do when you and Dad are fighting?"

"Oh, honey, that's not what this is about."

It was. I knew it, even then. I was being sent up the road so she and my dad could "reconnect." I was enraged, felt left out, unwanted. To make matters worse, my sister, my angelic sister, had had the bright idea of going to summer camp in the first place, though she was a Brownie and went to Brownie camp. My mom called around and found a bunk for me elsewhere during the same two weeks. I hated camp. I was passionate about that. Low ceilings, high bunks. A beam smacked me in the forehead every morning for thirteen days. The food was pig slop and the girls were catty, prissy bitches who came from money and wore lots of pink. I was out of my element. I didn't wear pink. Camp's only saving grace was the counselor in charge of the horses. Anne, always in jeans despite the heat, gave me extra lessons at no charge and made me stay to clean up after the rides. She must have known I was sad and set apart. The campers in my cabin all came from the same town. They all listened to Madonna and read *Teen Magazine* and *Seventeen*.

I'd come to respect my parents for taking those two weeks for themselves. That concentrated time salvaged their fragmented marriage. They were fighting daily up until that point. One time Michelle and I were home when my mom decided to play Frisbee with the items in the antique buffet. Michelle's knee scarred from where shrapnel of the good china had sliced her. "Nothing happened!" Dad was yelling. "I was delivering her mail like I always do and she invited me in for a glass of water. It was hot. I was thirsty. I accepted." He soon, fatally, stupidly, admitted that the woman was attractive and that he actually had fantasized about her. Melees ensued. The lesson: Never admit to fantasy. Doing so disrupted reality.

Dad kept denying the affair, and Mom smoldered when she heard jokes about the mailman's kid. And any time they had an issue they withdrew to the bedroom and "talked" right away so things didn't build and dishes didn't fly. I had developed the theory that all any fading couple needed was a quiet night and a good fuck to relieve tensions, to force out unrealistic expectations, or to get to the bottom of any suspicion. If that didn't correct matters, the couple was doomed from the beginning. When practiced well, sex was the secret elixir. I wanted to believe that. I had my body to practice on, but I hadn't had the opportunity or the time to test the theory with anyone else, not with any scientific rigor. I had other obligations.

The drug screen was taking forever. Finally, all tests in, Nurse Ratched called me to the counter. "You're healthy," she said.

Disbelief swept through me. Something had actually gone right. I looked for signs of *Candid Camera* or *TV's Bloopers and Jokes*. Nothing.

"So I can leave now?"

"Yeah, but keep away from the speed balls." She had some humor in her after all.

I strolled into the suffocating heat. I didn't carry any contagion that would taint the ice cream, and I didn't have to tell my dad I couldn't get the job. But more than that, as I stepped up into the stuffy tin TARTA, the idea that I'd be stuck in a factory for the rest of the summer, that I wouldn't be lounging at Bowman pool, fighting summer-camp kids for a place cool enough to pee, in the otherwise all-too-warm water, flattened me against the plastic bus seat.

Thirty minutes later, my bladder jostling and screaming for relief, I skipped off The Ride of Toledo and bolted for home. The Escort, short and stocky, shined in the driveway. Michelle could have picked me up. The bitch. She had flaked on purpose. Probably drove around the block so I'd have to bus home. And, she was in the bathroom. Strike two. Squeezing my legs together and jumping up and down, I slapped the door with my hand.

"I gotta go."

Her indifference to my swelling bladder passed through the door, "Go in the basement."

"There's ghosts and goblins down there."

"Piss in a jar for all I care."

"C'mon, you're only popping zits!" I yelled.

She swung the door open, glaring at me with her brown eyes. A red ring fading on her cheek where she'd been squeezing. Unzipping my pants, I dashed in, knocking her to the side.

"At least wait till I'm out!"

Such sweet relief.

"I passed the test," I said, dropping my dehydrated frame next to Michelle on the sofa.

"You're not the imbecile we thought you were?"

"I scored higher than you on the Iowa Tests."

She was not impressed. She scraped a fingernail across the pimple she'd been picking. I'd shared a bedroom with this one ever since she could sleep through the night. Three years younger and reading all the time, Michelle was destined for coke-bottle lenses, and by the looks of her pimple, a face pocked with scars.

"What are you talking about?"

"Drug test for work. Ice cream factory."

"You had doubts?" She squinted her eyes in a mixture of confusion and sass. Her fingers distractedly explored her face for more oil nodes.

I realized I was trying to confide in my younger sister, something I hadn't done since I was twelve, when I told her a dream about the two of us being taken captive during guerrilla warfare. We were put on the roof of a tall building and made to walk in circles. I broke out of the circle and ran off the side of the building. I woke up before finding out if I flew or fell.

"I was hoping for a disease so I wouldn't have to work."

"You're setting a bad example for me."

Up to that point, I hadn't thought that possible. Michelle was confident and comfortable for a sixteen-year-old. She was skipped when they handed out self-esteem trouble. The chances of her looking up to me were worse than Courtney being able to get a comb through her hair anytime in the next three years.

"Is that sarcasm?"

"Duh."

"What've you got going this summer?"

"Driver's ed and AP reading list."

I looked at her suspiciously. This was clearly a problem, because when she got her license, she would get car privileges, cutting into my privileged time. Tragic, too, because she'd use the car to hide out in libraries across the city.

"What do you care, anyway? As Dad says, you're up shit creek with no paddle."

We used to get along when we were younger. Now she scoffed at everything I did or said, thinking she was better than me, which she probably was. What I would have liked was to get her really, really stoned. Not just a first-time buzz, but bong hit after bong hit after brownie after cookie until she went daffy for hours, rendering her unable to read or think or judge me. That would have made me happy, though my parents wouldn't appreciate their angelic daughter spazzing out, running to them crying that her big sister made her smoke a lot of dope and she couldn't come down and couldn't think and feared she'd be that way forever, light, brain-fried, and not her deep, earnest, black-souled self. She did as much when she was eleven and choked on a cigarette I had given her. Her betrayal cost me nearly a month on house arrest. The little bitch asked if she could have a puff and crossed her heart and swore she wouldn't tell. That's when it all went bad between us.

"I'm your older sister. I do care," I said. "I care a lot."

She stared blankly, probably questioning the value of my existence, which, honestly, was okay, because she might actually come up with an answer that evaded me.

"Yeah, right. Why don't you just work at Mom's restaurant?"

Mom doesn't actually own a restaurant. She's a shift manager at the brick shithouse of a Frische's near the I-475 ramps on Secor. Second and sometimes third shift. Really carved into my high school social time. Before she got the job, my friends and I would hang out there for hours, drinking coffee and smoking cigarettes until someone threw up or got thrown out for being too disruptive.

"No way I'm working at that greasy pit."

"You can't hang around here all the time."

"Why not? You got a steady? You pop your cherry? That'd be great. The perfect plan. You get preggers. That'd put us back on equal par with the units."

She stared at me again, this time her neck bent in contracted derision. "Fuck off and die." She went back to the bathroom mirror.

5

"This," he paused for effect, "is a novelty job."

WAYNE. That was what the frayed iron-on patch over his left breast read. WAYNE R. With the white hairnet billowing like a cloud around his head, he looked like a clown. His red nose didn't help, either. I refrained from checking his feet.

"You all get it, right? The play on novelty? Novelty because it's new work for you. And novelty because we make and pack novelty treats? Anyway."

Eight of us, five in jeans and T-shirts, three dressed in white, head to ankle, sat around a cafeteria table, awaiting our orders. Seven waited for the tedium to set in. For me that had come long ago. We were told we were in the break room.

"You can lunch in here. Look around, people eating." He swept his arm toward the tiny room as if it were the wild plains of Africa and the time clock an exotic animal, the chairs undiscovered vegetation.

My seven cohorts of middling appearance and age looked around earnestly, as if they'd never seen such luxury. I was beginning to regret skipping out on college classes. Clearly, real life was, in fact, much worse. The pimpled kid next to me, sixteenish and dressed in white, listened attentively, nodding at Wayne, and cautiously, quietly repeating his words so as not to miss a thing. I pretended my ears weren't trained to hear the pitch at which Wayne spoke.

"That's the fridge. Label your shit."

Someone gasped. Heads turned toward a short, frail, middle-aged woman whose husband had probably just left her and their three kids, stuck without any prospects, having never had to work. The guy next to her snickered as did the bleach-blonde next to him. I was unmoved.

"Don't take anyone else's food without permission. If you have soft ears, this isn't the place for you," Wayne continued. He had the script down. "Over there is the punch clock. Every week you'll get a punch card with your name at the top. If you don't see yours, find a manager. We wear blue oxford shirts." Wayne pinched at his shirt. "That's how you can identify us until you learn our names. If you don't see your card, get one of us. We'll get you a blank card. Don't take it personally if you don't have one. That just means they screwed up upstairs."

Dissension in the frosty factory air.

"To punch in: turn the card this side up where your name is at the top, slide it in quick, then yank it toward the ceiling."

His careful directions sent me back to high school typing class and Mrs. Domino's Sesame Street speak: "Left hand, ASDF. Again, ASDF. Now right, JKLsemicolon." Her slow sounds rising and falling over each letter. Wayne must have been related to her. It took all my willpower not to kick him in the shins and run away.

"Make sure you hear a click. If not, it didn't register."

He had us all practice punching in once with a blank card, then for real. I wanted the group to maul me for getting myself trapped in the factory's iron teeth. When I clicked my card, I noticed the time. We'd been bilked twenty minutes' pay. Two whole dollars. People always complain about working for the Man. I finally understood why.

"It's four-twenty," I said. I had debts to pay.

Wayne looked at me with his Rudolph nose.

"It's four-twenty. We've been here since four. We're supposed to be paid for training."

Wayne's hard, blank visage denied that he understood the English language exiting my mouth. "We got started late." He turned away from me and headed for the inner door to the labyrinth of machinery and ice cream treats, white hairnets and white uniforms.

"The eight of us were here on time. *You* got started late."

Wayne pretended he hadn't heard.

"Yeah," a voice climbed from behind me.

Thank God someone's with me, a guy I might have gone to high school with. I couldn't be sure. He looked familiar in his round John Lennon frames. Didn't matter, though. His outburst helped us get our pay.

"We were here on time," a beady brown-eyed guy piped up. He was tall and thin and not unattractive. We exchanged knowing looks, though I wasn't sure what the knowledge was. He winked at me. I wrote the movement off as an involuntary tick.

Wayne turned back, snatched our eight cards from their slots, crossed out the time and wrote a four on each. He initialed them W.R. then crammed them into their holes and carefully avoided the glasses, the brown eyes, and my eyes. The three of us smirked conspiratorially. Ignoring our solidarity, Wayne carried on, "Ten dollars will be taken out of every paycheck for the first two and a half months for union dues. You'll get a union packet at the end of the day to take home and read. The packet explains our expectations of you and your rights as employees. You'll have to sign the last page and bring it back to us within the week. Hairnets must be worn at all times on the floor."

Wayne handed a box to my comrade who opened the lid and tugged a hairnet from the within. We each took one and covered our germ-infested nests. In this, we were all made equal. But the net wasn't thick enough to hold back my discordant thoughts. My mind raced toward other ways of paying my parents back: prostitution, drug-running, McDonald's.

"We have ear plugs if you want them. As you can see, the packers and operators wear white. You'll be sized for uniforms next week. Until then, if you've got white clothes at home, wear them." He held the door for us to enter our sanitary summer fates.

Cool air and the monotonous crank of machinery swallowed us. There were five separate machines lining the left wall. Stainless steel wheels and arms jutted from the slippery concrete floor. The space looked like a strange version of adult Chutes and Ladders or an industrial art exhibit gone horribly wrong. White and blue specks dotted the concrete gray room. Talking over a general hum and hiss of ambient noise, Wayne gave us a partial tour, explaining the machines and the products and what our roles were. In rhythm with the spin of a nearby machine, his words, the ones I managed to hear, went in one ear and out the other. He soon passed us off to Joyce, a petite, trashy woman with a gap in her teeth like the Wife of Bath's. She spoke in raspy tones over the steam and clangor.

"You are Type C employees."

Letters, not numbers.

"Which means packers. You get six seventy-five an hour. Time and a half for anything over eight hours. If you want overtime, let us know. Usually about halfway through the summer, the guys upstairs realize we're behind schedule and increase production, which means we work. It's not so bad if you need the money. Sucks if you don't. You get a two hundred dollar bonus at the end of the season if you last to Labor Day. Temps don't last long. One, maybe two of you will."

Eight thousand dollars sat like a yoke on my shoulders. Training was a four-hour tour with explanations and time for questions. Management didn't even let us lay our greasy skin on the cream. Everything was bleak. As soon as I could, I tore the hairnet from my head, punched out, bee-lining for home, which proved no haven. I wrestled with the sheets and the sounds of my dad's jangled snores and my sister flipping pages. The ceiling overhead scowled white and threatened to fall.

6

Four o'clock. I stood in front of the gray box. I punched in.

Behind me, Wayne breathed on my shoulder. "Did you hear a click?" he asked. After learning the tactics of a drill sergeant, he must have quit boot camp, come here, gotten a job as a packer, and moved up the ranks to manager, all the while honing his mediocrity.

"Yep. Clicked all right."

"I didn't hear a click."

My guess was Wayne was stubborn, and in his eighteen years at the factory had never worn the earplugs and was now nearing deafness. I showed him my card. Blue ink with sixteen hundred hours embossed in the right place at the right time. I hoped he wasn't going blind too.

He sized me up. "You look pretty athletic."

Apparently, the job required Olympics-ready employees.

"Go to Four."

"Which one's that?"

He glared at me. He knew I hadn't heard a word he'd said the day before.

"The first one on the left inside the door."

Machine Four churned out chocolate and strawberry Crunch Bars. A squat little man, almost as white as his uniform, scurried around frantically. He sported a gray mustache and a blue tag that read PAUL. He smiled impishly and barely made eye contact. He was the type of guy who looked when you weren't looking. He ran around the machine, checking buttons, fixing the wrap, pulling jammed bars from the metal pincers before they swung back around and new sticks tried to take their place, all the while watching the temperature and mix load indicators.

"On odd days," Ned told me, "we run chocolate. On even days, strawberry." Ned, a beefy man, with hound dog eyes, was one of the two packers Machine Four required. He stood heavily, all his weight gathered in his torso, and leaned into a metal tray where the bars, wrapped neat and clean, edged up toward his gut. There was so much of him that he barely moved when he packed the bars. "You grab eight. They come at you stacked stick to stick. Then you toss them in the box. The box gets twenty-four. Three rows tall. Eight in each row."

He, too, was trained in the art of the obvious.

The other packer, a quiet wallflower named Maria, popped flat cardboard into three-dimensional boxes for Ned to drop the bars into. Then she rapped a black button on what looked like an adding machine. A red slab of gummy tape spat out, an enlarged frog's tongue stuck in midair. She used this to seal the full boxes.

"You seen enough?" Ned looked over at me, watching Maria slap a tongue on another box. "We switch every thirty minutes."

"Sure."

Ned packed faster, and soon the bars were at the bottom of the tray. He stepped aside for my debut. Spotlight. I tried to count eight bars. Someone must have jimmied the machine. The bars advanced, marching. They spilled off the end of the tray and dropped to my feet. Ned grabbed a large box from near the wall and set it on a stool to my right. He threw the bars from the floor into the box, then some from the tray in front of me.

"Don't count. See the four on the left? Grab for just after that one."

My fingers wouldn't stretch around all eight bars at one time. I saw Maria's small hands. Fuck, if she could do it, I could do it. I grabbed nine. Too many. They flew all over the tray. I heard a mousy murmur from Maria. She was laughing at me. I threw the mess of melting bars into the box.

Ned nudged me aside. "Watch."

He was a natural. In no time, the tray was low again and he had emptied the box of the bars that hit the floor, working them stealthily back in. With such hands, he should have been a locksmith or a ladies' man. Maybe he was, but all I could think of were seven hours and ten minutes of this day, five days a week, for ninety days or even a lifetime. I saw myself throwing in the packing gloves, waving, as I exited the cool plant air into the Toledo heat and open sky.

Small Hands Maria didn't stick around to watch my ineptitude for a second day. Wayne had other plans for her. Beefy Ned, with his sloth's eyes, solo-packed the bars. Pop a box, fill it. Pop, fill. No one was slapping the frog's tongue onto the full boxes and sending them up the conveyor belt, through the box room and freezer, and off into the mouths of hungry Americans. Twelve lonely boxes of strawberry Crunch Bars were melting on the metal table when I arrived. I had to act. *Stat*.

"Oh, no," Ned said. He had turned sinister Wayne-like protector of the factory and all its ideals. He called me to the Tray of Death with two menacing curls of his gloved index finger.

Ambling around the table, I stretched my arms, cracked my knuckles, and pulled on my gloves, ready for surgery.

One box. Twenty-four bars. Three rows of eight. I could do it.

I reached into the tray, counted four on the left, pulled up, tossed bars into a box. I reached in again. Did I have eight? I thought I had eight. Doubt got the better of me. The bars crept up the metal arms, coming at me, challenging me. I recoiled. Bars hit the floor. I stared at Ned. He was not paying me any mind. His eyelids were so low I swore he was asleep. I loaded the slacker box on my right, the wrong box, the fuck-up box, with handfuls of excess bars. I watched the clock. Five minutes. Ten minutes. I managed to fill two boxes and slide them to Ned. Fifteen minutes. I filled another. Then another. Bars kept coming and coming. Twenty-five minutes. Another five and I'd be back on a half-hour sabbatical, in the stress-free world of taping. I managed two more boxes before my time was up. I looked hopefully, gratefully, toward Ned so I could give him the switch signal, but he was not looking my way. Stretching my fingers around another eight bars, I jammed them into the retail box. Then I lost count. Again. I bent to pick bars from the floor. More fell on my head, attacking me. I stood up and loaded the fuck-up box with more excess. I wanted Ned dead.

Forty minutes.

Forty-five.

Finally Ned noticed no boxes were gliding his way. He looked over to see me piling bars into the fuck-up box, loading it to overflow. He lumbered over, coming to the rescue, to resuscitate.

"It's been fifty minutes," I said as I passed him.

"Tough shit."

"C'mon, man, it's my second day."

"If you can't do it, get out."

I fumed as I taped his pretty, perfect-count boxes. I wanted desperately for him to fuck up.

Joyce stopped by to check my progress. She smiled her gapped-toothed smile at me but quickly dropped the façade of being nice to the newbie when she saw the heap next to Ned.

"What happened?"

Ned nodded his head toward me. Damned Brutus.

"Work 'em back in before they melt." She reached into the bottom of the box. "Fuck, the ones on bottom are gone," she said as if she'd lost a life. Ignoring me then, Joyce talked with Paul, the ghostly operator, while Ned, with the grace of a gunslinger, loaded many a box three rows tall. Joyce came back, heaved the fuck-up box onto her shoulder and emptied the mush into a nearby dumpster.

The day continued in the same manner for the next seven hours.

One of the problems with Machine Four was that it was right by the door to the break room, so anyone in there watched us. We watched too. Ned and Paul were pleasant enough to look at. They were competent. When I was at the tray, I created an all-out disaster. Bars were melting at my feet, and Joyce, shorter than me, was standing at my back, peering over my shoulder, glaring at my lack of progress. Her surveillance was making me a self-conscious wreck.

"This isn't a hard job." In addition to being very short, Joyce was very wise.

"You've had twelve years of practice. This is my second day."

"No lip. Pack faster."

"It's not lip."

"You want me to write you up?"

With arthritis grinding in my hands and my shoulders aching from hunching over the tray, I was back in junior high being sent to the principal's office. I was in hell. It really was other people.

"No."

Then Ned caught a laughing fit, his whole body rising and falling in thunderous shakes. Paul, squirrel that he was, kept running around the machine, checking gauges and gadgets. And there I was in my newly issued white uniform in front of the tray at minute fifty-two in the equivalent of solitary confinement.

"You don't get a break until you work these bars back in. You've already wasted too many." She tried to shake the surplus box. Being too full again, the box didn't move.

I groaned, certain that delaying my break constituted a violation of labor law. But I was young and stubborn and couldn't let those fucks keep laughing and yelling at me. I couldn't give in. The job was shitty and mindless, but I had some pride. Some. Then I thought, oddly, I had probably inherited such feeble pride from both of my parents. There was my mom, scrubbing sticky floors and picking up after teenagers and truck drivers, and there was my dad, toting a bag full of bills and meaningless advertisements. Both sailing through shitty, mindless work, yet doing that work year after year and doing it well. Then I had another thought: I was fucking doomed. Doomed to repeat the sins of my forbearers. I should have charged out of the door that first day, but for some reason I took a deep breath and braced for the bars' advance.

I packed and packed and packed.

The bars were relentless. I packed. More came.

And more.

Still more.

Then something happened.

Humiliation fell away. Ham-handedness too.

I had found the groove. Eight bars. Three rows. Slide to Ned. Eight bars. Three rows. Slide to Ned. The bars stopped dropping to the floor. Ned looked at me with open eyes. He nodded approval.

Joyce smacked me on the back. "You got it. Holy shit, you got it!"

I was one of them.

7

In a field the tiny head of sun stared down on us, warming our already warm skin. To the right a dense grove of trees blocked a cobalt sky. The shade looked cool and welcoming, but I had learned quickly the grove was infested with mosquitoes and gnats. To the left and down an embankment, the river was lazy brown and uninviting. A workday afternoon, the park was empty. Derrick took off his sweat-stained shirt. His skin was damp. His torso thick. His chest so white he still looked shirted.

"Do you think you'll reach a point where you don't want muscles anymore? Just want to be rid of them?" I was getting philosophical on Wednesday at noon. Plus, we'd smoked a fat joint.

"No way. I love feeling powerful. I like that I tower over people and intimidate them. No one fucks with me," he dropped down in the grass next to me and used the Frisbee for a pillow.

"You're nothing like that."

"Brawny on the outside, squishy on the in."

Not having been mowed in a while, the grass was tall and spongy. Longer blades scratched at my calves and stuck to my feet. We had been together an hour and Derrick hadn't kissed me. I kept expecting him to. Expecting to feel his Hulk Hogan self on me. I kept looking for his move, wanting to feel his weight, though the day was too hot and humid to be jammed up against each other making out, clammy skin sticking like Velcro.

"Just a big teddy bear," I said. "My first name's really Sara, but no one calls me that since my grandma started calling me Lee when I was five because Sara means princess and I'm 'certainly not haughty as all that.'"

"Sara."

"Yes, sir. What's a stupid thing you've done? Courtney and I once got in trouble at Franklin Park Mall for disrupting the peace. I kept darting in and out of the circular clothes racks, scaring all the lady shoppers. Courtney, drunk for the first time, couldn't help knocking over potted plants and shaking and trying to dance with the mannequins. We would've gotten off with a slap except she blew it when the mall cop asked if we were drunk. Do you know what she said? She said, 'No, man, you can't smell vodka.' The guy got into her purse and found four dwarf-size bottles she'd stolen from a hotel she went to with her parents. Her dad's a little into the drink so he didn't even blink at the bill. Is she still hanging out with Jake?" I asked. Maybe Derrick would tell me things about my friend since she wasn't telling me them herself.

"Yup. Jake says she gives the best head he's ever gotten. My theory is it's the only head he's ever gotten."

"She did look quite skilled."

We were both lying on our backs, knees bent toward the sky. Derrick's eyes were closed against the sun. "Everyone's different," he said.

"Are you saying you wouldn't appreciate such vigor?" All that pumping iron must have affected him in odd ways.

"Depends on the circumstances, but, generally, no. I like to be teased. I want it to take hours. Are you taking notes? I'm a rare breed. Kinsey will be calling soon."

"You can't keep it up for hours," I said and closed my eyes. The bright sun made orange spider webs of my eyelids. I wondered if Derrick was looking at me. I was playing a game, seeing how long

I could go without looking. Maybe I would sense his eyes on me, like when you know someone is talking about you even though their whispers were faint and unintelligible. "Can you? Is that what the supplements are really about? Is there a cult of weightlifters who can do this? Anyway, I should warn you now, I'm terrible at giving head."

"Jake said Courtney said she's been with nine different guys. Do you think that's a lot? Seven of them just from the nine months at school. That's like one a month. You're probably not terrible. Guys are bad at giving it to girls. They're the ones who need the most direction."

"How many have you slept with?"

"Two."

"Late bloomer," I said and immediately regretted my words. Derrick was twenty-four and buff and smart. He was kind. Maybe he wasn't into sleeping around. Maybe he was Mormon. "Are you Mormon?" I asked.

His face was turned the other way so I couldn't see his expression. The air between us went heavy in a way that was not due to humidity.

"You should put your shirt back on, you're burning."

He didn't move. "This is nothing. Do you know how many people died in last year's heat? Something like fifteen-thousand. From just the heat! Cost billions in damage."

"How do you know this shit?"

"How do you not? I read. I pay attention."

We lay in the heat. I imagined my blood boiling.

"You?"

"What?"

"How many have you been with?"

"Four." I flipped onto my belly. "Actually, I don't know if that's accurate. It really depends on your definition of sex. My cousin Samantha said the sex doesn't count if you don't enjoy it. She's been with zillions of guys, but only admits to eight. You want to know something else?" The words came easily. "I had this professor at school who was pretty sexy. She had thin calves and wore sandals or flip-flops all the time. Long corkscrew hair. Nice lips. I think I was attracted to her. Physically. Like, if she would have wanted to trade sex for grades, I would've gone for it. At first I thought it was just her intelligence that I was after, that my desire wasn't really a sexual thing, but more a mind thing. Then I decided it was only a sexual thing. But now, I think it was both. I had some fantasies about her. Those were better than some of the actual sex I've had."

Derrick had clammed up. Oddly I was yammering like a fool. Maybe it was the weed or maybe it was because I hadn't really talked to anyone about anything in a few days or maybe it was simply that he was easy to talk to. I could tell he was still listening. There was no hardness to him, no judgment. I liked that. I felt myself wanting to be closer to him, wanting contact. I leaned over and rested my chin on his chest. His sweat smelled good enough to lick. I kissed him. He didn't reciprocate, barely opened his lips, his tongue a shy snail in a shell.

"I haven't told anyone that," I said, wondering what such information said about me. Or what Derrick was thinking. That I was bi? I felt none of the heaviness or regret that I felt telling Courtney about Hailey. I felt like I was shifting around pieces of a giant, incomplete jigsaw puzzle. But then I was done talking about myself and my fantasies. I asked, "Do you think we can ever really know another person?" I was still on my belly, inched up close to Derrick, thinking he was just caught off guard and would lift his head toward my mouth. "Take Courtney. We're good friends and I had no idea she fucked so many guys. And the dreads. Those aren't anything I ever thought she'd go for."

"That's the thing, isn't it?" he said, an edge emerging in his voice. "We can't know anyone else. Not really. That's the shit thing with relationships. They're predicated on a foundation of mystery. We spend all this time trying to get to know someone only to find out they don't really want to know us." He looked at me squarely. "I should tell you, my girlfriend just broke up with me. Four years and she said it wasn't working for her anymore. What's that? *Working*. I'm not a fucking day at the office."

My lungs shriveled, taking my ego along. I felt like an idiot, moving in like that, thinking I was heading for a summer of afternoons at the park, evenings of ice cream, and nights anywhere. Thinking that I was heading into a summer of Fabio and poppers, getting stoned and eating stolen ice cream treats. I rolled onto my back, returning to my study of the sky. Thin, gauzy clouds rambled east and south, kicking fast and then holding steady because of the fickle wind.

8

A week of work went by. Days piled on each other and the machines whirred and growled. I thought of school and my predicament. I tried not to think about Derrick, or the reluctance vibes from his body. I hadn't seen him or talked to him since the day in the park. I felt foolish because I let myself want and then acted on my want. I threw myself into my work, thinking that if I gave it my energy, it would give back. I was a diligent dwarf whistling, "Off to work we go, we go," tossing novelties into the appropriate boxes like I had been a regular at the factory for years. Some days Wayne even seemed to sing along. One day he let me in on a secret. "You know, Lee, no one's ever caught on so quick. Usually takes at least two weeks on Four. You got skills."

My head swelled.

Ned pretended not to be listening. He had taken ten full working days before he wasn't using the sissy box to play catch-up. They'd used immersion therapy on me. Leave her be and run away. She'd make or break.

On his way round the machine, Paul stopped at my side. Harmless at first. "How's it going?" and "Hot day, huh?" Paul, despite his gray mustache, too-white face, kind eyes, and initial reticence bordering on undiagnosed mute, was a talker. Foul talk. Dirty jokes and dirt on folks. At some point early on after my mad skills shone forth, I had been deemed safe and was made privy to factory gossip.

On tape duty, Ned skirted off to the bathroom.

"He's got two kids, you know," Paul said, seizing his chance.

"So?" I tossed the bars.

"He's twenty-three," he said, standing next to me, not looking at me directly, but marking my response.

"Old enough."

"His girl's six. His boy's seven. Do the math."

"How old's the mother? Maybe she's robbing the cradle."

Paul looked at my tray as if the answer would spit forth from the inching rows. "I don't know." He ran off and started another ream of wrap.

Ned resumed his post. The tape machine jammed. The poor frog. But the jam wasn't catastrophic. Wasn't enough to shut down the machine. Ned lifted the lid and removed two gummy wads and the frog was croaking again.

"You married, Ned?" I asked.

"Three years."

I couldn't detect pride or pain in his tone. Three years was enough to be past the blissful, newness stage but not long enough to be loathing himself or his mate. Add kids to the mix, though, ones born pre-marriage, possibly to someone no longer in the picture, and the equation unbalances. I didn't see much wrong in Ned's case. He had a job, stuck around. He may have been missing some things but was probably gaining others.

"Kids?"

"Two, and one on the way. We're going for a football team."

"What's that, eight?"

"Eleven."

"Good god. I hope you've got a big house."

Paul was back at my side. "They're fucking each other." He threw his head over his left shoulder. "Quality Control Kathy and Craig from Seven."

"Is that news?"

Paul ran to his gauges. "Stay away from him. He's got crabs or scabs or herpes or something. I forget. I hear him moan in the pisser every now and then."

"Maybe he's jacking off," I countered.

Paul's pupils covered the blue in his eyes. He'd found a friend. "Fred, he worked here a few years back. Worked the cup machine. You know the one with the wooden spoons? Rumor says, Wayne walked in on him shootin' his shit into a few vanilla cups."

He was testing my limits. I didn't have any. Plus, his talk passed the time. Like a radio soap opera played in stolen snippets. He was safe as far as I could tell and had things to tell me, though I wasn't sure about their merit.

"They had to pull the trucks back in and unload." He stressed the last word with a deep baritone and grinned like a happy pumpkin. Of the things he yammered on about, I wished he would add a bit about how to get through a day without going batty in the brain or how to please my parents without much effort. Despite my efforts to whistle away the hours, to give it my all, the job sucked. My shoulders ached and my mind had too much room to roam. The constant buzz of machines, when not grating on my every nerve, lulled me into a stupor. I had heard pleasant fantasies of ammonia leaks and faulty freezing mechanisms and having to send workers home early. I prayed for one of these fantasies to bust reality open.

"Rotten stock, you know," he said, mock-serious again.

"Where's Wayne?"

"Why?"

"I want to ask him."

"You can't do that." His pupils grew dime-sized again.

By testing his credibility, I'd crossed a line, ruined his fun.

"Why not? He wasn't the one contaminating the product."

Paul went back to his batch and dials. I threw bars in boxes. Ned and his football-squad dreams, slapped the tape.

At six, Ned and I got ten minutes respite. At eight, we got thirty minutes freedom in the yard for lunch. I bolted for the side door to catch the last minutes of daylight. Kevin was on the weathered picnic bench. His slender thighs widened at the place where they met the table's edge. His booted feet dangled near the dirt and grass. "You're still here?" He lit a cigarette and held the pack out to me. He had worked at the factory the summer before and was back for more.

"Same as you. No thanks."

"Why don't you come to the bar tonight?" His eyes weren't on my eyes, but lower. He pulled long on his cigarette, his narrow cheeks caving even more.

I crossed my arms. "What bar?"

"*The* bar," he said, as if I should have already known.

"Not old enough." I looked at him. He wasn't bad looking. His beady brown eyes fit his lean, ruddy face. He had a swaggering kind of confidence, which would come off better without the white hairnet on his head.

"Everyone's old enough at this bar." He smashed his cigarette into the picnic table and hopped off. "How old are you, anyway?"

"Nineteen."

"You don't look nineteen." He drew something from his pocket, ripped a plastic wrapper open, and took a big bite. "Oatmeal cream pie," he said with a mouthful, answering my silent question. He shoved the remaining third into his mouth. "Think about it," he said. "I'm there most nights."

Through the glass door, I watched him shove another pie into his gob, then jab his timecard into the clock. Fuck. I hadn't punched out. I had to find Wayne. And just as I was edging off his shit list.

Wayne smiled like I was his five-year-old daughter. He initialed the card. "Try not to forget next time."

"I won't."

I was back at Machine Four a mere twenty seconds and Paul was at my side. "What was that about? With Kevin?"

"You're a nosy fuck, you know that?"

"Of course. Now tell me."

"You were right," I said, referring to the other night when Kevin had approached me three times. Each time when I was on tape duty. He stood close to me, closer than Paul or Wayne or Joyce had ever stood. His cologne hadn't mixed well with the aroma of strawberry Crunch Bars. And he was away from his station. Kevin was a boxer, which meant the full, retail boxes of Trix Pops, Crunch Bars, Yoplait Yogurt Pops, and other types from eight machines traveled to his area, which he bundled product into sleeves, shrink-wrapped, and sent to the freezer for more packaging and then pick-up. When the boxer didn't keep up, the conveyor belts jammed, pops and bars melted, dripping onto the walking mat. Anyone unfortunate to be standing on the mat during a jam would be hit with cold, colorful cream-shit.

Kevin had handed me an open box of Crunch Bars. "Your boxes aren't sealing."

"Huh." I eyed the box, slapped another tongue over the flaps.

His lanky stick-figured self strolled back to control central.

When I told Wayne, he couldn't find anything wrong with the red tape, with the boxes, or the conveyor belt. Second time I called, Wayne screwed up his face and shook his head. Third time, he didn't show. He thought I was fucking with him, girl crying wolf.

"You were right," I told Paul. "He was flirting."

"He's getting it on with Missy." It sounded like a warning.

"Who's Missy?"

"The bleach blonde with the roots on Two."

"How do you know?"

He grinned like a little boy just given a new toy.

At the end of the workday, after midnight, I was tired. A tired I had not known before. Like half my blood had been sucked from me. I couldn't imagine sitting in a bar, talking, laughing. Who had the energy? I didn't want to be out, but I couldn't sleep, either. My muscles throbbed, and I was nasty sore. I twitched when I lay in bed.

"Get settled already!" Michelle yelled.

"I'm trying."

"Try harder. It's bad enough you wake me up at one in the morning every night."

I shifted again.

"Work can't be that bad."

"Want to trade places? Give it a whirl?"

"You made your own fucking bed."

When I closed my eyes, ice cream bars advanced from every direction. My hands spasmed. I shot out of bed, wishing someone would rub my shoulders and massage my temples. Michelle turned her back to me. I thought of Derrick and his Incredible Hulk hands grinding me into dough. I thought of my mom who worked all night and slept half the day and still kept my dad in clean clothes and fed and happily fucked. I thought of the well-worn movie theatre in Marietta where I'd gotten a job, a place nothing like the factory's sanitized steel. The theatre played retro films and new releases, pornos on request, practically anything for special engagements, and war films and documentaries. The owner, a crusty old guy with a yellowing beard and a pronounced limp, used to tell me stories about Vietnam and war and how disappointing life is.

Unable to sleep, I went to the living room and turned the TV on, the sound low. Infomercials and *M*A*S*H* reruns. Next to the tube on a shelf of the entertainment center was a photograph, one of the few framed, not stowed away in a trunk in the attic. A summer shot. Mom in a swimsuit. Dad in trunks. They were riding a toy train around a small pond. She was leaning forward into him, her cheek resting on the back of his glistening shoulder. He was slender and smiling grandly as he pulled the T-bar to propel the train. He had a full head of hair. They were young. My age or just older. When I looked at their faces I didn't see the early lovers they used to be. I didn't see vigor. That must be a trick time likes to play.

Having finally dozed off, I was still on the sofa in the morning when my dad was getting ready for work. Dressed only in blue-gray shorts, his gut protruded painfully in front of him. There was no trace of the figure he cut twenty years ago. Michelangelo couldn't score away and retrieve the young body.

"What are you doing on the couch? Your bed not good enough anymore?"

I told him about the spasms and not being able to sleep.

"That's nothing," he said, offering no sympathy. He always had it worse. "When I first started at the PO as a clerk, I had to sit on a stool and stick mail twelve hours straight."

"You had lunch and breaks."

"Nope."

"It was a cushy government job."

He hated when I implied anything soft about his job. He, after all, had walked miles in the rain, his left foot throbbing angrily with gout. He hated the grind as much as I did and had been at it twenty years longer, but he had mouths to feed and bills to pay. There was something to say for that. He was allowed some pride, but hell if I was going to give it to him.

"Then, once I'd learn a zip, they'd fling me over to a new one and I'd have to start all over again."

"That's tough, Dad, real tough."

"Watch the sarcasm. Knowing zips inside-out kept you in diapers and in school." He shot me a look so hard I couldn't remember the last time he smiled.

"I didn't need 'em when I was four," I said, trying to keep it light.

His jaw still set, he played along. "Talk to your mother about that one. She stopped breast feeding you yet?"

"A year ago."

"About time. When do you get paid?"

"Next Friday."

"Why not this Friday?"

"Haven't worked a full two weeks."

"I want to see that money soon as you cash that check."

"*I* want to see that money. See if it's really worth these aching hands."

"Couch. Bed. You've got choices now. Try the streets. No skin off my teeth. That'll teach you it's worth it."

Man, he turned it on quick. And often. So often I was beginning to think he'd never really kick me out. He could have done so ages ago. Still, there was something behind his threats I didn't like, something that twisted around inside me, firmly squeezing at the fattest tube in my gut.

9

During the first two weeks, new employees usually gained five to ten pounds from sampling the product, which we weren't allowed to do but did anyway because no one cared. We didn't even get a tsk. Most of the managers had worked up from packer to operator to manager, so they knew what being low on the pole felt like. The thought of eating the sugary cream sickened me. I knew just where and how it came to be, which was from powdered, dusty mixes in plastic bags in cardboard boxes. I managed to avoid adding extra pounds to my belly.

One afternoon in the break room, others sucking on Popsicles, I was content with a peanut butter and jelly sandwich when Jeremiah, the freezer man, handed me a paper he had written. He didn't stay long because he was dressed in Carhartt coveralls and the outside temp registered ninety-two degrees. He didn't like to have to strip down and dress back up. A theology student at a seminary in Indiana, Jeremiah somehow thought me a kindred spirit because I had gone to a religiously affiliated school. We had had a couple of conversations the first week. Now he wouldn't leave me alone.

The paper was twenty-eight pages. I counted "Jesus" nine times in the first paragraph. "If you'd like, we can talk about it over dinner. But I think you'll find my argument that Jesus, having lived in what's now the Middle East, roaming deserts and whatnot, could not possibly have been white. He had to have darker pigmentation to have survived that climate. It's evolution, really. The body adapts. There's no way he looked like that Swedish guy who played him in *The Greatest Story Ever Told*." He paused, eagerly waiting for me to contribute. When I didn't, he rocked back on his heels and said, "My treat, of course."

"Hmm," I said, noncommittally, pretending to read. I'd been hammered with enough Catholicism to know I'd feel unbearably guilty if I told him to fuck off. "Let me read this before we make plans." So long as you weren't caught, lying produced less guilt than telling the truth.

"Okay great." The Abominable Freezerman waddled back to his icebound lair.

I stuffed his paper in my locker and returned to Four.

"Summarize this in fifty words or less," I told Michelle when I got home. She was uncharacteristically planted three feet from the television, ruining her eyes. I held Jeremiah's paper out, but Michelle didn't flinch. "It's a college paper," I said seductively.

"You flunked." She liked to remind me of the obvious.

"Not mine. Some guy's from the factory. " The TV screen shone a panel of blue. "What are you watching?" I dropped the paper in her lap.

"I'm setting the VCR for Dad since he refuses to learn how himself. What's in it for me?"

"Personal edification."

Normally Michelle read anything she could glide her eyes over, but getting something from me made the glide hitch and stutter to a halt. "You know your ABCs," she said. "You summarize the thing." She pushed a series of buttons on a remote.

"Make sure you have it start before the show. You know how he hates to miss the beginning," Mom said, coming in from the kitchen. She took the paper from Michelle's lap. I wondered how she could read with the black bags under her eyes getting in the way. She forged ahead though. "What is this? The first paragraph's all about Jesus."

"Jesus the philosopher? Jesus H. Christ on a bike with Muhammad and Buddha on scooters? Jesus Jones?"

"Michelle," Mom warned.

"No, the standard Biblical Jesus who has been misunderstood for centuries," I said, ignoring Michelle and risking a fight at the same time.

"You girls. Haven't those Catholic schools taught you anything?"

Michelle and I shared a sisterly we've-got-secrets-galore look. Mom didn't know half of what Catholic schoolgirls got themselves into.

Michelle raised an eyebrow. She looked at me and asked, "What makes you think I'd be into this?"

"You're into everything."

"Looks like a fine paper. You should both read it," Mom ventured, handing it to me. "Will we be meeting this Jeremy fella?"

"Did you read that first paragraph? He's arguing that Jesus was a black man," I said, not caring what Jesus looked like.

"What about Derrick?" Michelle asked.

"Who's Derrick?" Mom, trying to be a part of our lives.

"What do you know about it?" I asked, feeling the bricks stack inside me.

"I know he calls here," she said. "Sometimes collect."

"It's probably true that Jesus had a darker complexion. Cleopatra was the same, right? You know, when I was your age things were different. Any boy used to have to meet my parents before *anything* happened. Before he could call, before we could go to the movies, even before we could go to church together. It would have been different if we'd lived in a big city. Everything was changing. Civil Rights and the Feminist Movement." She became conscious that maybe she shouldn't continue.

"And?" Michelle and I said in unison. We both saw the potential. Our parents were still in their twenties in 1969.

"Then I no longer got their permission." Mom twirled a lock of hair between her fingers, twenty-something again and discovering things about herself she never thought possible.

"Why didn't you get their permission?" Michelle prodded, futilely. Whatever lesson my mother was trying to impart was forgotten as the thrill of that time rushed through her.

"The world opened up in many ways. Vietnam was going on. Protests. Kent State shootings. Music. America was upside down and I'd just met your father."

Vietnam made me think of Yellow and Rudy in Marietta and what they saw and did at my age.

"And none of that mattered. I mean, it did, but it didn't."

Interrupting our female bonding session, Dad's "Nancy!" bellowed from their bedroom.

"Coming! So whether it's Derrick or Jeremy, you just take those fingernails and scratch out what little place you can for yourself."

"So the moral is, love conquers all?" Michelle and her perception. I was thinking about my fingernails. After years of chewing, I'd finally started clipping them properly. They were straight and short. Not much scratching could be done.

"Love's never enough, but it helps," Mom replied and jumped up to find Dad.

When I thought about my parents, love wasn't a word that came to mind. Servitude did. Compromise. Beige. But love? That deep, tender feeling of affection and solicitude or that crazy intense sexual passion? Neither of these applied properly to what went on between my parents. There was a time when I thought I would have done anything for Courtney. That was the closest I'd come to love. I supposed love was supposed to soften the hard edges of the world. I couldn't see it doing that. And then there was that watery love of

Jesus—spiritual and selfless and a model for humanity. I crinkled the paper. I didn't want to experience Jeremiah's mush. "What do you want?" I asked Michelle. "For reading the paper."

She scoffed, answer enough. Money facilitated any type of exchange between us. She wasn't a money-dragon like my dad, a capitalist at heart. She was pragmatic with her time, wanting to read what she wanted to read. I wouldn't bother with the paper. Eventually Jeremiah would stop coming around when I quite obviously ducked into the bathroom each time I saw him.

I gave up and went to the kitchen to find dishes crowding the moss-colored Corian countertop. Dishes, another condition of my parole. Doing them by hand was a drag, but an inescapable one because my parents didn't own a dishwasher. My parents' simplicity wasn't a deliberate Thoreauan choice, having something to do with sucking marrow. Their simplicity was born of middle class necessity. Private school for the kids or steam-cleaned dishes for us? I understood their reasoning, but I would have given up a year of Catholic school and plaid uniforms and selling chocolate bars for the ease of loading and emptying as opposed to scraping and scouring and drying and stacking. But in order to live and eat under their roof, I had to fulfill my duties. Minions would have done a better job, taken some pride in their work, and cost less, but I scrubbed and scoured, trusting my newly adept packer's and dish-soap hands would be soft as a dolphin's nose. Ten minutes into a scrubbing groove, Michelle reached in front of me and switched the water to cold before filling a glass.

"Excuse you."

She drank, staring at me through the glass with the stone eyes of a gargoyle. She refilled the glass and drank again, again staring eerily at me, a small sisterly death wish in the air. It was going to be a great weekend.

Saturday, more dishes. The dried, crusty whites of eggs caking the lips of plates. Rain pelting the roof. Much needed rain, but damn did it make the house stuffy. By Sunday I couldn't bear it. The house was small and getter smaller. Michelle occupied the bedroom with her battery of books and reticence. On the couch, gut jutting like a beached leviathan, my dad flipped from the *Grand Ole Opry* back to ESPN. His thumb linked to a satellite connection, he pressed the button at the exact instant a commercial came on. He dozed off, snoring immediately. When I tried to slide the clicker out of his kung-fu grip, he twitched, muttering, "I'm awake. I'm awake," and clamped down harder on the remote. Half a second later, he barked another snore.

I thought of calling Courtney, but couldn't bear losing an eye to her hair. Plus, everything felt weird between us and she was probably busy being naked with Jake. My stomach turned as I started to wonder if I was jealous. I'd been thinking of her a lot. Was I hoping that Courtney and I could be something more than just girls who were friends. Girlfriends? Was I hoping to drop into a new layer of intimacy? I couldn't be sure. I unthinkingly chewed my lower lip as my head got light and airy. What I did know was that I wanted to tell her more about Hailey. That after Hailey vandalized the mall, she vandalized me. Not that day, but later. She drew all over my body, making her mark in a thousand different pens and fonts. Within me, she unleashed confusion and doubt and pleasure and guilt and chaos. And all the while seeing, feeling my own body, for the first time, I started to think, yeah, what we're doing is art. Yeah, I'm beautiful. Hailey couldn't be broken. She didn't have the least self-doubt hang-ups. She was daring and open. She talked about everything. She was curious about everything. She had surplus energy I didn't have. I asked her why she wrote on walls, plastic humans, in bathrooms and why she wrapped mannequins like mummies.

"Lots of reasons. Ever heard that expression 'read the writing on the wall'? It's a Biblical thing. Book of Daniel or something. A mysterious hand appeared and wrote on the wall while one of the kings was eating. That night the king was killed. So the writing is a warning."

"Of what?"

"I don't know. I just want them to wake up."

She also liked the rush. The rush when you do things you're not supposed to. The charge and the feeling of power, like a big secret issuing forth. You against the world. You, you, you.

I liked the feeling, too, after her certainty wore down my fear and nervousness.

We hung out almost every day for a month, doing things like vandalizing bathrooms or leaving cryptic notes in the pages of books at libraries and stores. Lying on the red comforter on the floor of her room, we listened to Run DMC and Bad Brains cassettes and Hailey told me how much she hated Whitney Houston and her blue eye shadow but loved her curly hair. I got red-faced and warm when Hailey would switch cassettes and play 2 Live Crew and have me tug strands of her hair through a plastic cap and told me the pain felt good. She made me feel nervous and special at the same time. We stole cigarettes and Mad Dog from the corner store and smoked and drank in the woods behind the bowling alley. For whatever unspoken reason, we steered clear of each other during the school day. We only had one class together and opposite lunch periods. Still, I felt awkward sitting in class, like there was a spotlight on me and everyone knew I was doing bad things with the weird girl who talked too much in class to everyone's annoyance.

And then there was the other rush.

"You ever kiss a girl? It's hot. In seventh grade I used to go out in the woods with these kids from the neighborhood and play spin-the-bottle. The rule was, no matter who the bottle pointed to, you had to kiss. French kiss for at least thirty seconds. I don't know if the rule had to be that strict. It was really creepy one time when

Jimmy Hayden and his brother Kyle were there. Jimmy spun it and it landed on Kyle. And they kissed. They had to. We made them. And then, when Kyle spun, the bottle pointed to Jimmy. As if once weren't enough. Neither of them came back after that day. Kyle's in juvie now, keeps getting himself into trouble. I think the whole thing really fucked him up. Anyway, there were a couple girls there that I kissed a few times. I liked kissing them so much better than kissing boys. There was always something I didn't like about kissing boys. Like their breath smelled. Or their lips were cracked. But kissing girls? Wow. When it was my turn to spin, I'd always try to spin it just right so it'd land on Erica. My body ached for her kiss. She had full lips and wore tight shirts. Like she *liked* her body, you know? I never thought too much of my crush at the time. I just knew I liked kissing girls. I still looked at boys. It's only been in the last year or so that I've come fully to own my identity. Lesbian, you know? Sounds so much better than dyke. It's foreign. Erotic. Exotic. The word, I mean. Anyway, I'm in good company. There are lots of lesbians. K. D. Lang, some tennis player. Madonna gets it on with girls and boys. Gertrude Stein. Virginia Woolf. Emily Dickinson. Djuna Barnes."

She was always talking.

I wasn't a talker. I never thought I had much to say. But, that summer, when there was no one around, when Courtney spent all her time in Jake's crotch, I wanted to talk. I wanted to tell her more about Hailey. I hadn't told anyone else a thing about Hailey and was beginning to think things disappeared if you didn't acknowledge them. Experiences became a dream, a passing one-night stand, foggy in the particulars. I decided Courtney was out with Jake on another lust-filled bender. Escaping into a stupor was so tempting. Sucking on a joint of stupidity.

Movies were a steady friend.

Dad heard the car keys jingle. "What do you think you're doing?"

"Taking the car."

"Think again."

"C'mon, I got a job."

He considered this. "Not good enough."

"You know, getting back on track and all."

"Put the keys down."

He was such an asshole. I threw the keys on the coffee table.

"Walking's good for you. Get home early."

"I don't start until four tomorrow." I was whining, something I hadn't done in at least a month. "And I'd be able to get home earlier if I had a car."

"Have that girlfriend of yours pick you up."

There it was again: *girlfriend*. The syllables sounded foreign, like a hard Russian word jammed into an English phrase. I didn't say anything. I didn't want to invite a discussion. I didn't want to debate Courtney or Hailey with him. I dismissed Meg O'Connor from my mind, too, though talking about her would cover sexual confusion and what I did at school. Just what I wanted to talk about with my dad.

O'Connor's was one of the few classes I attended faithfully second semester. I wasn't particularly enamored with the Greeks and their boy-love, but I was drawn to O'Connor and her deadpan, ironic lectures. As if in a trance at the front of the room, she walked from wall to wall, either looking at the window, not out of it, but at the glass itself, or down at her feet, at her pink toenails. She always, always wore flip-flops, walking her meditative path, her black mid-neck corkscrew hair bouncing in slow motion as she discoursed with herself. "Today, feminist philosophers do philosophy. We'll cover three issues. One, the myth of the detached observer." O'Connor couldn't have been more detached nor any less observant. "Two, feminist social critique, wherein we lambast oppressive institutions." Like the one that provided the means for her pink nail polish. "And three, feminist ethics, the inclusion of emotion into ethical decision making." I'd listen to her lulling voice and hidden jokes, and inevitably ravishment scenarios would spring fully formed into my head. The lost teachers opened themselves to daily fantasy, chastisement, and even sometimes, occasional admiration. I knew I'd never teach.

If I had told Dad about O'Connor disrobing in my mind as she walked the classroom, sliding out of her linen pants to reveal a pink thong that matched her toenails, would it have brought us closer? Would he have let me take the car? Would he have liked the quiet librarian who let her hair down and fulfilled with equal vigor every fantasy of her twenty-three students?

I turned the handle on the door, trying to leave Courtney and Hailey and Meg tucked quietly away.

"Hey!"

"Hey, what?" I wasn't going to make it out of the house alive.

"A horse walks into a bar. Bartender looks at him, says, 'Why the long face?'"

With the door open, the warm night beckoned.

"Heard that one at work today."

"You work with a wild bunch."

"Don't be late." His eyes were on the TV.

"I'll have the car back before you have to be to work," I said, half-serious, but playing it straight. With one foot on the welcome mat, I was almost free.

"You're not funny." He glowered at me, then checked the table for the keys. "And you're letting the cold air out."

No dishwasher, but central air. What did Whitman write about contradictions and multitudes?

Outside, naked, philosophizing Meg joined me on my walk to the theatre, her pink nails glowing in the dark.

O'Connor proved more cognizant of her students than I had suspected. She paused mid-trance, mid-lecture one afternoon and barged in, fully clothed, on one of my fantasies. "Lee Bauer," she'd said, "enlighten us with your thoughts. You have a dreamy look on your face."

I was struck dumb for three reasons: she knew my name; possibly she had a window on what was playing in my head, a mind-reader that one; and three because I couldn't see my face to know why she'd stopped class to ask.

"What look?" I said, almost adding that pedagogical theorists should consider the inclusion of mirrors in the classroom, but didn't because that would've betrayed my fantasy and polished the window she already had into it. My face was already red enough, and I was trying to become one with the hard desk.

"See me after class," she said, striding right back into her lecture. "Moving into Irigaray, who deconstructs how women have been conceived throughout philosophical history, we learn that woman is other, less than fully real, less than and/or the opposite of Being. Irigaray considers Freud, who saw female sexuality as deficient, as lacking…"

Mild panic swept through me. Instructors had pulled me aside before but only to warn me that I was in terrible straits and about to fail their classes. I wasn't failing O'Connor's class. I had squeaked out two papers on the Dialogues of Plato and Greek Mythology and was planning to write the final research paper. I was considering The Myth of Er, my thesis being that many people are called to do nothing. The accomplishments of ninety-nine percent of Americans would support my argument.

After the class cleared out, O'Connor sat in the desk in front of me. She shifted her body sideways to face me and crossed her right leg over her left, pointing her pink nails my way. "Don't be alarmed, Lee. I just wanted to run something by you, hear your thoughts. I think it's about time this university offered greater support to fifty-four percent of its student population. I would like to start a women's group on campus. Your role would be to petition the student government and administrative services."

"Sounds like a lot of work."

"Listen, Lee, you're a bright kid, a bright young woman. Your papers are astute. You just need to get more involved to keep you on track. What better way than this?"

I sunk in my seat. I hated being called a kid and told what I needed. Besides that, O'Connor couldn't have had more than ten years on me and her big pink toe was beginning to annoy me.

I ground my molars. "I'll think about it."

"Don't think too long. Your sisters are depending on you."

Sisters? I was a TV junkie in the seventies and passing through puberty during the Reagan years. According to plan, I'd now be graduating as a complacent college kid sometime in the nineties. I hadn't thought anything about women's issues since Geraldine Ferraro was on the ticket for the White House, and even then I didn't think much about *that* other than, Huh, cool. There was no way I was going to step into Meg O'Connor's path and follow her into righteousness.

"Sisters. Right," I said, grabbing my books, and moving for the door. O'Connor's class soon became one I "got involved" in avoiding, notwithstanding losing my fantasy candy and the possibility of getting into her good graces. I couldn't help wondering why the hell she'd chosen me. I was not a good feminist, and I was very lazy.

Before O'Connor, I'd never given women's concerns or politics much thought. Her corkscrew hair and fine feet mesmerized me enough to strip her down and engage in my own version of sexual politics, but then she had to go and ruin her class by focusing on me. I tried to lose interest and not think about her anymore, which was hard. For some reason I couldn't *not* think about her. After Hailey, I hadn't thought much about sex, let alone concocted elaborate fantasies. But O'Connor ignited my imagination, sexual and otherwise. If nothing else, the fantasies were fun and passed the time. They didn't mean one thing or another, only that my imagination worked. Or so I tried to tell myself.

I considered what telling my dad a snippet of such intimate details might be like. I'd be forced to watch his pale face shift into some nameless emotion I wanted to avoid. My dad was, after all, the same man who cancelled cable for a month after walking in on Michelle and me watching *The Hunger*. Michelle and I had been sucked into the show by the utter adolescent curiosity about violence and sex and other worlds. Plus, I was just starting to listen to David Bowie cassettes. I thought it might be fun, just for a second, to feel a bubble of power and see the utter shock on his face, when I revealed a small fraction of just what goes through my head.

Across the street from the Secor Frische's where Mom was undoubtedly serving coffee to high school punks, loomed Showcase Cinemas with its five theatres, wide, cushy seats, buttery popcorn, and overpriced shitty Hollywood blockbusters. Showcase was nothing like the theatre in Marietta with its thin, fraying and stained carpet laid over cold concrete floors, its musty seats and scratchy sound system. The crusty old owner wore what looked like pee-stained facial hair. Yellowbeard. I'd started calling him that in a fit of inspiration after he'd called me Kid for three weeks despite my attempts to get him to use my actual name. He was born in West Virginia and had settled in Ohio's oldest city after the war because he liked the brick streets and wanted to find the tunnels of the Underground Railroad, rumored to run from the Ohio River over to the Ankorage House.

"Fucked thing is," he said, "whenever I dig into the ground, it's damn hard. So any tunnels, even ten feet long, without the right 'quipment would take months. I also wonder 'bout a few things. Like, if there are tunnels, where'd they put the dirt so no one'd see? And how'd they breathe down there? And how'd they stop the wall from cavin' in? I've seen war. I been in tunnels and foxholes. They're small. They choke you. You get in 'em as a last resort."

For as long as I'd known him, I couldn't ever quite tell when he was messing with me.

Yellow—I'd shortened the moniker in a moment of stoned brilliance because it sounded funny to me—played art films, requested triple Xers, and the very occasional new release. He'd put up anything for special engagements, even family-birthday or holiday-blurry home video. He had a fondness for documentaries too.

"Ohio River divided slave states from the free. That's another reason I didn't go back to Wheeling. History. Fucking America."

Yellow, paler than goose feathers, claimed his great-great grandmother was a runaway slave, which helped explain his obsessions. So did Vietnam. He was a borderline conspiracy theorist. Mostly I liked the guy, though he had breath that could suffocate a sewer rat. We had a silent agreement: he never asked why I wasn't in class. I never asked him to brush his tongue.

"Kid, welcome back!" he'd say, leaning toward me over the counter. I put my hand to my nose as if scratching an itch. In fact, I was trying to block the stench.

"What's playing today?"

Sometimes he'd wink and say, "Something real special just for you." In other words, the same two films that had been running for the previous two weeks. By the fourth visit to the theatre, I'd learned to ignore any insinuations in his tone. Yellow had his theories and perversions, but he was harmless, all talk. Or so I believed then.

One class I'd succeeded in passing first semester was English. I explicated John Donne's divine poems in a manner that the teacher found "compelling and insightful." He was a hippie-turned-prof who hit on me eight times in the first two months, averaging one hit per week. Like Yellow, he didn't seem to care that I wasn't in class, even his. Not only did we bump into each other on campus, the days I did emerge from the dorm, we also bumped into each other at the theatre.

"Shouldn't you be in class, Bauer?"

"Should, Jim," I answered. Though he insisted his students call him by his first name, he consistently called us by our last names.

"Why aren't you?" He pushed his black plastic Buddy Holly glasses further up his nose. Had he used contacts, he would've been a handsome guy. The glasses ruined his face.

"*Terms of Endearment* is playing for a second week." Untrue, *Rain Man* was. I wanted to catch his reaction.

"You must have missed that one in the eighties."

"Yeah, considering I was still in diapers then." Also not true, but I liked to keep him guessing.

"At least I know where to find you when you're not in my class."

Whenever I made him think about the difference between our ages, which wasn't really all that much, he'd cut the talk short and scurry off in his corduroy jacket with fraying blue elbow patches. He was so affected.

The other class I passed that semester was math. Not much to say about that one. I can add. Second semester successes, if you can call them that, were Bs in intros to philosophy and psychology.

Thinking of Yellow and school and my failure, I could feel my face sour. I tried swallowing and wiggling my cheeks. The ridiculous exercise didn't help.

I stepped up to the cashier table at Showcase. "*Field of Dreams*, I guess." I dug in my pocket for my life savings.

"Just one?"

I looked behind me. Emptiness.

"Yes. Just one."

The cashier slid the ticket across the counter, careful not to touch my hand, afraid my solitude was contagious. People in Toledo don't do things alone. They couple.

In the dark theatre, gum glued my feet to the floor. With my shirt-sleeves pulled over my hands and my arms resting on their supports, I settled into an anonymous seat in a middle row, ready for two-plus glorious hours of escape, my final cigarette before the factory firing squad riddled me with holes.

I couldn't escape.

Kevin Costner's boyish face and snaggle-toothed innocence mocked me. The tall Iowa corn razed to a field of dust so that he could be reunited for a game of catch with his father. The audience was quiet with couples sitting closer than usual, mesmerized by a man's foolish pursuit of a dream. I became acutely aware of the empty seats adjacent to me and the lack of Courtney, who possibly wasn't lost and drifting as I'd thought, who hadn't flaked, but just maybe had ridden easily into the next phase of her life, following her own dream, whatever that was, doing something I hadn't yet done and wasn't sure why I couldn't. She had ridden into a fashion statement that said something about her inner life, even loosened it up some, and I hadn't changed an external thing, but was shifting like mad inside. To top matters, I, feeling utterly and ultimately alone, was in a dark theatre watching a movie about a guy who builds a baseball field. I watched the movie through because it wasn't terrible enough to prompt me to leave, but all I could think about, aside from the sticky floor and the stale popcorn and my parents' disappointment, was the character on the screen who had a good life and a wife and brother and several ghosts watching out for him, whereas I had a fine life and two empty seats watching me.

10

"I'm moving to Alaska," came the words from Courtney's mouth. No hello, no hug, not even a nod. In the four-by-four foyer at the factory between doors she didn't crack a smile to let me in on the joke. She may as well have just punched me in the stomach. "Come with me," she implored.

The air was stale and the people in the break room were watching us through the window. "Let's go outside."

We walked around the side toward the picnic table. Sprawled across the top were the blonde and a few others, staring toward the sky. One of them pulled on a cigarette, lighting the air like a fire-fly. Courtney and I cut across the street and into an alley between houses. We stood opposite each other, leaning against the back walls of strangers' garages.

"You're my best friend and I think it'll be great."

"Really? Really?" was all I could push from the absence in my mouth.

"Yeah." She nodded emphatically. I was unconvinced. All of sudden I felt like Courtney was just someone I used to know, a classmate I might make awkward conversation with at a reunion ten years from now.

"I feel out of place here," she said. She lit a cigarette and tried to run her fingers through her mangled hair. "I have to get out. I just have to." She waved her lit stick through the air, looking left and right as if anticipating someone she didn't want to see. "It's too small here. I'm bored. I'm young. I want to see things. Travel. Don't you want to?"

Sometimes Toledo felt small and stagnant, but that had nothing to do with the town. Not feeling compelled to hop around the country and meet people from different places, I couldn't relate to what she was saying. People were the same anywhere and I had enough trouble fitting into my own skin.

"I don't know. I've never really thought about leaving and I don't have any money. You're probably just going through a funk of some kind. Wait a while." I wanted to touch her arm, relax her disturbed state.

"I'm dead serious, Lee. I'm leaving today. It's unbearable here, at home. Ever since I quit basketball. My parents. My brother. There's nothing here for me." Courtney inhaled long and hard.

"Why not just go back to school early? You liked it there." I wondered if I'd suffered a head trauma, I was so confused. "Why Alaska of all places?"

"Come with me. Come with us."

"Us? Are you talking about Jake?"

"No, no. Billy, this guy at school. He's on his way. We're gonna get fishing jobs." She paused, considering something. "He's really funny. You'd like him." She carried on her appeal. "Look around, Lee, flat, boring. Superstores and shopping malls. I need a change. *You* need a change. For chrissakes you're wearing a hairnet."

"It's sanitary," I said.

"This is a small town with small minds. Alaska has mountains and freedom and simplicity. A totally different way to live."

"You're delusional. It's not going to be as easy or as fun as you think. I thought college was going to be a grand palace, but it turned out to be a shack in the woods. Don't let your imagination override common sense. There are bears and burly, mean men and cold and darkness. I hear it's so cold there! Seriously, what's going on? Are you pregnant?" I couldn't read her at all. Only her agitation and frenzied eyes. She wasn't telling me something. I thought maybe I should go with her, if only to get three hours out of town, realize our mistake, and turn back.

"Nothing's wrong. If I don't leave now, I'll get stuck. You're stuck. You're so fucking stuck." She looked at the garages in the alley around us, shadowing us. "You're working in a factory. You'll end up another mass-produced product like the rest of the humanoids in this town."

Everyone thought the novelty items came out the same. The Icy Pops. The sandwiches. The Crunch Bars. It wasn't true. The composition of any two vanilla Crunch Bars wasn't ever the same. The quality control people spoke of acceptable bandwidths of variation.

"We've gotta take a lesson from Roy. Anything you want, you gotta go for. C'mon, come with me. It'll be like old times. I know we've been a little off lately. I've been wondering what's gotten into you. You take everything so seriously these days. It's time to loosen up and make some memories."

Her agitation reminded me of junior year just before I got expelled. She was on my porch, frantic, shaking, couldn't get a word out. Her brother had killed himself in the Chambers' garage with a sawed-off shotgun. Courtney found him. No one else home, she ran immediately to my house, four miles in sandals. I was the calm, the axis of her spin. I called her mother and the police and stayed with her. Sometime since, I'd been pushed out of her circumference. I didn't know how to get back in, or if I wanted to. She didn't remember things the way I did. Details were lost. I was beginning to think we were incompatible. High school bound us in ways unavailable to us now. Our individual lives weren't tethered by nuns or drugs or school or even Toledo.

"You don't want me with you. I'd just be in the way."

"You won't be, you'll see. Yeah, there's the thing with Billy, but he's really funny. We'll find you a woman up there or more likely a really effeminate guy, one or the other. Come on, just like old times. It'll be great."

"Do I have to grow dreads?"

She groaned and looked away.

"I don't want to go back to who I was." Though I wasn't sure that girl was much different than the one standing before her.

"You won't. We won't. We're brand-new."

"What would I do?"

"Chop the heads off of fish! What the fuck does it matter? We'll figure it out. Whatever you do won't be any worse than whatever the hell you do in there."

"Bloody fish heads versus ice cream?"

"You know what I mean."

I did know. I started to consider if I could get home, pack a bag, and sneak away without a blow-up. "Can't we go tomorrow? There's no way I'd get out of the house tonight without someone stopping me."

"Now or never."

"Who's car?"

"Billy's."

"This is insane."

"That's what makes it brilliant! When we're eighty, we'll look back on this and laugh at how stupid we were."

"Who is this Billy? What's his deal?"

"You'll see. He's got a little bit of a troubled soul, but he's great."

"How are we paying for gas and food?"

"So you're in? We've got the gas and food covered. We've got it all covered until we get there. Just don't worry about it."

I stood, weighing it all in my mind. Courtney and I close again sounded great. Seeing America. Feeling a part of something. Long days in a hot car. Courtney's lumpy dreads falling like dead vines over the back of the front seat. My parents' fury. A strange, funny boy named Billy belching out the window. Car sickness. Courtney and the belcher fucking in a tent by the side of the road. Me watching Courtney and miles of corn. Me wanting her to see me and want me. Oceans of America. Courtney and the belcher disappearing to another town in Alaska. My parents' worry. The money I owed them. Some mountains and small towns. Some laughs. My body aching with stiffness from hours in the car. Disappointment. Regret.

Then I saw clearly Courtney's impatience and vacant eyes. I was standing directly in front of her, feeling myself fade, my body becoming transparent. Soon I'd blend with the white wall of the garage and she wouldn't be in Toledo to notice even that.

"Come on, already."

She kept throwing the idea at me offhandedly, like it popped into her head and popped out of her mouth before she thought it through. The invitation was a surprise, given the distance I felt between us. I hadn't imagined that she'd still want me around to that extent. Maybe she did. Maybe she wanted some part of Toledo with her. I'd never considered living anywhere else, at least not seriously. My parents and sister were in Toledo, my memories and my life. For all its flaws, it was home.

"I can't go. As tense as it is at home, leaving's too much of a fuck-you to my parents." Though Courtney was lost to me, I liked knowing she was around if I needed her. I liked that I was near if she needed me. Given time, we might pull toward each other again like filings to a magnetic field. She wanted adventure. That was clear. She didn't want to go anywhere, without someone familiar. She must have known I wouldn't go.

"You're going to regret this." She hugged me earnestly and briskly kissed me on the mouth. "I'll send you postcards."

Like that, she was gone, and I was left alone in the alley, back to the wall. Twenty minutes passed. I was supposed to be back from lunch. I was late and I didn't care. They could have my job. The only person I'd been close to, gone. Another ten minutes. Twenty. Once again, all I had was the wall to hold me up.

The last three hours of work ticked by slower than a turtle's crawl. Paul must have sensed my dark mood because he wasn't dashing by between mix loads to tell me something seedy. Even Ned opened his droopy eyelids to peer at me in wonder.

When I got home to the quiet house, I didn't feel like sleeping. The night would be night anyway. TV couldn't calm my bewilderment about Courtney and it couldn't ease the sense of loss in my chest. Maybe she was reaching out to me or more simply just trying to drag me by my hair into whatever tangled mess she had with Billy. I suspected there was something to him. She hadn't mentioned him at all. Drugs. Depression. A sorry home life. There were endless ways a person could be baffled and broken. I imagined she was trying to save him. I could clearly see all the mistakes and mishaps that lay ahead for her and I couldn't do a thing. Like she couldn't do a thing for her brother, then or now. In a time like this I'd have called her to help me sort it out. As things stood, she'd be wrapped around him, an anchor causing them both to sink. I grabbed the phone and went to the front porch.

"Hello?" Derrick whispered, hoarsely, drowsily.

"Were you actually sleeping?"

"Yeah, yeah. I think so. How are you?"

"Courtney left."

Rustling noises came from his end. "Yeah, I know," he said. "Jake's heartbroken."

"Sorry I woke you."

"It's okay. I didn't think you were ever going to call. I'm glad you did."

I hadn't thought I'd call, either, not after that day in the park, but sometimes even a stranger's voice was preferable to the one in my head. Derrick told me all about a new supplement he'd recently tried, one that gave him more energy for a longer workout and also oddly helped him sleep better. I half-listened. The other half imagined Courtney somewhere on some long road across the continent, headed northwest.

11

Punch in.

Punch out.

Punch in.

Punch out.

12

Pinheads was not a swanky, happening place. The air was dense with smoke and the juke played so low the crack of bowling pins being knocked around provided its own rhythm. Two old men were hunched over the bar, planted on stools they'd known all their lives. There was no TV for them to watch and they didn't talk. Still as statues except for the occasional lift of glass to lip. An old pool table, its felt wearing thin, divided the managers and machine operators from the packers. I was still in my whites. Everyone else had changed in the locker room before leaving. Behind the bar, a body-builder with tattooed biceps and a happy patch of chin hair stared impassively at me while his fist twisted a rag in a glass. "How old are you?"

"Twenty-one."

"ID?"

"Lost it down at school last month. Haven't had time to get it replaced." I would be twenty before year's end.

"She's cool, Gus. Works with us at the factory," Kevin said, coming to my aid.

"I can see that from her get-up. What do you want?" He still doubted my age, but was either annoyed by Kevin's thin, smug mug so close or simply didn't care all that much one way or another.

"Vodka tonic."

A solid choice. Gus started pouring.

Kevin introduced me around. Head cocked, the blonde smacked her gum. Her eyes traveled head to toe and back down again, sizing me for a catfight or some kinky three-way. I couldn't be sure. No one was talking. Didn't they have *anything* to say? I sipped my drink, trying to remember why I'd come. Then I remembered: Courtney was gone and Derrick wasn't into me. I had sorrows to drown.

Wayne tugged me over to his table. "I want someone to meet you. Kris, Lee. Lee, Kris. Lee's our star packer on Four," he boasted, showing me off as his prize pet.

On the other side of the pool table, the packers, still not talking, gaped as I sat down in the chair Wayne pulled out for me. I'd crossed a line.

"On Four, huh?" Her voice was deep, almost raspy.

"Kris' been away on vacation," Wayne said. "Factory's not the same without her."

I felt oddly disappointed that she was one of them.

Paul watched us over the upper arc of his glass. "Call her 'College.' Summer money. Once and done. Here and gone." Though he was casting me off in front of Kris, I knew from his gossiping in my ear that he liked me. His tone betrayed a sliver of admiration.

Kris eased back in the wooden chair as if it were her sofa at home. In front of her was a glass of water, out of place amidst the bottles of beer. She didn't seem like a factory clown with rosy cheeks from the cold within, no Midwesterner settling in to practicality as the years settled around her waist and thighs.

"She's one of us. She's a union girl." Joyce tongued her gums. A cluster of empty glasses in front of her. "You like the fact'ry, Lee?" She asked, dropping a syllable.

"It's okay. Pretty mindless."

"Hate it myself, but don't know no different."

I shuddered when I saw myself in her shoes ten years down the road. If this was what the union does to women, I didn't want in.

Her teeth didn't bother me. Her jaundiced face and sagging shoulders did. Her dead eyes did. I was sure the factory had everything to do with how she looked, though from Paul's insinuating words, domestic troubles factored in as well.

"She takes after you," Wayne said to Kris. "Better watch out or she'll have your job soon."

"She *can* have it," she said with an easiness about her, a sense of being comfortable in her clothes. She was thin and strong. Her solid thighs filled her jeans, and her blue tank top revealed the makings of tennis-ball biceps. Could've been a weightlifter or an aerobics instructor. I preferred to see myself in *her* shoes in ten years.

Paul pushed himself from sitting to standing. "Who needs another?"

Hands went up all around except for Kris'. Nobody chided her or gave a second look. She was half-reclined in the chair, in her worn jeans, tank top, sandals, looking around the room, half-listening to the murmur. Her long brownish-blonde hair, blue eyes, buttery, copper tan a stark contrast to the predominant wrinkled, pale skins nearby.

"Kris works second with the rest of us." Wayne finished the swill in his bottle.

I couldn't picture her long hair bunched into a hairnet, and I didn't know what the hell to say. "What machine?"

Being the gentleman he was, Wayne answered for her. "She's not on a machine. We call her a floater. Knows all the machines, so helps out wherever, but isn't management." He kept her in place, below him. Kris smiled at me as Wayne talked. I thought maybe I still had my hairnet on and that was what she was smiling at. I touched my head. Not there.

She was a floater, and I was a flaker.

She must have been Wayne's pet at some point. He was slightly starry-eyed. I drank my drink.

A bit of cream on his upper lip, Kevin twirled a cue stick behind his back. "Hey, I need a partner for pool. You have to break," Kevin said. "I suck at it."

"Get someone else," Missy said. At first I thought she was referring to me, but then she pointed at her table where a girl was leaning heavily into the dark paneling. "Partner's about to pass out."

Missy racked. I stepped up to the cue ball and gave it a jab. The cue cracked the triangle, and three balls found pockets.

"Wow," Kris said. "Watch out."

Then I missed the easiest shot in the world. Kris took my stick and silently pocketed ball after ball. I didn't get to shoot again. Kevin and I stared glumly at the green felt and the solids left on the flat field. Though she hadn't done a thing, Missy gloated.

"Again," Kevin said, grabbing the balls two at time from the undercarriage, lining them up in the wooden triangle.

Missy leaned over the table. Her blonde bangs falling in her face, their black roots shone under the table's bright overhead light. The cue crashed off the right of the apex and plunked into the corner pocket.

"Rack 'em!"

"What are you talking about?"

"Scratch on the break and you lose," I said. I felt a sudden, unfamiliar competitive rage.

"Nooo," Kris said.

"Is there a rule book here?"

"That's ridiculous. A scratch is a scratch."

"Not on the break," I said, looking to Kevin and the blonde for confirmation, which they didn't offer. My voice had risen an octave. I wanted things my way. Being invested in something so trivial felt strange.

"Let's just play it out. The quarters are in."

"Fine by me so long as you know you lost."

Kevin shot and dropped two balls. Up again, Kris didn't miss a shot. She finished off the table, re-racked, and re-broke, sinking several solids.

"You could let the rest of us play," I said.

"Then I wouldn't get to see your scowling face."

"I'm not scowling. I'd just like a chance, is all," I said. I *was* scowling, feeling miffed like a five year-old who wasn't getting her way. First the competitiveness, now this. Who the hell was I?

Kris tapped the cue. The ball bumped three rails, rolling to a stop behind the eight. I had no shot.

"There you go," she said. "You wanted a turn." She smiled wickedly.

Kevin and the blonde were standing next to each other, their elbows touching, watching impassively. The game meant little to them. I took the stick Kris held out to me, tauntingly, and crashed the blue tip into the cue, sending balls whirling around the table. Two solids disappeared. I was inadvertently playing for her team.

"Slop."

"I had no shot." I shrugged, the competitiveness just as quickly smothered by defeat, and handed the stick back to Kris.

"That's not very sporting."

The blonde fired away recklessly. Then Kevin missed. Kris smiled smugly at me. She shot with precision and ran the table. "Two to zero," she said.

"One to one. The playing it out doesn't count."

She handed the stick back to me. "Thanks."

"Nine ball?" Kevin asked. He put quarters in the tray and slammed in the silver tab. I was so angry, I couldn't answer.

Two-thirty and many vodka-tons later, I turned my key in the lock and opened the door. Dad was asleep on the couch, an afghan pulled over his legs. "What the hell?" he sat forward. "It's three in the morning."

"Overtime." Careful not to slur.

"Did I hear a car?"

"One of the guys brought me home."

He rubbed his eyes. "What's that smell? Cigarettes?"

"Smoke from the break room. It's horrible in there. Worse than a bar." Still fuming from losing the pool matches, I didn't want to fight with him. Further ridicule and disappointment wasn't what I needed.

He was too sleepy to notice or question more. "You bring me anything?"

"We're not allowed."

"Yeah and we're not allowed envelopes or tape from the PO," he said, his eyelids falling shut again. "Some guy called. Derrick?" he murmured as sleep took hold again.

The noon sun cut through the blinds, tanning stripes on my legs. I hadn't slept so hard all summer. Though groggy, I was anxious to get the lowdown from Paul on Wayne and his muscular minion.

"Who?" he yelled as he fixed the wrap.

"Karen. Karen and Wayne. She was at the bar last night."

"You mean Kris?"

"Oh, yeah, her." Kris with a K. Wayne had made special mention of that.

Hands on hips, head facing the floor, Paul thought hard. "Nothing between 'em."

Ned didn't pay much mind when Paul and I rumored the mill. He had figured a way through the eight-hour day that we weren't able to find.

"Nothing at all?"

"Nope."

"What's her story, then?"

He hawk-eyed me. I was more inquisitive than usual.

"She was drinking water," I offered as explanation.

"Yeah, rest of us don't get it either. She doesn't drink much. Been here nine years. Started on third, worked that two years. Then second, where she's still at. I don't know much about her. Does side-jobs in the morning. Remodeling, painting, wallpapering. Heard she does good work."

Nine years. I was shocked. Couldn't fathom myself being here that long, or Kris, though I knew little about her. Her lack of weary eyes and her flat belly set her apart.

"Yeah, she mentioned a second job last night," I said. "You were chummy with her all right." I skated another box to Ned. I couldn't believe Paul didn't have anything for me.

"Why? Because I sat next to her?" Paul got defensive when I insinuated. "I'm a married man." He flashed his ring-less hand. Jewelry wasn't allowed on the floor. "You were the chummy one. Talked to her quite a bit." Jealousy, subtle and slender, escaped his lips. He was overacting with his slow, too-deliberate speech, and he was trying to throw the insinuations back on me. His normally ghost-white face was flushed. He knew something, but wasn't talking. Just what the something was, I couldn't be sure. Still, his surfacing scruples surprised me. "Why do you ask, anyway?" He straightened a row of wrap, not offering anything else about anyone.

"Same reason you tell," I said. Gossip slowed other thoughts. Metal arms went round. The bars came out.

At lunchtime, Kevin was waiting for me at the picnic table. After devouring an oatmeal cream pie, he took my hand. His palm was warm and a little sweaty. He was cute when he was nervous. An inch of his thin hair stuck straight up in the wind. We walked through the parking lot and cut through an alley. Headlights chopping Toledo twilight, a car pulled forward. "Meet Gene."

"Hello, Gene."

"Get in."

Two guitars and amps were strapped in the belts of the backseat. Gene seemed harmless enough, so I slid across the front seat and straddled the stick shift. A dimple emerged in Gene's right cheek. He didn't speak. He drove us in circles around the neighborhood, shifting gracefully, avoiding my inner thighs. Kevin dug into the glove box.

"You smoke dope, right?"

That was what all the intrigue was about, a small canister of green leaves in the glove box.

"Sure, but what about the drug tests?"

"They never do those after the first one unless you show up drunk or fuck up a machine or something." He handed me a joint.

I considered Kevin's expectant brown eyes, then lit the joint and inhaled. I wished he would have let me into the club the night before when I had terrible cramps. My uterus could have dropped to the floor and I would have kept packing.

After lunch, the factory was an entirely new place. New, but not any better. Metal dinosaurs swelled from the cement. Packing while stoned presented new challenges. I couldn't calibrate the speed of the bars and nearly succumbed to the sissy box. The hum and crank of the dinosaurs assaulted my ears. I heard voices: Wayne's, Joyce's, Dad's. I had no idea what they were saying. I couldn't listen and pack at the same time. Paul gave me knowing frowns, but didn't speak. Not a rumor escaped his lips. He had had his day with drugs, had given them up six years back when he crashed his car and broke his arm, keeping him from work for six weeks. The fear of car wrecks didn't stop me, though. I didn't drive often, and I didn't care if I couldn't work. Dad couldn't say much about a broken arm. At Icy Bites, about the only thing you had to have was two functioning arms.

Next day. Same time. Same channel. Meet Gene. Hello, Gene.

Day after that, no Gene. Kevin's Jeep, two joints tightly rolled and a box of oatmeal cream pies. Twenty minutes. Enough time to get back, get a drink of water, use the bathroom, squeeze the Visine, punch in.

I poked my fingers into Kevin's bone-thin thigh.

"Really, I can't feel that."

"You can't feel it because you're stoned." His legs appeared skeletal in the white uniform pants. No meat. I wondered how Derrick's legs would feel if I poked them, firm and solid. I could have bounced a quarter off them. I surmised I would've been able to do the same with Kris'.

"No, it's from an accident. Most of my right leg is numb."

I pushed harder. I pinched as firm as I could, trying to make him pull away. I prodded, like he was a brother trying to pull one over on me. I indulged him, but I wasn't going to fall for his small caper. He couldn't fool me. I didn't believe his leg was numb. We circled the block a couple more times until we were laughing so hard at something we couldn't remember.

Back inside, the weed weakened and didn't ease the eight-hour shift. Instead, time turned miserable and long. Eight hours felt like ten and twelve. Minutes became plow-horses dragging their burdens. My mind slowed. The walls closed in. The metal arms snatched for me.

13

Country music swaggered its trite lyrics at us as Kevin and I entered Pinheads, scooting past Joyce, waltzing by herself. Kevin headed for the bar. I lingered near the pool table.

"Ready to lose again?" came a voice from behind that made me freeze and lose balance. Kris.

"No, you're clearly the shark in the house," I said matter-of-factly.

"My teeth aren't nearly as sharp. How about darts?"

My body was suddenly very warm despite the icy air from the blasting AC. I tried to shake my limbs free of a chill. "Sure," I said. "I've got the elbow angle and wrist flick perfected." I demonstrated awkwardly. Kris smiled, perhaps at me, not with me.

"I'll take you on," Paul said.

"Let's go."

I'd only played darts once before in the basement at my cousin's house. Paul had to explain the rules of Cricket and show me the throwing line. He was up by forty points.

"Your form looks like it could use some work," Kris said.

Down eight slots and fifty-eight points after Paul's last throw, I was feeling exceedingly warm and red-faced. I was beginning to grow angry. "Yeah, well, you'll be the last person to work on it," I said, then, "and anyway, I don't want to crush Paul's ego right off the bat. He should feel the bitter loss only after a long hard battle."

"Playing with his emotions. Smart strategy."

"Emotions?" Paul said, saving me from biting back. "What the hell are those?"

"Are your quarters up for the next game?" I asked Kris, a note of challenge in my tone.

She dug deep into her front left pocket. "I don't know. Should I tangle with perfection?" She stepped in front of me as I was about to throw. She thumbed her quarters into the holders.

"It's only a game," I said, dismissively. I could've done damage right about then. Kris' taunts were too much. I hated losing, and two nights in a row might have tipped me into fury. I threw my third dart. It stuck in the outer black frame. The night was not going my way.

"Pool's only a game, but that's not the song you were singing the other night," she said.

"Once you get to know me you'll see I'm full of contradictions."

Two massive arms wrapped around me. I told Derrick he could find me at Pinheads if he ever got bored in Bowling Green. He must have been bored because the massive arms were his. They were comforting and loosened my mood. I introduced him to Kris and Paul and saw Kevin watching us from beneath the bill of his cap.

"Hey, you work out, huh?" he said to Kris, shaking her hand.

"Little bit."

"What's your routine? Do you take supplements?"

I went back to the throwing line.

"Five or six miles a day and a few sit-ups and push-ups."

"That's it?" he said. He stepped back to take a better look at her. As he did he bumped into Kevin.

"Watch it, man," Kevin said. He and Derrick were the same height, but opposite in build. Kevin was a scrawny puke. Put the two in a boxing ring and Derrick would drop him in the first few seconds.

"It's cool, my bad. I'm Derrick." He stuck out his hand. Kevin had no choice but to take it. "Dead fish. Firm up. Shake like a man!"

Kevin yanked his hand back. "You up for some pool?"

"Sure, *man*," Derrick said. He winked at me.

"Your boyfriend, I presume." Paul said, in on this gossip firsthand for once. He flung three darts. Bang! Bang! Bang! Winning the game. The machine's red and white lights flickered madly and muffled cheers emerged from its speakers.

"Damn you!" I yelled.

Kris retrieved Paul's darts and reset the game. She stood at the line, elbow at a ninety-degree angle, her firm triceps parallel with the floor. She was wearing a tank top again, quietly showing off her arms. Her first two darts cut the air for the bull's eye. The third missed the board completely, etching a tiny hole in the cheap paneling.

"Slop!" I said and grinned, promising myself I wouldn't go red in the face and stomp around if I lost. It was only a game, I coached myself.

"You trying to trash talk me? I'll tell you now. It doesn't work. I've had years of experience with jokers like you. I'm unflappable."

When her turn came around again, I whispered to Paul, "What'll get her? What's her Achilles heel?"

Twirling the tip of a dart, he shook his head. "She doesn't have one. Believe me, I've tried."

"You're failing me, Paul. You'll be stripped of your gossip king crown if you don't come up with something."

"Really, there's nothing."

"Dethroned."

Kris' last toss put her in the lead by three points. I couldn't let her beat me.

"Youth shall prevail."

"Screw youth. You need some practice, kid."

Kid sent blood rushing to my eyeballs. "I'm no kid. Do you know what a kid is?"

"A goat," Paul helped.

"I meant it with the utmost affection," she said without inflection. I couldn't tell if she was as competitive as I was or if she was messing with me.

"The hell you did." I wrenched my darts from the plastic board. We were tied. I saw Kris check the scores and mark out which numbers she needed for the win. She was caught up. She didn't want to lose, either. She was probably not used to losing, and I'd thrown her. I had to calm down. Center myself. Focus. I was surprised at how worked up I was.

We fell into silent competition, toeing up to the edge of the tape, checking our elbows, flicking our wrists. Our eyes constantly checking the red-lit scores, which were too damn close. I threw each dart expertly, angrily at the board, yes, but at something else. The straight shot of the dart pierced the chaos I felt inside. The dart had a clear trajectory and center goal. The dart had purpose.

Another six shots like this, then, "Ha! Ha!" I yelled loudly. I couldn't contain myself. I threw my hands in the air and strutted around the bar, triumphant. Paul and Kris threw for second place while I headed over to the packers. Glaring at me from behind her pool cue, Missy dampened my glory.

"What's the problem?" I said, cockiness coming through.

"Fuck you, Lee."

"What the hell's your problem?"

"Go back to the other side."

"What?"

"We're summer help. They don't give a shit about us."

"It's fun for now. No love lost."

"Whatever," she said, back at the table for her shot.

Paul and Kris were still tossing for second. I looked over at the pool table and the packers. I didn't know any of them very well. I was surprised to find myself upset that they'd brushed me off. They should have been encouraging my victory. Derrick caught my eyes and shrugged his empathy. He made Kevin look like a roughly drawn stick figure.

"Good game," Kris said, holding out her hand, a far better person than I. We shook and she sat down. "What are you smiling at?"

I'd been caught in the act. "It's kind of silly, but I'll tell you anyway. In thirty years Derrick's going to look like the Michelin Man or Poppin' Fresh Doughboy. Kevin will still be a stick, though a stick with a paunch if he continues to drink like he does. Missy's hair will be that same mishmash of black and blond, but her face will be yellow from smoking so much, oh and she'll be tattooed and dating a Harley man. More rough and skanky than she already is. Paul, in thirty years, will be just the same, though his skin will be droopier."

"He'll have bushier eyebrows."

"Completely out of control. Joyce?"

"Same," she said. "What about that guy over there?"

"The one who looks like Dave Thomas from the Wendy's commercials? He's really a priest who's been defrocked. He comes to the bar to drink his impulses away."

"And you?"

"What?" I said, though I'd heard her clearly.

"What about you in thirty years?"

"I have trouble imagining past next week," I said, staring just over her right shoulder toward Kevin and Derrick at the pool table. The boys were whispering about something and then leaned their cues against the table and went outside.

"My brother used to say he'd be dead by twenty," Kris said.

"Was he?" I looked at her earnestly, catching the fullness of her blue eyes.

"He's thirty-five now and married with three kids."

"That's not dead," I said, stupidly.

"You don't know my brother. Do you want another drink?" she asked.

"Better not. I think I have to drive Doughboy and Stickman home. What is the good life, anyway? Do you think it's partying like a rock star groupie, doing risky things, living it up or marriage and kids and a steady job?"

"I guess it depends what you consider risky. It's never an either/or thing."

"I suppose not," I said, again stupidly. I was having trouble forming thoughts and articulating words. Kris leaned back in her chair and crossed her legs at the ankles. I couldn't figure out how to sit. She was so at ease, and I was back to trying to find solid footing. Then I said, because I couldn't help it, "It's really too bad you lost that game."

"Victory, like happiness isn't a sustained feeling. It comes and goes."

"Thank you, Zen master."

Gus cried last call. We didn't move.

"You'll see."

"You speaking from experience?"

"What else is there?"

So as to avoid drawing attention to his weaving, Derrick cautiously maneuvered his rusted Pacer through Toledo side streets. "I don't like him. The one with the tiny eyes and the Little Debbies."

"Kevin? He's all right," I said lazily, foregoing deeper analysis.

"This probably comes across like I'm jealous and all, but I'm not. Can I ask you something? Since Lynn left me, I've been questioning everything. So, that night at the party, did you like the kiss?"

"Really? That's what you want to talk about?"

"I'm for real here."

"I did like it. What makes you think I didn't?

"Your mouth was really dry."

"We'd been smoking weed all night."

"Cotton mouth aside, you just didn't seem to dig it. Other girls I've kissed liked having my tongue in their mouth and they liked putting theirs in mine, like a duel or something. And then they do something with their hands."

"Like shove them down your pants?"

He grinned, remembering such hands. "Not always. It's not required. Hands can go anywhere, like on my neck or in my hair or on my lats. It's when the hands stay at the woman's sides that I know. And," he hesitated, looking at me carefully before continuing, "when we were watching Courtney and Jake go at it, I leaned into you, you didn't respond."

"So?"

"I had the biggest hard-on ever."

"Seriously? Don't take it personally. I didn't, I didn't notice. It must have been the drugs. Or maybe watching my best friend give head to a guy she just met kind of took the wind out of me. And you know, I haven't even masturbated in—Jesus, I can't remember the last time. Is that what happens when people work full time? They don't have sex anymore because they're so tired?"

"You're not upset, are you?"

"That you had a happy hard-on watching my friend suck everything out of Jake? Nah, doesn't bother me one bit."

"You're not mad or weirded out that we're talking about this? Look, I'm sorry about the park. I was in a weird mood, thinking about Lynn and all, you know?"

I didn't know. He and Lynn had been together four years, and had lived with each other for half of that time. My longest relationships were seven months and three months. The second one lasted that long because his parents were away for part of it and we had the house to ourselves and were both willing to take advantage of the solitude and each other.

"One more thing," he said. "You're not still interested in me, are you?" He loaded the statement in such a way that I'd be even more of an idiot if I said yes.

"I guess not. You are more like a brother."

"Don't say that."

"Why?"

"Because that would make your sister my sister." He clicked the car's headlights off. Blackness spilled over us. I felt like there was a bowling ball in my stomach. I waited for the inevitable. "You mind if I go out with her?" he asked, delivering.

"She's sixteen."

He shut the engine off. "Yeah, but she's smart as fuck and good-looking."

"How do you know?" When had he been sneaking off with my sister? And where was I? Better yet, where was my dad to grill her about this and ground her for life?

"I stopped by one afternoon when you were already at work. She was sitting on the porch, reading a biography of Georgia O'Keeffe. I told her about camping out west where O'Keeffe got a lot of her inspiration. We talked for a few minutes. It was nice."

"You didn't get her stoned, did you?"

"No."

"Christ, Derrick, she's sixteen." By defending Michelle's honor so ardently, I'd channeled my dad.

"That's only four years younger than you and eight younger than me. Miniscule. And don't tell me I can't get her stoned, you were doing way more when you were her age."

"That was me, though." The logic made sense in my head, conveying it to others was another matter. "It's different."

"Let her make her own mistakes."

"I'm willing to do that, provided those mistakes aren't coerced."

"I wouldn't make her do anything she doesn't want to do. I'm not like that."

"You have my blessing, then, I guess."

"You're not into Kevin, are you?"

"Are you going to date him too?"

"He's got terrible weed. And he's a scrawny jackass."

"Duly noted." I opened the door. "Just don't fuck with her head." I started to close the door, but stopped. "On second thought, don't let her fuck with yours."

After a few hours of pool and smoky air, after Kevin patted my ass and chatted with Missy, after I finally beat Paul at darts and babbled with Kris about the future, and felt bad for Derrick because he couldn't talk ice cream shop, the only light that was on was Michelle's nightlight.

"What are you reading?"

"What do you care?" Defensive teen angst. If Derrick wanted to put up with that, he was welcome to it.

"I'm your sister."

The priss didn't look up from her book as she said, "Doesn't mean we have to bond. Circumstance is the great illusion of life. It obligates you to things you wouldn't otherwise do or say."

"As long as we are circumstantially stuck with each other, we should make the best of it." I could work the jargon.

"You stay on your half of the room and I'll stay on mine. And don't write in my books." She threw a phone number at me.

"Don't go stealing my boyfriends."

"He's an oaf."

She didn't want to talk and I did. I was buzzed and free with my feelings, and she, having read some things, probably had some things to say.

"We can at least be cordial until you go off, write a great American novel, get famous, and forget about me." Hunched over the edge of my bed, I untied my shoes.

"Fame is overrated." She turned a page.

"How would you know?" I kicked the shoes under the mattress and undressed.

"Read about it."

That was how she knew everything. She refused to actually experience life. I couldn't fault her too much. She was only sixteen and not much went on at that age. I'd approached most of my life through a cloud of marijuana. I secretly hoped Derrick wouldn't change too much of Michelle's inexperience. Then I hoped maybe he would. Some of Dad's focus would finally shift to her.

"What are you going to do, then?" I pulled a T-shirt over my head.

"Finish college once I get there."

"Yeah, one of us probably should."

"You could go back." She placed her book next to her on the bed. I was making progress.

"Can't afford it."

"Knowledge has no price."

"The hell it doesn't. School isn't a magic ride to life-security. Look at me, I'm in debt to my eyes."

"I'm not talking about school. I'm talking about *knowledge*."

"You know what knowledge does? Knowledge makes you realize how dissatisfying life is. How fickle. And that you're alone. Despite anything, just you in your own body. All the time. Your own head. Forever and ever. You may know a lot of things, but you know nothing. So you're alone and you've got nothing to do, so you go to the bar or smoke a joint or see movies and try to pretend things are otherwise." I slid between the sheets. We didn't say anything. Michelle watched me.

14

Michelle and I were flung to my mother's parents' house when Dad and Mom needed a time-out from us or from each other. During those visits my grandmother and I pieced puzzles together at the kitchen table. Sleeping Beauty. Pinocchio. The Dwarves. Not paying attention to color gradations, I was always trying to jam the pieces together. "Gentle, dear. They'll fit," she'd say. Sometimes I didn't have the patience to sit with her, but my grandpa's stories tended to nudge me into stillness.

"Yep, all right," he'd say, "you're Libbey stock. All of Toledo is. 1800, Toledo was a western frontier town. 1900, it was a bustling port city. Edward Drummond Libbey brought glass and class to Toledo in 1888. Libbeys were good stock. 1901, they started the art museum. My pop nailed the first paintings to the wall in one of the rented rooms. That was a side-job. He was a construction man. You know, he once told me about a colored fella he worked with."

"Don't tell *that* story," my grandma interrupted.

But he did, to her chagrin.

"One day, the Colored looked him up and down and all around and said, 'Boy, you is overfed and under-fucked.'" My grandfather smacked his gut. "German food'll do that to you," he said. From behind my grandma's back he winked at me. His wide-mouthed chuckle shook the table. He patted grandma's shoulder. She squeezed his hand. Their affection for each other was natural.

Forty years with the same person. I couldn't imagine getting through two.

I was thinking about this, packing away like a good monkey, able to turn off my mind for brief bouts, letting it drift without pause. Courtney was in a different state entirely, and I couldn't get her back. Not that I necessarily wanted to retrieve our high school shenanigans or her dread-being. Derrick was now probably lying in the grass with my sister. I thought I was getting used to Court being gone. In fact, I was finding my own niche with the factory crew—getting stoned with Kevin and playing games with Kris. And I was repaying my parents dollar by dollar, slowly earning back their respect.

Joyce was staring at me. I removed an earplug, pretending that was why I hadn't heard.

"You want overtime?" She was starting to like me. "Just hang out when your shift ends. We can put you somewhere."

"You know how she got that gap?" Paul mimicked giving a blowjob and loosening his teeth. He was starting to annoy me.

"She was born with it, Paul. It's called a diastema."

"College, you're moody."

"Am not."

"How late were you out? Your boy not satisfying you?"

Irritability surged through me. Working eight hours and some-times more, side by side, day in and day out, could make Gandhi throw a punch.

"He's not my boy, Paul."

"Then what's up your ass today?"

"Your pencil dick."

I tried not to imagine Paul's penis. I found the idea of him naked akin to the idea of my dad naked: something that should never, ever happen. But I was annoyed and not about to take the comment back. Joyce's deformity, which wasn't a deformity at all, just a noticeable gap, didn't look that bad. Paul's suggestion—at once sexual, violent, not feasible, and not funny—disturbed me. He'd crossed a line, one I was surprised to find I had. His riding people's physical defects and personal flaws was getting old.

He shook his head and walked back around the wheel.

Ned and I switched and switched again.

Paul came close, his shoulder brushing mine. "You know," he said, "we all have our shit. You're nothing special."

"Yeah, I do know," I snipped, throwing the bars too recklessly. "I'm just in a bad mood. You should understand that. Sometimes you don't talk for days, and I never say a word."

He softened, if only a little. "Kris is all right. She's a good friend. Joyce is all right too, most of the time. In general, people here are good people. Lemme tell you a story. Few years back, before I worked this machine, an old guy worked it. Had for years. He got a call one afternoon, something about his wife being sick. He missed work the next few days. This was a guy who never missed, rain or shine, hell or—so we come to find out his wife died. Fought cancer for something like eight years. And this guy came to work every day from being at home with her or at the hospital at her side. He had to come here, work doubles, be away from her just to pay for her treatment. Well, so, his first day back after the funeral, he was wearing pajamas. Pajamas! The guy was lost, but you know what? No one said a word. We let him work his product and punch out. People here, you know, Lee, I just like to keep myself occupied. The mind rolls. It can turn on you if you don't let it latch onto something." He half-smiled, barely revealing teeth.

I looked away. My hands continued to throw bars. He was right. I knew he was, but in that instant I didn't have a peacemaking bone in my body.

Ten minutes before quitting time, Kevin's hand was on my lower back. The feeling wasn't the comforting, brotherly touch of Derrick.

Kevin's tobacco and oatmeal breath slid into my ear and down my neck. I liked his beady brown eyes, but not much else. Yet I wouldn't talk myself out of him.

"You coming out tonight?"

I thought about another night of the same shit. This was how whole lifetimes passed by. "Working a double," I said.

"Fuck that. There's a late night party to hit when the bar closes."

Another night. Same shit. Being with Kevin allowed me not to have to step out of myself. I could laugh and drink and smoke myself daffy. I could stay on my limbo cloud. I didn't have to grow up in any real way. "I need the money," I said.

"Whatever. Find me on lunch tomorrow."

I nodded, and pushed another box toward Ned.

Third shift was fun if you liked standing lazy-eyed and slack through an extra eight hours. A new round of workers made the night turn counterclockwise. Third-shifters either furled into themselves or laughed hysterically. Two poles: anti-social, possibly psychotic introverts and super-social, possibly psychotic extroverts. Where I fit in depended on the night.

I was in the back, hour three into third shift, hour eleven on the day, when it hit. Toxic shock. I was a dead woman. Headache. Nausea. Cramps. The fucking cramps! I'd forgotten about my tampon, as usual. But it had remembered me. Moisture. And I was wearing white. The regular bloodletting, though supposedly beautiful and unique, was the one thing I hated about being a woman. I couldn't care less about centuries of oppression. If such barters were possible, I'd trade motherhood for a life without periods. In an instant, I'd trade it.

I had to get to the bathroom and uncork, but I was working on Two, where, if you didn't keep up and a Popsicle got by, it jammed the box machine, which got nasty sticky, and the whole line had to be shut down. I didn't know what to do. I watched the clock, wrestled the hands to lunch with my mind. It didn't work.

"You look kinda pale," the operator said from behind the wheel.

I nodded. If I spoke, I'd pass out. A Pop advanced toward the box machine. I hopped left, catching it in time. My womb didn't appreciate that. A manager walked by.

"I need my lunch now."

"You got twenty minutes. Hang in there." A third-shifter by choice, he worked the dark hours so he could deal with fewer people. He didn't hear me and didn't want to.

"I mean now." I glared at him. "Just a bathroom break."

"What? You expect *me* to pack?"

The task was only for two minutes. He probably thought the apocalypse would come the second he lowered himself to my job.

"It's an emergency."

"Your hands aren't broken."

I wanted to kick him harder than I'd ever wanted to kick Wayne, who was an angel in blue compared to the lone third manager. I hated my job more than anything in that moment. Instead of unleashing my fury, I started talking. "See the real problem is I'm on the rag. I've had a tampon in for hours."

"Gross. I don't need to hear that. That shit ain't funny."

"I'm not trying to be funny. I'm trying to reason with you. There's this thing called Toxic Shock Syndrome. Happens if you leave a tampon in too long. There's a strain of bacteria that can start during menstruation. It causes flu-like symptoms—fever, vomiting, headache, a nasty rash."

"You're making that up. Toxic Shock's like a reaction to a chemical spill. You girls are always using that to get out of everything." He started walking away. "I'm not falling for it."

"It can kill me." No response. "Fuck this," I said, leaving the Popsicles to their sabotage. "Yo!" I tapped him on the shoulder as I skidded around the corner toward the door. "You're it." The manager rushed back to Two.

"You better be dead when you get back!"

I wished I was. I wouldn't have to return to his stubbly-faced sneer and the cold, hard Popsicles that came one after another without end.

In the bathroom, I pulled the string. Soaked through and through. I only had a spot not even the size of a dime on my panties. Imagination. Gets you every time.

15

At the end of an endless shift, Paul and I glared at the sign. We were ready to tear the bold font from the wall. "Does that really mean Saturday *and* Sunday?" I asked, but he grabbed his lunchbox and left. No last minute gossip. No after-work beer. He was pissed. I was too stunned. The sign was poison. I looked for an antidote.

Kris whistled through the door. She reached her tan, taut arm in front of me to punch out. "Overtime pay," she said. "Covers my vacation and then some. C'mon, I'll let you beat me at darts."

I followed her vanilla-honey scent into the locker room and clumsily dialed the numbers on my lock. Still whistling, she removed her polka-dot hat and a heap of blonde-brown hair fell to her round shoulders.

At Pinheads, Kris' long fingers propped beers in front of Joyce and me. Joyce was drunk already. Their table eerily empty, the packers had other plans.

"Can't the union do anything?" I asked, twisting the bottle by its neck.

"It's in our contracts," Joyce said, not quite slurring but about to. "They can require us to work up to fourteen mandatory days a year above our five per week so long as we're paid time and a half for anything over forty hours." She drank down half the beer in one smooth tilt.

I wouldn't have signed the contract they did, though I had signed a summer one, signed my summer life away, without reading it. I vowed to pay more attention to things.

"It's only one weekend," Kris said.

Joyce slugged back the other half of her beer. "You're a little too chipper to be losing a weekend." She lifted off her seat toward a full one.

"But I'm gaining two nights working with you." Her sarcasm stalked Joyce to the bar, but her eyes were on me. She smiled. She was doing that a lot.

"I've already worked two doubles this week," I said. I didn't want the factory controlling my life, deciding my weekend activities. Forty hours was enough.

Kris had spent half the night fixing something in the freezer and her cheeks were rosy from it. Her blue eyes looked kindly on me. She held up her Budweiser. "Cheers." She had heard it all before. There was no point. We clinked bottles and I resigned myself to a lost weekend. We sat quietly for sometime, overhearing Joyce's cackled laugh at the bar while she did a few shots. With my free hand I dug into my pocket for a quarter. "Scoot back," I said, sliding into the seat next to Kris.

"Why?"

"Just scoot back."

She did and I leaned closer. I was going to bounce a quarter off her thigh, but when I felt warmth radiating from her skin and when I smelled a welcoming soapy scent mixed with her scent, I couldn't move.

She looked at me. "What?"

I didn't have words.

After working all weekend and ending it with another double, nearly comatose, I walked in at eight-thirty Monday morning to my mom waiting for me. After eight hours on third shift dealing with drunks, she was usually in bed by eight-ten. Instead, she was smoking a cigarette at the kitchen table. Whatever she had on her mind wasn't good. She never smoked. On the tabletop spun a small black tube, a little bigger than a cigarette. Mom's bags were darker than ever.

"Morning," I said cheerily. No use.

"What the hell is this, Lee? You said you were done with the drugs. We sent you through rehab. Spent all that money. Gave you a year at school. Is this what you did? Is this how you spent our money those nine months? I can't believe it. Can't believe you'd do this to us."

The black object was my one-hitter.

"Where'd you find it? I haven't seen that thing since high school."

"Where did I find it? I found it!" She slammed her palm on the table. "You know damn well where it was."

"Seriously, I haven't seen that thing in two years."

"Don't try to talk yourself out of this one. It won't work. I've had too much practice."

"Give me a cup. I'll piss for you right now." Forgetting somehow, until the words were out and off my little red lips, that I had smoked a joint with Kevin not more than twelve hours ago and that I probably would again today on lunch and that I had been pretty steadily stoned every evening for the last three weeks or more and that I had my own storehouse of THC gathering in my fat cells just waiting to be found out. "Dump your coffee. I'll piss in that cup," I said anyway.

"Watch your mouth. I can still wash it out with soap, you know."

"I'm nineteen, rounding the corner to twenty."

"I know," she said, heavily, such defeat in her tone. "When are you going to act it?"

"You're just like Dad. Two broken records."

"If you'd grow up, things would be a lot easier."

"I told you, I haven't seen that thing for two years."

She looked at me, searching, wanting to accept that. "Why should I believe you?"

At the beginning of the summer, I couldn't adequately explain how I'd spent my year at college, not with any reasons my parents understood. I couldn't explain my fascination with O'Connor's pink toenails or how I got involved delivering digitally re-mastered tapes and tiny pills I didn't know about. Explaining why she should trust me now was like trying to explain color to someone who's been blind since birth.

"You haven't used this at all, lately?"

"Open it. The resin is years old. There's nothing fresh in there."

She unscrewed the tarred cap. "It does smell musty."

She put the device down without screwing the top back on. She looked at me in a way I didn't recognize. Later I decided her expression was one of distance and suspicion, a look you'd get from a stranger who wants nothing to do with you. Usually she caved and we returned to status quo—ignorance, denial. She sighed and tossed the one-hitter in the trash. A pang of guilt swept through my stomach.

16

"They have brains smaller than peas, like any other fish, but they're smart. People have been hunting them longer than any other North American trout, so their instincts are more highly developed and they're harder to catch."

"Who *hunts* fish?"

Flowing out of Bellefontaine, snaking through west central Ohio and dumping into the Great Miami River, the Mad River was one of the state's only trout rivers. Kris and her housemate, Susie, a petite, energetic woman who ran a popsicle machine first shift, and Kevin and I were camped along the Mad's banks, eating Tony Packo's hotdogs and drinking beer. Kris had planned the trip, inviting along all the second shift workers who'd worked the previous weekend. The four of us were the only ones who showed. Kris and Susie had driven down in Kris' brother's beat-up RV. I bumped along State Route 33 in Kevin's Wrangler. His dad was a thirty-six year employee at the Jeep plant and foreman for seventeen of those years, so Kevin got a prime discount. Sitting on the Jeep's jumping shocks for three hours had given me a headache, and campfire smoke against my corneas didn't help it any.

"Could you stop poking at that? The smoke burns my eyes."

Susie was paying no mind, so intent on telling us about the damn trout. "If you don't let them know you're there and your lures match what they eat, *when* they eat, you can catch them all day long."

This was our weekend away from the windowless factory. We wanted to be outside for as long as possible, but the sky was an angry mess of clouds and intermittent rain. Campers at the other sites had doused their fires and called quits on playing weekend Lewis and Clark. We were watching the rain, trying to wait it out and not panic, running for cover.

"How do they know you're there anyway?" Kevin said. "Fish can't think."

"Instincts. Years and years of instincts. So completely refined now. You might say instincts are a form of thinking, but really it's the nature of the fish to know."

Kris tilted her lawn chair toward me and whispered, "You think she's making no sense, wait until she gets stoned."

"I bet she's funnier."

"No, no. She's wound up now, that'll make it worse. She'll talk your ears off. You won't get any sleep."

The sky quit hesitating and rain came down cold and fast. Kris collapsed her chair and tossed it under the RV. The rest of us followed her lead. She and Susie ducked into the RV, and Kevin and I crawled into his Coleman, which was tiny, made for midgets. My feet pushed against the walls. Cramped and lying close, we zipped into our separate bags. My head was still throbbing from the drive down and my eyes were seared. Breathing Kevin's air made me feel more trapped.

The RV's headlights went on, shining through the nylon shell. "What do you think that's about?" Kevin asked, blinking away the light. "I bet they hit the button by mistake. Hey!" he yelled. "Turn off the damn lights!"

His screaming tore into my headache, intensifying it. "There's no way they heard that."

"Hey!" he screamed louder.

I clamped my hand over his mouth. "They can't possibly hear you. Not with this rain and being inside the RV. And they could have music on."

"It's annoying," he mumbled. Hot air pushed between my fingers. I took my hand back.

"They'll figure out they're on." I rustled in my bag, trying to relax. I tried to breathe deeply, get some oxygen to my brain, but the air was too stuffy. Rain began to collect on the tent's fly, sagging it toward us.

Kevin sat up on his elbow. "The lights won't bother you?"

"I've slept through worse."

"I don't intend to sleep," he said.

He looked at me and my chest sunk in. My head ached now with annoyance and regret. I'd done this to myself, crawled right into this claustrophobic hut. Kevin shifted closer and kissed me. His lips were dry and thin and his tongue didn't feel like a tongue, but more like a finger or dry stick swabbing out my mouth. The RV lights were still on, like someone was trying to see our shadowy forms. Kevin put his hand beneath my shirt. "Wait," I said, stopping the quickly advancing hand. He didn't take it off me, but kept his hand right where it was. I had followed him around on lunch at work. I had sat in his Jeep and greedily smoked his weed. I had gone to the parties and bars he liked to go to. I had let him rest his hand on my knee on the drive down. I had watched him buy condoms at the last gas station. All of it. I had let it all happen. I guessed I had hoped we wouldn't get around to this moment.

"Shit, relax," he said, as if I'd hurt his feelings. "You're not a virgin, are you?"

"No."

Rain pelted the tent walls. Beads of water dropped from the fly.

"What's the problem, then? Usually I don't wait this long. If it's your period, I don't care. I have paper towels in the car."

That surprised me, his not minding a painted dick. Right now, though, sex wasn't top priority for me. In fact, sex wasn't a priority at all. Since the Derrick rejection, minor as it was, I wasn't feeling a need for a screw. And three weeks didn't seem long to wait to have sex with someone you just met and weren't so sure about. Kevin was good for a drink and a joint. We had forged an easy, mindless alliance, and here he was fucking it up.

"I don't like tent sex," I offered blandly, untruthfully, but I was more than willing to expound on why the close quarters and hot bags dehydrated me and sucked desire from my body. I hoped Kevin would take my words at face value and leave me alone.

He rolled on top of me.

"Tell me you want it." He was hard. Even through the down bag, I felt his cock. I looked at him, trying briefly to talk myself into giving up ten minutes. He looked fine: trim, tanned. He had a full head of hair, though receding some. Headache notwithstanding I wasn't into having sex with him. More than that, I was starting to feel nauseated and I lost my ability to breathe.

I pushed him off.

He was red-faced and his teeth were clenched. His arms shaking. I think he wanted to hit me. He crashed back into his pillow, deciding his next move. "Fucking lights," he said.

I lay there scared, angry, feeling stupid and alone. I felt the tension in my legs. I'd been holding them together tightly. I tried to relax a little, but my whole body trembled. I took a breath. I listened to the rain assault the nylon. I tried to figure a way out if he tried to mount me again. The cramped tent made escape almost impossible.

"What's wrong with you?"

I didn't know where to begin. A shrink would have had a hard time narrowing the possibilities. "There's nothing wrong with me," I said, without conviction. I was tired.

"So?"

"We don't know each other that well," I said, sighing. That had never stopped me before and it wasn't the reason.

"Sex is a way to get to know someone," he said.

"Yeah, but not from the get-go." Either he was a jerk or I was getting prudish and old. I tried to be a little more open. "What are you looking for?" I asked, for once trying to get to know him.

His eyes squinted. "What do you mean what am I looking for? Isn't it obvious?"

"From me. What do you want from me? Do you want a relationship? A fuck-buddy?"

He looked at his hands as if they were unfamiliar objects. "Yeah, sex," he said. "That's a start."

"Anything else?"

Silence. Confounded. Sex was all he really wanted. Sex and some food and a few nights out would make a life for him.

"I've been getting you stoned a lot."

"So I owe you, is that it?"

"What do *you* want?" he asked. "Do you even like me?"

"I don't know what I want," I said, truthfully. "I'm a little lost right now."

He looked at me, his face screwed into disgust and misunderstanding. I thought about how to explain myself so he would understand. I didn't bother, though, because a part of me didn't think he could.

Kris' voice came through the nylon shell. "Hey! It's raining pretty hard. Do you two want to come in here? I don't want you to get carried down river!"

I jumped up and scurried out of the tent, grateful to be out of the awkwardness, grateful to not have to answer the same questions I asked. Kevin followed and we left the tent in the rain and scrambled into the camper's tight quarters. Susie was asleep already on the top bunk. In her flannel boxers and cotton T-shirt, Kris inched in below her.

"Do you know the headlights are on?" I asked, laying my bag on the floor, head near the front seats.

"Shit. No. Thanks." She hopped out of bed and shut them off. "Would've drained the battery. Disaster."

Kevin flopped over and pulled his bag high. I zipped in to the chin again. I looked at Kris, whose eyes questioned me about Kevin. I shimmied in my mummy-sac, and wondered if Kris had heard anything above the rain pelting the roof. Her eyes beamed concern more than curiosity. She knew something, but wasn't saying. She curled half-fetal around her pillow. For a brief second I imagined myself as that pillow, her arms tight around me. She felt good holding me steady in a comfortable closeness, natural, something I was sure I hadn't felt before in just that way.

The Mad River wasn't raging, but I was stupid enough to test its depths anyway. Three joints in, Kevin and I paddled down-rive. He sat in the back. I sat in the front, Sea Breeze sloshing in the plastic bottle between my knees. Vodka, cranberry, grapefruit. Who said Wheaties was the breakfast of champions? In the other canoe, Kris and Susie drank their way through a case of Budweiser, Susie downing two for every one of Kris'. I tried to start a splashing war with my paddle but ended up dropping it in the water. Kevin paddled after it like a madman. The lost paddle penalty would have been forty bucks and a lecture from my dad. The morning sun shone its laughing face.

"You should just drink beer if you can't hold your liquor." Kris pulled her oar through the water. Her round shoulders braided into muscular arms.

"I'm holding it fine."

Her biceps twinkled tensely on the backstroke. I was beginning to think she had an amazing body.

"Yeah, but nothing else."

I drank big from the plastic bottle.

"You're not gonna be able to walk up the hill to the bridge."

I craned my head around toward Kevin. "What is she talking about?"

"The railroad bridge. She told us about it last week. You climb up the banks, jump from the bridge. Forty-five foot drop." Either he was ignoring the previous night's lack of events or he was humoring me. "You said you'd do it."

I was no daredevil. I had only been to Cedar Point twice in my nineteen years, and both times I camped by the exits to the rides and waited for everyone else to deplane. But with vodka in my veins, I was ready to drop the forty-five feet from the bridge. If cool and controlled Kris did it, I could too. I was, after all, destined to take her job. Why not her glory as well? At the shore, I hopped out, trying to back the canoe up so it didn't float away.

Kevin dug his paddle in the muddy bottom. "I'll stay here," he said. As far as I could tell, we'd made a silent agreement to leave last night alone and make the best of today.

"Wimp."

He craned at the bridge. His fear gave me extra incentive. I could show him up too.

"Somebody's gotta stay in the canoe."

"We'll hold it for you." Susie was on my side. Her arms thin and pale, prone to burn.

Still, he declined.

Brain loose from the liquid, body limber from the weed, I braced for battle and trudged up Bunker Hill. My knees muddied as I slipped on the wet bank. My head spun and my stomach churned at the reality of what I was about to do. Extreme sports weren't for me. I should have been in a car staring out the window at the flat American countryside in Nebraska or Illinois or anywhere else on my way to an Alaskan cannery to chop the heads off fish, not on this messy bank heading to a high bridge, about to dare my head into a forty-five foot drop.

Kris yelled, "Look for the red arrows!"

On the rail, two spray-painted arrows pointed at each other about a foot apart.

"That's where the water's deepest!" She'd reclined in the canoe, laughing, a queen holding court.

I looked down over the rail. "You did this?"

Kris was removing her shirt. "Two times last year!"

Kevin's voice rose from below, "But she's nuts." The punk. He was supposed to be supportive. He was supposed to be up here.

I wanted to turn back. The drop was fucking long. I dreamed of the hazy heaven of Courtney's car window.

"Can you see the bottom?" Kris again. She had her sunglasses propped on her head. Her blue swimsuit accentuated her tan and drew out her eyes.

"No!"

"That's a good thing!"

Thank God there was a monsoon last night.

I stepped over the rail. This time as I looked down I didn't see Kris or Susie. I saw the brown water below me. I saw through the water. I saw a boulder. I saw my leg wedged beneath the boulder or my neck breaking on it. I felt my lungs pound, ready to burst because I couldn't breathe.

"You want a three count?" Susie, rooting for me and dousing herself with sunscreen, didn't bother to look up.

I looked to Kris, smiling with the full knowledge of what was ahead. The lip of her blue trunks nestled beneath her pelvic bones. "One!" she yelled.

I jumped.

My feet shattered the water's sheen with a smack. My ass hit too, and immediately burned. I was deep in the Mad water and out of breath. I shot toward the surface, where I gasped for air.

"Do it again," Kris said, feigning indifference, but smiling at me.

I climbed the cliff. At the top, my gut mutinied. I scanned the sky and the tops of trees. I briefly wondered where Courtney was, what peaceful activity she might be involved in. I was decisive and all action. I walked on the ties of the bridge, stepped over the rail, and plummeted, down, down. No three count. No words. I simply jumped, and I hit hard. Again. Feet, then ass. I swam for the shore and stepped like Aphrodite from the depths, newly reborn, feeling unstoppable. Water weaved through my long hair and trickled down my back.

"Your shorts are ripped." Even glassy-eyed, Kevin had keen powers of observation.

A wedgie had exposed my left cheek, transforming my suit into the worst of thongs. I wished Kevin weren't along. I wished for just us three women, laughing at the female form.

Kris didn't say anything. She sat with her pink lips and perfect teeth in a half smile, her blue eyes glowing against her blue suit, knowing my ass hurt because hers had felt the same a year ago.

Not fun. Not a dare. Some kind of spite or inner demon, some kind of inner shift, drove me up the mountain and off the bridge a third time.

With the fire stoked, its heat and shadows flickering off our faces, we brought our chairs close, but I couldn't sit down.

"What's the problem?" Kris asked, in mock concern. She knew.

"Hemorrhoids?" Susie asked. Sometime in the afternoon she had conspired with Benedict Arnold. "You're kinda young to be getting those little buggers."

I couldn't sit down. I walked around the fire like an old man, making faces behind their backs. Kevin passed me a joint. I was all too glad to smoke, and hoped it would numb the pain. It didn't. It only made me sleepy and stupid. I handed the joint off to Kris.

"No thanks."

"You don't smoke?" Kevin's beady brown eyes with red whites went wide.

"No."

Nine years at the factory, and she'd avoided this trap. Others had habits or obsessions of some sort that kept them going. Kris didn't drink herself into oblivion. She didn't smoke herself silly. I wondered what drove her, how she made it through the machine with her head intact.

Kevin, staring at the sky, sucked at another joint. He didn't say much else, not that he ever had anything of import skidding through his head.

"Have you ever?" I asked.

"There was a time, yeah. But some things happened and I decided it wasn't for me. Makes me feel stupid, silly, like my head is only air."

Susie relieved me of the weed, then inhaled and promptly giggled like an eight-year-old. "I just pictured cutting open Kevin's head and finding nothing but a full balloon," she explained.

"Why *my* head?"

"Lee and Kris think too much. They're silent brooders."

For as batty as she was, Susie was perceptive. I kept up my slow circular march. Kris' eyes arched around the circle, following me.

"Kris is like a wary brown trout," Susie said. "Avoiding all the lures the rest of us chomp at."

"I just don't like a foggy mind."

"She runs like a trout swims. Hey! Wouldn't it be funny if she breathed water? We'd have to keep her in a tank and take her to the ocean to run."

"How much do you run?" Kevin asked.

"I'm no Zola Budd, but I manage twenty-five to thirty miles on a good week."

Kris' muscular, tan legs were glowing under the fire's light. I'd hate to get caught in her figure-four leg-lock. I walked around the fire some more on my own legs, which were putty, and my butt cheeks burned.

"Zola who?" Susie asked.

"Professional runner who ran barefoot."

"I bet she had the worst corns." Susie cringed, curling her feet under the chair.

Kris looked at Susie. "Did you call to check on Ari?"

"She's fine. Having fun."

Kevin was zonked, his face to the stars, cheek muscles slack, eyelids heavy. His stiff silence made me want to kick him into speech, into some sort of personal recognition. I didn't care that he only wanted me for sex. I cared that he couldn't reason out why. I cared that he spent his days and nights blitzed, stumbling through life coated in dense head fog. I cared that he was wasted and wasting his life. I cared because I was doing exactly the same.

I circled the flames, looking off into the woods, the muscles and fat in my ass alive in the world. My eyes kept veering toward Kris' profile. Her hair hung loosely past the back of the chair. Light from the fire gently licked at her jaw. Her cheeks were rosy from a day in the sun and sitting close to the fire. Her warmth made me want to touch her shoulder where it met her collarbone, follow the sturdy ridge to her breastbone. The impulse was strong and my body warmed, though I was several yards from the fire. My chest was surging with heavy delight and I felt a physical ache to move closer to her.

I said, "You didn't tell me I'd bruise my ass."

"I told you to hit the water feet first, not ass first."

17

Sunday night, I was carefully lying on my side, watching an episode of *Growing Pains*. Mike Seaver's at a party where everyone's doing cocaine. He's torn up about it. Can't decide. Should he, shouldn't he? He's had good parenting, but the peers press in. Finally, he leaves the party and drives around late into the night. His father is angry when he gets home past curfew, but Mike tells him what happened and that he said no, and his father, played by Alan Thicke, hugs him. I imagine Alan Thicke as my father, the sensitive, affectionate, neo-Freud. I'd be his shining apple. We'd live in that big house with hardwood floors. We'd analyze things in kind ways.

In reality, I was spread out on shaggy carpet from the 1970s. The walls weren't lined with books and paintings, and my father wasn't in his office-study with a patient. He was out playing poker with other mail carriers. He hadn't hugged me in years. Not at my grandmother's funeral. Not when I was eleven and flipped over the handlebars of my bike, trying to hop a curb to get onto the sidewalk. My mother was no Maggie Seaver, either. She didn't have the golden locks or the confidence. She wasn't assertive. And that night, she was putzing room to room, tidying and sighing.

"What happened to your thighs?" she asked, having spotted the many shades of purple coloring my seat.

"This isn't another 'you're big-boned but you better watch it' lecture, is it?"

"No, Lee, look at your thighs! Honey, what did you do?"

Muscles stiff from climbing the hillside three times, I slowly got up, Mom watching me with concern. In the bathroom, I stood on the side of the tub, high enough to see my ass in the mirror. My legs were dark blue and black, with a bit of pukey green. "Bruise from the canoe trip," I said, hoping she wouldn't ask for details.

"Honey, that's an odd place. Something didn't happen, did it?"

"Nothing out of the ordinary." The bruise was massive. I pushed at the darkest blotches. The sting from the previous night had morphed into a dull pain.

The front door opened and closed. "I'm home," Michelle called.

"Hi, honey!" Mom said. "With Kevin, I mean," she said to me, severe, yet reluctant. She didn't want to deal with a prospect so grave. I didn't either. The thought of talking intimately with her made me uneasy.

"No, nothing like that." I hadn't even considered that she worried about my safety because I hadn't either. Kevin was pretty harmless, usually spaced out on weed or talking sports when he was drunk.

Mom searched my eyes while hers rounded with fear.

"Oh my god!" Michelle said, catching sight of my hip in the mirror.

"Dramatic much?" I said, stepping down from the tub edge.

"Do I want to know the story?"

"Probably not."

"Jesus, what happened?" Michelle stared at the inkblots on my legs, reaching out to poke at the darker one.

"It wasn't a man? You would tell me, right?"

"No, it wasn't a man." A woman drove me to jump. "I would tell you," I said, though I wasn't entirely sure I would. Sex was a hard enough issue to discuss with parents.

She didn't move. The frown wouldn't leave her lips and the bathroom felt too small for three people. Michelle poked at my thigh.

"Ouch!" I yelled, knocking her hand away.

She jumped back, and I laughed.

She smacked me on the arm. "Bitch."

"I jumped from a railroad bridge," I said. I watched my mom's lips curl under and her eyebrows lift. "A few times. It was a dare."

"When someone tells you to jump off a bridge, you're not supposed to."

"Why would you do something like that?" Mom asked, looking into my eyes for a clue. Her face wrinkled with age and concern. "It's so dangerous. You have no idea how deep the water is. There could rocks or any manner of things. You could be paralyzed!"

I didn't know what else to tell her. That I was trying to prove something to Kris? That I was trying to impress her and later wanted to curl into her in the lower bunk? Mom could deal with the idea of a man as the culprit. Moms prepare themselves for that, but not for their daughters to come home with other women. Though I wasn't planning to come home with Kris, I was just thinking about her more and more. Or was I? Was my jumping from the bridge a mating call? Hey! Look at me! Look what I can do!

"I was having fun."

"Your idea of fun needs to be rethought."

"I'm fine. It looks bad, but it doesn't hurt."

Michelle pushed at the bruise again. "It's huge. Look at all the colors. It's like you've got an electromagnetic spectrum tattooed poorly on your thighs."

Mom toggled into sassy mode. "It doesn't matter that you're fine now. I don't want to get a phone call in the middle of the night or the middle of the day or whenever that you were knocked unconscious by water after jumping from a hundred feet up. That's such a stupid thing to do, Lee!"

"It wasn't a hundred feet," I said, turning to Michelle, hoping to deflect some of my Mom's energy. "Where have you been?"

"Out."

"Out with who?"

"Whom," she corrected, knowing fully what I was trying to do.

"Well?"

Michelle and I looked at Mom, wondering which one of us she expected a response from.

"Just be careful. Think a little more before you do things."

"You were with Derrick, weren't you?" I asked after Mom was gone into another room. "You said he was an oaf."

"He is," she said, smiling and poking harder.

Monday afternoon, back in the persecution. The bars came, as they always did. They wouldn't leave me alone. Someone snuck up behind me. "Ms. Bauer, we need you to take a urine test." I snapped my head around. Kris' perfect teeth grinned at me. Deepening her already deep voice, she said, "We have reason to believe you engaged in some unethical behaviors this past weekend." Her blue eyes sparkled in jest.

Exhaling fully, I smacked another two feet of tape on the box in front of me. I feigned a five-year-old's whine. "My ass is still bruised."

"I didn't throw you off the bridge." She swaggered off into the lower office, then around and about the plant. A faint smell of honey and vanilla trailed behind her. I didn't want her to go. I wanted her to take Paul's place and run the rumor machine.

Paul hip-checked me. "Heard you tied a few on and threw yourself off."

"How are you in the know that quick?"

"Satellites." He ran around, flipped a switch, came back. "You have a good time?"

"Yep. You missed out."

"Family obligations." He raised his shoulders in helpless defeat.

"And you, Ned? Why weren't you and the wife and the team there?"

He didn't look at me as he loaded the boxes. "Taneesha had to go to the hospital. She miscarried."

"Oh, my god, I'm so sorry. How far along was she?"

"Four and a half months."

"Is she okay otherwise? I mean her health?"

"We'll see. She might not be able to have another. Too risky or something."

His dreams of a big family were gone just like that. I had no idea what he was going through. Even the thought of having kids of my own turned me off, especially when I imagined them turning out like me.

"I'm so sorry," I said.

He nodded.

Paul didn't know what to say, but he did wait a few minutes before asking me, "You get it on with Kevin?"

I dropped the eight count I had. "Wedding bells and commitment chimes. True love."

"You better be fucking with me? Are you fucking with me?"

"Yes."

"Well, don't. That guy is bad news. I usually don't like to tell people what to do, but don't get too into him."

His gruff concern was charming. Paul didn't have to worry. I didn't plan on getting into Kevin at all. For once, not feeling the need to reassure Paul, I brushed him off. He let it drop. He had other trout to fry.

"You know Fred in shipping?"

"Seen him."

"He still lives with his mother."

"Is she sick?" I asked, knowing he wouldn't tell me anything if it weren't juicy.

"Ask me how old he is."

"How old?"

"Thirty-two."

"Cliff Claven was in his forties."

"That's TV. The guy makes thirty-six grand a year and still suckles Momma's titties."

"Titties are nice to suckle."

Paul cocked his head like a pup, like I'd spoken a command he'd not heard from me before. I cocked mine in consideration. Freud was indeed alive and well. My eyebrows squeezed hard. I had no idea why I'd said what I said. I tried to cover it. "Or so I've heard."

"Uh huh."

"What does she get out of it?"

"I'm not going there," Paul said, and he didn't. He glanced at my breasts and went back to his mix and sticks.

An hour later Kris was back. So was a familiar physical ache. I caught myself staring at her breasts. Must be C cups, maybe bigger. I started to wonder if I was looking at her like I sometimes caught Kevin looking at me. Why did it matter anyway? I couldn't remember thinking about Hailey similarly. I was too fraught and tangled in the whirl of my body coming alive and my mind leaving me. There was no sense of aesthetic appreciation with Hailey. Maybe that's what I was feeling for Kris. She was a beautiful woman. The looking was about symmetry and proportion. I was fooling myself and I knew it. When she spoke, my eyes found an appropriate object, a stranger's face. Kris had a trainee in tow.

"Lee, this is Shelly. Show her your magic."

My mind wasn't quite on factory work.

Shelly was tiny with tiny fingers and a dull sheen to her eyes. I gave her my best, but she wasn't going to make it on Four, where I was the expert. Four was my machine. She handled the frog's tongue fine. Everyone did. But time was up. Time for the tray. She approached.

Her eyes saw double or half or not straight. Bars flew into the sissy box like dirty gym socks into the wash. After ten minutes at the tray, my protégé, Shelly, started to cry.

"This is not a job to lose it over. Really." I stepped to the tray. "Just watch."

His days as Jedi Master over, Ned was glad Shelly wasn't his trainee. I had to get her to stop crying. "Where'd you go to high school?"

"St. Ursula."

Ugh. The other girls' academy. From money.

"What are you doing here?"

"I used my parents' credit card to fly out to see my boyfriend. They don't like him very much. He lives in Arizona. I know, you're thinking it's crazy, but he's worth it." She smiled a shy smile. "I have to pay them back."

I tossed bars for a few minutes. "What'd you do in high school?" I asked, deciding I didn't want to hear about love woes or money problems. They were all too familiar. But I couldn't help wondering if my parents knew her parents from way back.

"Studied, went to class. What do you mean?" Her confusion arrested her tear ducts.

"What did you like to do? I mean really enjoy. A sport or something?"

"I played the flute for the marching band."

Great. A band dork. But she had something. The only thing I had in high school was the ability to piss off the nuns at Catholic Girls Academy.

"Then you've got agile hands. You can retrain them, expand their talents." I couldn't believe the shrink-speak spilling from my mouth. Shelly should be playing at the Parasol with the Toledo Orchestra, not wasting her life in the metal labyrinth, a virgin sacrifice to management minotaurs.

Kris checked in. "How's it going?"

She'd been standing behind me. I shook my head sadly, and considered making a request that Shelly be paid to play the flute over the intercom. I rethought that because, frankly, she might not be any good, and if she were, she might send us into worse stupors.

"Take over, Shelly. We have other tortures for Lee." Shelly's eyes went black as sin. I walked off, not unhappy to be doing so, but feeling sorry for Ned who'd have to return from retirement.

Paul watched me leave his machine. "Hey, College, looks like you're moving up in the world."

In her confident strut, Kris led me to an erector-set for adults. Two metal arms extended from a central nozzle and formed a V. A conveyor belt spread out from the lower left of the nozzle. A mini wrap machine folded around the belt a foot down the way.

"I hope you've got agile hands."

I was at once imagining my agile hands on her naked breasts. Meanwhile I stared at the metal robot. I was fearful it was an evil Transformer. I really should have been banned from the TV.

"We're bumping you to minor operator."

"So I'm a B employee now? Do I get a gold star?" My body was charged, being so close to Kris. She smiled, showing her great teeth. White and straight. "This is the cookie machine. It makes ice cream sandwiches. You're going to run it."

Some other schmuck was stuck on Four and I was proud to be rid of it, to move up the ranks. Ready for a change. Maybe the factory wasn't so bad. Just when things were turning stale, sour, other challenges presented themselves. But as I threw the first row of cookies on one of the arms, my insides tightened. I tempered my thoughts to keep from turning two months into twelve. Exactly how the others fell into the bronze handcuffs, I figured. They mistook a small step for a giant leap, and then never minded that the staleness returned and seeped into their pores, their beings.

18

The asphalt on Sylvania Avenue had been torn into rough grooves in preparation for repaving. When this would happen was anybody's guess. The road had been in a shredded state since I'd gotten home for the summer. Large holes in the asphalt revealed the original brick from decades back, which was a shame. The red would have made the landscape more interesting. As it was, the Escort's low undercarriage didn't appreciate the rough road, holes, and patches of brick. And though he was driving with painful slowness, Dad couldn't avoid the deeper potholes pocking the street. The muffler kept scraping and grinding against the road.

"You should really get that fixed."

"You should mind your own business." The steering wheel was forcing its own groove into Dad's gut. He didn't need to get car fixed. He needed a new car. "So how much?" he asked, driving me the eight-tenths of a mile to work. He'd measured the distance.

"Seven-twenty-five. Fifty cent raise," I told him, proudly.

"You won't see half that. Matter of fact, you won't see half the half of that. Government'll take one half and I'll take the other."

"Say that five times fast."

"Go collect your fifty cents," he said, pulling in front of Icy Bites' powder blue door. "Hey, wait!" he said. I leaned in through the passenger window. "A duck walks into a bar orders a drink. Bartender comes back with it. Duck says, 'Put it on my bill.'" He was having a good day off.

Stepping into the line of white-panted and white-shirted factory workers, awaiting the piddly five digits our lives had come to, Kevin nudged me with his shoulder. "Hey, what's going on?"

"Getting my check."

"I know *that*. I mean after."

"I gotta cash it and give it to my dad."

"Skip that. I got something better."

I was surprised he was still willing to let me smoke his dope after I hadn't put out. I said, "I can't. He'll have my ass."

The secretary was wearing a smart blue suit and a big smile. "Bauer, Lee," I told her.

"ID, please." She beamed.

I passed her my license and signed for the check.

"We've got an hour. Run an errand with me," Kevin said, like a little red devil on my shoulder. "It'll be fun. I swear." Seeing my questioning look, he said, "Forget about the other night. We'll just hang out."

"I don't want to go anywhere dressed like this." I was in my work whites.

"That won't matter where we're going."

"I shouldn't get stoned. I'm running the sandwich machine now. I need a clear head. At least until I get the hang of it. And I've gotta get to the bank."

"We can stop at the bank. We don't have to smoke. Like I said, just an errand."

An hour to kill. Boredom had led me unthinkingly into nasty corners before, but that didn't stop me. Kevin huffed as I ran into the bank, telling me to hurry up. I stuffed the envelope with the cash for my dad into my pocket, and we were off on Kevin's errand. The Jeep cruised down Monroe Street past the art museum, its glinting copper roof forced my eyes back to the urban drear. Wind whistled against the ragtop and a few miles later we were in the gothic, Victorian grandeur of the Old West End. My grandfather had worked on some of the houses. He told me that "in the late 1800s, early nineteens, that part of town was *classy*. A visual buffet. And that's just on the outside. Inside, some of them houses have five-six fireplaces, a dozen bedrooms, and second floor porches. Sloping roofs and towers. Nothing like the crap being built today. The wars ruined domestic architecture in this country." The houses were huge and beautiful, but the farther we drove, the less appealing they became. Roofs were caving. Houses were boarded up with cheap ply. Gang graffiti was everywhere. The rich had gone to the suburbs to live in sterilized conformist communities, leaving the rest of us with this.

Kevin crashed a front tire into the curb where nearby garbage disfigured the lawn. I noticed what had to be gunshot holes through a few windows. There wasn't a squirrel or bird in sight.

"This is a drug run, isn't it? We're running for drugs." Disbelief set in, paranoia too. My eyes scanned for signs of a sting operation. "I don't mind smoking your dope, but I don't want to be involved in the pick-up."

He charged ahead of me around the side of the house, climbed through a window, and up a back staircase. Anger set my jaw. I hated being trapped. I followed him.

"Hey, man, c'mon in," Axl Rose's look-alike said, opening the door to us. He eyeballed me. "I'm ready for you in the back."

"Stay here," Kevin said, as he and Axl disappeared into one of two rooms.

My feet were planted, and I fought the urge to throw something. There was nothing handy to throw, though. The apartment wasn't the mess of bottles and syringes and bullies I'd expected, rather a Spartan space with only a couch, a table with two chairs, and a small radio on the floor against the wall playing *Paul's Boutique.* The table was piled high with black-and-white photographs. "Who the hell are you?" a voice broke into my study of the pictures—shots of trees and fields, dolls' heads, and junkyard objects arranged to look haphazard.

I turned toward the source of the voice: a wiry woman in leather pants and a tight brown tank top. A biker bitch if I didn't know better. She had long red hair and an armful of tattoos. She was as remarkable as the photographs. The air in the room shifted, charged magnetically. I was charged and stunned, certain I was watching a digitally re-mastered movie of my life. None of it seemed real.

"Hailey?"

"Sara Lee Poundcake."

"You know I always hated that."

She was skinnier than I remembered, her breasts not nearly filling out her shirt. I had to search a little to see them.

"We always hate what's good for us."

"How are you?" I asked, my body assaulting me with the thrill and chaos I'd felt rushing through me when I was with her.

Just a couple years ago, after she'd told me about playing spin the bottle, she'd said, "Kiss me. I'll show you what it's like." My head pounded, and at first I didn't think she was serious. Like she was testing me. Like it was a game and I was her plaything. My stomach cart-wheeled toward my throat, and just as she was about to turn away, I lunged forward, the force of my mouth, face, head, body, pushing her to her back on the floor. I kissed her. Kissed her first out of anger, out of impatience, out of just wanting to shut her up. Out of annoyance and awkwardness. And then because I could. Because she didn't stop me. All of this collapsed into something I didn't have a name for at the time: lust. I grabbed her, in all my fear and anger and confusion, I grabbed fistfuls of hair, wrapped her with my legs, squeezed, pulled, wrestled her near. Hailey met every move with the same force, the same velocity, her tongue searching, her body reaching. I had no idea where the energy or the will to act had come from. All I knew was that I was awake, so awake. I was fire. I didn't want Hailey to say another word. I didn't want her to start analyzing or scrutinizing, so I kissed her more and, clothed still, slammed my pelvis between her parted legs, as if fucking her. Hard, like I'd seen in movies. My face burned and my stomach was doing jumping jacks in my throat, in my head, everywhere. My throat was terribly dry, and there was a rushing heat in my crotch. The movement wasn't enough. I couldn't bear the inner tornado. I couldn't stop. I shoved my hand down the front of her pants, and feeling warmth, wetness, feeling Hailey's legs open, I moved into her with two, then three fingers.

She made it possible. She made so many things possible.

"You live here with this guy?" I asked, trying to swallow everything down.

"Questions, questions."

"How are you?"

"Fine," she said, coldly.

This was not the Hailey I knew. That Hailey was always talking about art and the impossibility of God. Talking about hunger as the heart of *Last Tango in Paris*. Talking about how certain songwriters had to die, Ian Curtis, Janis Joplin, Nick Drake, David Savoy, because, really, how could someone who feels so deeply grow old with any semblance of grace? Their lyrics would bottom out and just become empty sounds. Talking about polyamory as the most logical and emotional response to relationships. Talking about tedium and just how little people make of their lives.

That Hailey was exciting. Before her, I hadn't been interested in anything. I wasn't a performer. I didn't go out for sports. I didn't read or even care all that much about music. I stood back looking, acting, being bored. If there was something I liked, truly enjoyed, I played cool. Otherwise I was doomed. If I allowed the smallest fraction of excitement in, I was setting myself up for terrible, searing disappointment. Hard as it sometimes was, keeping my emotions in check was the goal of my teenage years. I'd learned early, if I put some small part of myself out there, it came back tangled and bruised, irrevocably deformed. Then what was I supposed to do with it?

"Are these yours?" I asked, referring to the photographs. I was stuck on one in particular that had wires and wheels and rims and bars, bent and twisted and reaching. Some looked angry. Others looked like they were suffering. I looked toward Hailey for an answer and realized that's what I'd done all along when we knew each other. I followed her. Everywhere. She was leaning back, arms crossed tightly on her chest, watching me. "Seriously?" I said. "You're going to be like this? We haven't seen each other in three years. It makes sense we might be a little curious about each other's lives. You have to admit we did know each other pretty well at one point."

"We have experiences. People come and go, passing in and out of each other's lives all the time, reaching all sorts of levels of intimacy. It doesn't always mean anything. It's just how it is."

There was a little of the old Hailey, but with a sharper edge.

I used to love listening to her go off about whatever, unless it was me.

"You've got to stop backing down from the world. This is it, you know. This is your one fucking go-around. Make the best of it. Try every fucking thing you can."

I hated her lectures. "Why are you so fucking mean?"

"It's not mean. It's realistic."

"I think you're wrong. Totally wrong. I mean, yeah, people do come and go, but they leave a mark. You, for whatever reason, just don't like to admit it."

"Listen to you, all grown up, finally saying what's on your mind."

"Seriously, are these yours?" I asked, pushing the photos around.

"What's with all the white?" She walked into the kitchen. "Religious shit?" Drawers and doors creaked open and slammed shut.

Hands hidden behind her back, she came over to where I was standing at the table. Sweat and incense oozed from her body.

"I'm working for the man," I said, patting my back pocket with its stack of fifties.

"Which man would that be?"

"Icy Bites, the ice cream factory. Anyway, whether they're yours or not, they're really good." I was surprised by how caught up in them I was. The photographs were interesting enough to distract me from the past. I wanted to keep looking at them and understand them better.

"What do you know about it?"

"They're striking. This one looks like a Picasso, all fragmented with something weird going on with the light." I didn't know how to talk about what I was seeing, but for some reason I wanted to.

"All right, I'll play along," she said. "They are mine. I'm in town for a few days. Ted's just a friend. I live in Chicago and go to school there at the Art Institute. And these have nothing to do with Picasso. Think more along the lines of Kandinsky and the essence of objects."

"His name is Ted?" I looked around incredulously. "He doesn't look like a Ted. I'm surprised you're in art school. I thought you hated all that institutionalized crap."

She stepped uncomfortably close to me, as if she was about to kiss or knife me. "A lot of the thoughts we have at fifteen are naïve thoughts." She stepped back and a flash went off. For an instant all I saw was red. Then Kevin and Axl, I mean Ted, shaking hands. "Drop by later," Kevin said, over his shoulder, ushering me out the door, dazed by the camera flash and the strangeness of seeing Hailey again. I couldn't help but think she looked good, a little on the thin side, but good.

I punched in. Employee B. Wayne accosted me. "Where've you been? You were supposed to have this machine going twenty-five minutes ago. You're supposed to call at least half an hour before your start time if you're going to be even two minutes late."

"I'm fine. Family's fine. Thanks for asking." I pushed past him through the inner door into the din of the machinery. It was the first time I'd been late all summer. I wasn't about to grovel or explain. Wayne must have realized this because he stopped snapping at my heels.

Two hours until the shift was over, Kris perched herself on a stepladder near the erector-set. Twirling blue-handled pliers in her left hand as I flung cookies onto the arms of the contraption. Her vanilla-honey breasts had been replaced by Hailey and the black and white photos of delicate metal.

"What are you doing here?" she asked. I heard accusation in her tone.

"Making sandwiches."

"Here, at the factory. In Toledo. You could be doing anything."

She almost sounded like Hailey. *Do anything. Do something.* I slit the seam on a new box of sandwich wrap and cut too deeply. Irritated, I threw the first few sheets in the trash.

"I've been hearing that a lot lately."

"Well?"

"I owe my parents money."

"For what?"

I rolled a sleeve of cookies onto the left side of the V. Too hard, a few broke. I picked them out and set them aside. For what, I had no idea. I was making a mess of my new position.

"You crash their car?"

"I owe them for school." I fed the wrap into its slot until it took and I slid the ream on its peg. "I didn't do so well this past year."

"What happened?" She adjusted her polka-dot cap.

My mind went to Hailey. There was Hailey. Fucking Hailey. Fifteen and fucking a girl. It was wrong. It was right. My head was bitterly twisted. My stomach exploded into butterflies whose wings too soon felt torn, shredded. I had no idea who the hell I was, especially after she dumped me "to see other people." Hailey was the beginning and then I lost myself in Courtney and screwing around, smoking, drinking. It was a way to feel alive in the world. At school I was on my own.

"I flaked."

The roll of wrap got thinner and thinner.

"You flaked?"

I felt my chest sink in.

"What does that mean?"

"Means what it means," I said, not wanting to be interrogated by anyone anymore, least of all Kris. "Like a shrug. I just couldn't do it."

"What kind of lame excuse is that?"

The excuse *was* lame, but I couldn't begin to explain. "My parents don't buy it, either."

"Huh."

We sat quietly for a few minutes while I ran the machine. My mind darted from Hailey to Courtney to the floundering person I was, to the dawdling one I'd become.

"You know, I never went to college because we didn't have the money for it. Well, that and other things happened." She leaned forward, elbows on knees, watching me work, maybe watching for my response. She clapped the metal tips of her pliers together. "My parents were farmers. Liked to be outside with their hands in the dirt. My dad couldn't sit still to read the morning paper. Except having his hands in the dirt dug up nothing. How much do you owe them?"

"Eight thousand. My dad usually leaves me with a little spending money, though."

"That's kind of harsh."

"I guess, but I blew it pretty bad. I let them down. Again."

"Again?"

"Long story," I said.

"Why'd you go in the first place?"

"I guess because it was expected of me. I didn't really know what else to do."

Under the cranky sky, Kevin waited in his Jeep by the factory door. Paul's warning rang in my ears, but I was wired, so I let it ring. I had an extra fifty cents to burn, and Kris wasn't going out. I coasted onto the passenger seat of Kevin's car. Kevin drove west on Sylvania, not the route to the bar. Extracting a joint from his ashtray, I lit up and passed it to him. Back and forth we went until I melted into the passenger seat and dropped out of the present tense, returning only when we pulled into a quiet neighborhood in the land of the one-story houses. Kevin parked in front of a small house with closed curtains. From the curb I could hear music, even faint murmurs.

"Whose house?" I asked.

"Missy's."

I didn't think Kevin had friends outside of the plant employees, except Gene, whose stick I hadn't straddled in ages. When we entered the house, rumblings of laughter came from a back room. The doors down the hallway were all closed. Lounging in the main room were the usual three packers whose names I'd never committed to memory, except Missy's, whose name, thanks to Paul, I couldn't help but remember. I plunked down on the couch. Kevin squeezed in next to me. The dark roots on the crown of Missy's head held my attention. Lifting her head, she pinched her nose and sniffed hard. A bill slowly unfurled on a CD case on her lap. White powder dotted the plastic cover. A small vial rolled off. Her hand swooped, snagging it before it hit the floor.

"Nice get." Kevin was watching her too.

"Everything go okay?"

"Yep."

"Except he made me late for work," I added, feeling left out of the secret circle.

Missy ignored me.

Six separate nostrils wrapped around the end of the bill before it reached Kevin. AC/DC squealed from the speakers. Though I wasn't tired, I needed to sleep at some point. I didn't need a further boost. And I didn't need a hole in my head any bigger than the one already forming from weed and the spin of machinery and the deafening harangues of my dad. The four packers, Kevin included, issued a collective stare when I passed the CD to the next person.

Kevin had his dead snake of an arm around me. "I thought you were cool with this," he said. He jumped up and switched off AC/DC for Great White's ... *Twice Shy*, which was just as screeching and painful to the ears.

"Sure," I said.

He flopped back down next to me, dead snake in tow. "Hit it then."

"I'm good, thanks." I didn't feel like a fight. And though I didn't like his reproachful tone, I didn't say much else. People were going to do the hard shit, regardless of the dangers. That didn't mean I had to. The occasional joint and the occasional drink was enough, even if Mike Seaver would never date me because of it.

"You ever tried it before?"

"Once, but it was laced into a joint."

"What's the point of that?" Missy asked.

"I asked the same thing," I said, trying to play along. Maybe I should have told them I had a nose allergy, and that anything that went up there got sneezed right out, but I didn't. They seemed like a humorless group.

"That Kris is over at your machine all the time," said a packer with stringy black hair and a pasty complexion.

"Yeah," I said. Bland agreement felt like the right move.

Stringy continued to give me the stink-eye.

"Thing breaks down a lot," I said. We were headed for a heady stoner's conversation.

"You know she lives with Susie and Susie's kid?" Stringy continued, insinuating. That Susie worked first shift was about all I knew about her outside of her campfire chattiness.

"Yeah, they split the rent."

"That's not all they split," Kevin said.

The third packer snorted a laugh. "Ask her who Melissa Etheridge is."

Then I got what they were getting at, but there wasn't much to get. People engaged in all sorts of sordid and noble and strange or inane activities. So what if two women shared slippery fingers? Doing so was probably more fun than doing drugs every night with the same crowd in the same basement. I thought of Hailey, imagining her up in their faces at the first suggestion of judgment. She wouldn't let their ignorance pass. She'd get an orgy going. Not me. I wanted to be somewhere else with someone else. With Kris, I realized, which both soothed and frightened me and pissed me off because she was likely with someone else. All her time hanging around my machine was just that, aimless loitering to pass the time.

"Everyone knows who that is," I said, beating down my irritation. "A Bruce Springsteen wanna-be."

The coke-speckled CD case went around the room again.

"What's the story with you two?" Missy said, her eyes zipping back and forth at Kevin and me. The white puck up her nose had obliterated her fears.

I didn't bother to answer. She had more of a story with Kevin than I did and besides, I didn't know for certain if she meant Kris and me or Kevin and me or someone else entirely. Not giving a shit, I wasn't following as well as I could have been. And then I seemed to be the center of attention, a place I wasn't comfortable in. I liked the periphery. But they'd moved the walls closer as if they'd plotted something secretly because I wasn't them. Fangs bared, the pack was circling.

"We're just hanging out. Patience and all that." Kevin winked at me.

At such a lovely and intimate moment, I saw myself wrapping my arms around him, sending my tongue shooting down his throat. I'd straddle his lap for better positioning, deeper tonguing. Letting him and the rest know just what was going on. Instead, I plucked the joint from his fingers and inhaled very, very deeply. My lack of response dispelled the air of agression. The ratty black-haired packer and her cohort sojourned to the kitchen for shots of tequila. Across from us, Missy stabbed at Kevin with her eyes. She wasn't getting what she wanted, and my presence was the reason why.

"He's just using you," she said. As warning or threat, I couldn't be sure. She was talking to him but looking at me.

"Shut the fuck up, Missy," Kevin said.

Glass shattered in the kitchen. Laughter followed. Missy didn't blink. "You're an asshole, boning your way through the plant."

Kevin clenched his teeth, but didn't say anything. Missy closed her eyes, rolling back into the music and into her individual emptiness. My own brain was fried. I couldn't connect thoughts, puzzle out what the others assumed about me and whether it was true and if it really mattered. I wanted to know who else from the factory Kevin was with, if only to have one up on Paul. But I didn't bother with that either. I asked Kevin to take me home.

The dead snake on my shoulder twitched. "Dude, I can't drive right now."

Her legs jouncing, Missy trained her eyes, hawk-like, upon us.

First Courtney's disappearance, then the run-in with Hailey, now having to deal with Kevin. Topping the pile was the idea of Kris with someone else. It was all too much. My insides raged. I needed to do something. I needed to get out of there. "Hand that over," I heard myself say.

"The kid finally wants to play," Missy said, plucking the case and coke from a nearby seat. She cut two large lines, and presented them to me.

I sniffed hard and fast with my left nostril, then with the right. A sharp spike flew up my nose into my frontal lobe. I sat back and the spike induced a generalized bleed. The inside of my head filled with a hard warmth, and every nerve sang with electricity. My eyes widened to the aerate the transformation. I saw Axl-Ted and Hailey. Hailey Berger with her red hair and fine tits and half-smirk of derision. There was a fist in my head and a vice on my heart. For three years I had ignored everything I felt with her or about her. All those feelings were suddenly boiling to the surface.

Axl-Ted took the case from me.

"You two are just in time," I heard Missy say. "This chick, here, has just outdone herself. We're waiting to see if she passes out or starts turning cartwheels."

"And how does it feel?" Hailey said, staring me down.

"You want in on this?" Axl-Ted asked. Her nose took over.

The coke surged through me. I felt as big and bulky and strong as Derrick after a hard workout, stronger even. I could have thrown the couch out the window, and Missy too. "Feels fine," I said, playing cool. "But I think I need a drink." In the kitchen, the Tequila bottle was half-empty. The lights were out and broken glass winked from the floor.

Stringy Hair poured me a shot. "You know, we thought you were a bitch at first, but you might be all right."

I swallowed the shot, which slid down surprisingly fast and smooth, with no cruel aftertaste. "Always stick with your first instinct," I said.

Stringy Hair slugged from the bottle and left. Her friend followed, obedient. I leaned against the counter, arms folded tight across and into my chest. My whole body rigid. My heart and head thumping erratically.

Hailey and Ted came through the swinging door, with Ted nearly yelling, "His work is totally religious. Those stupid strips are God AND man as a single stream of light. Old Testament Adam is Adamah is adom—red and dam—blood. It's all Hebrew-connected."

"Can you believe the shit this guy comes up with?" Hailey asked. "Hey, you're still in white. She's all white." She lifted herself onto the counter. "The picture of purity. She's a goddamn living zip right out of a Newman painting."

Though I'd changed into a different shirt, I still had my white work pants on. "You're still black," I said. "Inside and out." She looked remarkable. Fucking remarkable. Feeling that about her irritated me. Something went lacing through my spine when she looked at me, and I was filled with sudden desire despite how awful she'd been to me three years ago. There was no doubt she had made her mark. I poured her a shot. She drank it down. I poured her another. She drank that one down. As I was pouring the third, she hopped off the counter, taking the bottle from me.

Ted looked back and forth between us, shook his head, mumbling, "End of conversation. Just like that. You never take me seriously," as he headed into the other room.

"I do take you seriously, Teddy," she yelled after him. "You know I'm with you on the whole spirit-man-earth thing in Newman and it kills me that Mapplethorpe's dead, but have them turn this white-trash crap off, would ya? Hey, more white. It's a theme."

I had no idea how to speak their secret language, navigate their private universe. I wanted to, though. I wanted to be able to fake-argue about strips and whoever the hell Mapplethorpe was. The liveliness of the mystery attracted me.

"What's your theme?" she asked me.

"My theme?" I resumed my crossed-arms post against the counter.

"You haven't changed. A safe that still needs to be cracked." She shook her head. "I tried. Your story," she said. "What's your story, philistine? Everyone has one. Why the hell are you working in a factory?"

"Good pay. Good benefits. What *should* I be doing?"

"Everything. Anything. There's a whole fucking world out there to be had."

She pulled a baggy of pills from her pocket. She lobbed a tablet into her mouth then looked at me, considering. She took another pill out and placed it on her tongue. She stepped in front of me and uncrossed my arms, pinning them behind my back. It was too late to resist. Not that I would have. She smashed her mouth against mine, kissing me hard and tonguing the pill into my mouth. She held me against the counter, her lean, strong body against mine. My spine rippled with electricity, with the old thrill, with a new one. I pushed into her as much as I could from my pinned position. "Swallow it," she said. She released my hands, but didn't back away.

"What is it?"

"Only one way to find out."

I kissed her. The kiss was a battle of tongues, angry and fast. She bit my lip. I bit hers harder. We kissed hard for some time, reaching toward the back of each other's throats, until finally we needed full breaths of air. She loosened her grip on me and slid her hands down my back onto my ass, around to my hips, holding there.

I could feel my lower lip swell and I tasted blood.

"I do remember that about you," she said, a wicked smile teasing her cheek. She ran her other hand along my neck down to my pounding chest and held there looking at me. After some time she pulled a folded paper from her pocket. With no light in the kitchen, I barely made out an indistinct, white oval right of center. The picture she'd taken of me.

"I wouldn't keep that one in your portfolio," I said, snatching it. I folded it up and put it in my pocket.

"*Portfolio*? What, you think I do this for anyone other than me?"

A white column of heat pulsed through the notches in my spine. It must have pushed forth from my eyes because Hailey said, "That's the ecstasy." We were kissing again. Another battle, this time more familiar but no less exciting. I could have kissed her like that until my tongue collapsed from exhaustion. She bit me again, drawing me deeper. "There are parts of you I miss," she said. "I think this is the one place you let yourself go."

I'd not thought of it that way before. I lost and found myself kissing her, and previously fucking her. "I suppose you're right."

"You ruin it when you talk."

"I could say the same about you."

We locked pelvises again.

My body wanted more, wanted to feel her skin against mine, but my head sirened the opposite. We'd had a good time together. She took me to a hidden field, then left me there to find my way back. "Look, Lee," she'd said. It'd been days since we'd hung out and I was going crazy. "I want to have experiences with other people. We're way too young to be locked into each other." She went on about having told me in the beginning that she was polyamorous. "This has run its course." I called her. I left notes in her locker. She shut me out, coldly, completely.

Despite the memory I kept kissing her.

"What the fuck?" Kevin with the perfect timing.

I sucked at my bloody lip. I was alert from the coke, dreamy and gooey from the X, and a little fuzzy from the booze. He threw the Jeep keys at me. They hit the edge of the counter and dropped to the floor. "Go start the car."

"Chill out. Everything's all right. We're just having some fun."

"You said you were ready to go home."

"I was until Hailey showed up. We go way back. She's an old friend." I kicked the keys back at him. He picked them up and threw them at me again, harder this time. He missed. Hailey grabbed the tequila bottle and whipped it against the wall next to Kevin.

"Fucker!" he yelled, running at her. "I always hated you, bitch!"

My legs were gravy and I was having trouble understanding why he was so mad, but I managed to push him away. He grabbed my arm and wrenched it hard, setting me off balance. I slipped and fell on my side, knocking my funny bone and cutting my elbow on the glass. Oddly, none of it hurt. It felt like a cat had scratched my arm. I started laughing.

Kevin looked down at me. "You're a fucking tease."

"Oh, Kev." I smiled. I couldn't help it. "We're just hanging out. Don't be such a prick. Have some X. Go sleep with Missy." I got up and grabbed a paper towel, cradling it to my elbow. "It's all good."

"You never told me you were a fucking dyke."

Not knowing why and unable to suppress it, I started laughing again.

Hailey snatched the keys from the floor.

I tried to get my breath. My heart pounded and I thought I blew a rib. "Yeah, sorry about that," I said. "I didn't think you'd let me smoke your weed if you knew."

Hailey made for the door. "Hailey, don't go," I said. "We have catching up to do." I smiled at her with what I thought was a dreamy look. With so many substances in me, I really had no idea what my face was doing.

"Fuck this," Hailey said. "I don't want any part of your little break-up." She was gone, and I didn't want her to leave. I shook my head at Kevin for fucking it up. I wanted him to disappear. I wanted the last month with him not to have happened.

"What the hell is your problem?" he said. Frustration creased his face in wavy lines. He rattled a chair hard against the tile floor, gripping so hard his knuckles went white. In ten years this would be his defining moment.

"Two people can hang out without sex confusing things," I said, and wanted to believe it, but found myself continually confronted with contrary evidence, "like buddies. Like me and Derrick. Derrick's a good guy. You can be a good guy."

Gene came into the dark room. "Everything all right in here?"

"Gene, man, Kevin is angry."

Kevin stared straight into my eyes. "You're a cunt." With that, he left.

The fall, the torn skin, and the fight made me feel tired and detached. My hard head and bloody lip and sliced elbow made me long to be away from Kevin, away from the pack, and ready to be in my own bed listening to my sister snore. "Gene, you're a good guy and a good driver, but fuck all this. This is all crazy, don't you think? I don't know what I'm doing. Do you know what you're doing? It's like it's all a bizarre maze of mutual loneliness."

The streetlights had long since cut off for the late hours of the night, the early hours of the morning. My elbow had stopped bleeding, and didn't look as if it needed stitches. My shirt needed to be laundered though. Any ecstatic feeling I was feeling from the pill I had swallowed was gone. If I ever saw Hailey again—just the thought of her sent something whipping through my pelvis. The kiss and her hands squeezing my ass. The memory had a surreal glow. I wasn't sure it had happened at all, and at some level regretted that more hadn't.

But the heat didn't end there.

"Where the hell have you been? It's four in the morning."

I didn't say anything, just closed and locked the door.

"What's wrong with your arm?" Dad asked, accusingly.

"It was bleeding," I said, as if it happened all the time.

"I can see that. *Why* was it bleeding?"

"I fell."

"Damn it, Lee. What did you do?"

My head was losing its hardness and starting to clear. My body still jittered as if cold, though I wasn't. "I don't want to fight, Dad. Whatever answer I give sets you off, so it really doesn't matter what story I tell."

"Where's this week's money? I checked the account."

I reached into my back pocket and pulled it out.

"This some kind of joke?" He was holding Hailey's Polaroid of me.

My stomach surged and mind spun, circling for what I'd done. It hit me—Hailey's glorious and treacherous hands on my ass. My heart resumed its flurry of drumbeats. "I don't have it," I said, stupid, defeated.

"What do you mean you don't have it? Where is it?" His voice rose. "Are you doped up?"

"I'm not doped up. Listen, let me borrow your car. I think I left it somewhere. I'll go get it." He started to object, but I cut him off. "I'll go get it."

He stared hard at me. "You've got forty-five minutes. Don't make me late for work."

"Okay. Okay."

Furious at Hailey, feeling betrayed by her again, all over again, I got in the car. I retraced the route past the art museum into the Old West End where Kevin had taken me earlier. The neighborhood looked even more broken-down in the dew and morning light. I knocked on the door, yelling, "Hailey! I need my money! I know you took it." My heart pounding, my head a hive of dying sparks, I slammed my bodyweight into the door. It didn't budge. After several futile attempts like this, a neighbor down the hall poked his head into the hallway and said, "Knock that shit off. Try the damn fire escape if you need in so badly." Which I did. I got to the window of the bedroom. It was locked, but I was desperate. I rammed my elbow through the glass, breaking the scabbing skin afresh, and reached through and twisted the lock. The bedroom was a single mattress on the floor, some clothes piled in the closet. No one was home yet. I found a note on the table: *Outta here Ted. Thanks for the hospitality. See you in Chi-Town next time you're through. This one's for you.* Next to it was the metal-works photograph I'd been captivated by earlier. I grabbed it and made my slow descent out of the apartment. Elbow throbbing and bleeding again, I sat in the car for a few minutes, thinking maybe I could just drive to Chicago. Maybe I'd catch up to Hailey. Maybe I should go back into the apartment and look for money. There had to be money in there. Maybe. Or maybe, more likely, I was just a foolish idiot.

"Well?" my dad said as I entered the house. He was sitting at the table reading the paper.

I rubbed my forehead. "I don't have it."

"You don't have it."

"I didn't spend it on drugs. I didn't gamble it or drink it away. I was stupid. It's gone. It's just gone."

"You *lost* it?" Incredulous, he looked at me closer, eyes resting on my fat lip. "What the hell did you get yourself into? Fighting like a teenage boy? I work five, six, days a week for years, providing for you and your mom and your sister, trying to set a good example, trying to do right by you. And what do you do? You fritter it all away. Every damn day for the last twenty-three years, I sling those letters."

"Oh, c'mon, you've got the easiest job in the world."

"You wouldn't last one day."

"I'll bet my check on it."

"What?"

"I can easily do a day. I'll bet my check."

"Take a shower, get dressed."

"What?"

"You said it. You owe me a check," he said.

When I got out of the shower, my elbow was still bleeding. "Dad?"

"Let's go."

"We have to make a stop first."

Reluctant, he drove to the urgent care where I got eight stitches in my elbow, making him late for work, ruining his perfect attendance for the year.

"Used to be a day I'd do anything for you," he said. "I don't know who you are anymore."

"Makes two of us."

In the wizened light of the employee area of the post office, I was six again. I felt three feet tall, standing in front of his coworkers with a fat lip and a sore and stitched elbow. I should have kept my mouth shut. He loaded up his truck and we were off. At the first street on his route, he cranked down the emergency brake.

"Let's go, Lee. We don't have all day."

"What?"

"Get your ass out of the car, now."

"But my elbow," I muttered.

He stared me down.

I got out because I didn't know what else to do. He hefted the mailbag onto my shoulder. I lost an inch in height. The fucker was heavier than I'd ever imagined.

"You match the address on the envelope with the one on the house," he said.

"This illegal. You know that, right? A federal offense."

"Get going. And by the way, we're adding the urgent care copay to your tab."

"Of course you are."

"Hit it."

And I did. In all my disbelief and anger, in all my fatigue and pain, I did. I marched from house to house, my dad following behind me. When I finished that bag, we went back to the truck for more mail and another swing. We didn't speak. Weariness weighed on my shoulders. The last of my buzz evaporated. I crashed. A dark, heavy veil pulled over my brain and draped my body. That, mixed with the humiliation of walking in front of my dad, carrying the load he'd carried for twenty-plus years, broke me. My eyes welled. I looked to the sky to keep the tears from falling. I knew I was done. I was done screwing around with Kevin. I was done popping pills and smoking dope. I was done fighting with my dad, with myself. If it meant never feeling like that again, I was willing to walk the straight line.

19

I would like to say that that was all that happened. My summer adventure. My low point. Stolen money and a make-out session with a biter who'd taken my virginity years before. A humiliating day as a mail mule. I would like to say that that was enough to compel some self-reflection, to get me moving in another direction, in any direction. That I made good.

It's not that simple.

Never that simple.

I am here, yes, and you're reading this damned thing. Judging me, judging my misdeeds, misadventures, and my rendering of them. "Be candid. Be critical. Be true," was what you'd said. Halfway through, I thought, man, this guy must be a voyeur, reading such drivel every year, twice a year, even. And I also thought, immediately, that the assignment was silly. The whole idea of a memoir—a life account— written before age sixty, at the minimum, is absurd. I mean, c'mon, very few lives are that interesting, period. And then to think that a twenty-year-old has anything to say? Even more absurd. Twenty. Still victim to mood swings and hormone fluctuations and acne. Still victim to MTV adverts and pop songs and the idea of true love. But then, here it is, all this ink to cover one summer in a lifetime of summers to come. I admit, the game is fun, the game of writing all this out, making sense, choking on my own lint. I know now that this is more than an exercise in writing a memoir, that the real point is to explore the nature of the narrative and what it reveals, because that's what's at the core of psychotherapy: the story. The story told, then reframed in the storyteller's mind. And conversely, psychology —character—is what's at the core of literature. What people do and haphazardly don't do and outright refuse to do. The telling dampens inner turmoil and establishes control in the teller, gives some semblance of stability to identity. The telling and retelling answers questions and solves problems, allowing for distance and sequence, which aren't available in the moment of the happening. The telling allows us to change not what happened but our emotional attachments to and our current understanding of what happened. The telling allows, perhaps most important, redefinition. They're ultimately all we have, the tales we tell ourselves.

There is more to the story, and more redefining to do. The story isn't as simple as a few plot points leading to an epiphany, subsequent change and some kind of ever-after. There's always something more. Something left out or ill-conceived.

Back to the telling.

20

Kris' large Chevy, functional for her side-job slabs of drywall, two-by-fours, and tools, had a two-foot console that placed a chasm between us. In my parents' Escort, I was always bumping hands or nudging arms with the shotgun rider. In the van this wasn't possible. I bridged the divide with my eyes, watching Kris' fingers guide the wheel. She'd driven us a short distance on the interstate and exited into Point Place, which borders the northwestern part of Maumee Bay. Houses were crammed together and fenced in. Her van was out of place amidst the small cars, three with flat tires and major dents. She parked near an embankment and reached behind her for the six-pack of Coors Light she bought after work. She looped a finger into a plastic ring and let the cans dangle. I followed her tight runner's frame over a knoll and out a narrow breakwall, two feet wide and about eight feet long. We were at a small inlet of the bay. A few football fields to our right was a docking area. There was no movement. The boats were in. Kris eased herself down, hanging her legs over the side. I inched closer, dreading a dip in the water, and sat next to her, hip to hip. I was distracted, yet my body vibrated, like it was filled with nervous bees.

"I intend to get you good and drunk so you'll spill whatever's on your mind," she said. "You've been unusually quiet all night."

I drank the beer and listened to the waves crash against the stone.

"I've seen you drink. Will three beers be enough?" She opened a can. Foam rolled over its sides. She sipped quickly then handed it to me. "Nice out here, isn't it? I like it. Like the ocean."

"I had this dream last night," I told her. "It's one I've had before. I'm on fire. My arms and legs are burning, but it doesn't hurt. I watch with this weird detachment as my arm burns and a line of flame crawls up my shoulder. My hair bursts into an orange-like sun and I'm laughing. Then the dream shifts and I'm in a hospital and someone's yanking bandages off me. My skin is rough and dry. Large smooth white scars bubble against these long, leathery lines. And my hair hasn't grown back in. And then I'm standing outside the hospital and people won't look at me. They walk wide arcs around me and I just stand there, waiting, but there's no one to pick me up."

"That sounds awful."

"Do you believe dreams mean things?" I asked but didn't wait for a reply. "I don't know. Mine are always pretty weird and I can never really figure them out. You know, if they're supposed to mean something. But I know about this one. Or at least I think I do. When I was at school, I started going to this movie theatre. A lot. So much that the manager—he had these thick forearms and a scraggly beard going every which way—started telling me stories about Vietnam. And then after that, he said I spent a lot of money there and wondered if I wanted to make some." I paused, considering if I wanted to rehash the story.

"Go on," she said.

"The theatre was just a small two-screen thing that played whatever the guy wanted to play. Some smut, but mostly old black-and-white movies. I figured he needed a projectionist or a counter person. He was the only one I'd ever seen working. He asked me if I had a car, which I didn't. So he said he had a bike that I could ride, said the job was delivering stuff." Kris was gazing at me, rapt. "Are you sure you don't mind me rambling on about this?"

She took a sip of her beer, looking at me. "Get on with it already."
I told her the story:

"Job's delivering stuff," Yellow said.

"What? Like newspapers?"

Unsure if I was joking, he darted his eyes from the left side of my face to the right. "See, the last kid graduated. He ran for four years. You're a freshman. I figger you'll be around the next four." He looked around the small foyer, and then slid off his stool. "Come round the counter. Lemme show ya."

I followed him up some stairs, past the two projection booths, through another room, and down more stairs to a door. Yellow didn't need to dig tunnels underground. He had his own maze in the movie theatre. He unlocked the door and pulled the cord to a single bulb in the center of the room. There was a computer at the back and videocassettes everywhere else, stacked floor to ceiling. Each tape had a white label with black numbers written meticulously on the side.

"You want me to deliver videos?" I said. I pulled one out and looked at it. No title, no words, just the label and number.

"I get videos in for some people around town who order 'em. Since I'm running the shows here, I can't deliver the tapes. Can't be two places at once." He looked at me gravely as if he'd just made an astounding philosophical leap.

I caught a whiff of his nasty breath. "Why don't I watch the counter and you deliver the tapes?"

"I got a bum leg. Besides that, customers would rather see a pretty lady like you knocking at the door. They liked Tim fine, but I think they'll like you better."

My stomach turned. I wasn't sure if it was his tuna breath or the insinuation. I needed money. Calling my parents again wasn't an option. Yellow held the alternative.

"Why don't they go to Blockbuster like everyone else?" I asked.

"Blockbuster don't deliver."

"What's on the tapes?"

"You just deliver them and don't worry about that."

I looked around the room. There must have been over a thousand tapes, all with their secret, careful code. "Is this illegal?" I asked.

"I fuck Uncle Sam any chance I get. It ain't illegal in my book." He pulled the string and the room went dark. "Five bucks a tape. Under the table, of course. You'll do it?"

"Yeah, I'll do it."

The next day, riding Yellow's rickety old Schwinn bicycle, I delivered a backpack full of videotapes to four people who each opened their doors cautiously, peering out from the centimeter sliver. "What's your name?" they asked. When I told them, they opened the door an inch, just barely wide enough to slide a tape through. I held tapes out and fingers like miniature pincers crept through the crack, snagged the tape, and disappeared behind the door again. It happened like this for three weeks straight—the same four houses, the same four pincers, and the same doors closing in my face. After ten days I had to collect the videos and return them to Yellow. I made eighty bucks a week. I got some exercise, pedaling through the windy, hilly brick roads.

But my curiosity wasn't satisfied. "Why can't you tell me what's on the tapes?" I asked one afternoon as I loaded another set into my backpack.

Yellow shook his head and didn't say a word.

I shook mine and headed for the door.

"Don't let Rudy give you any shit."

"Who's Rudy?"

"You'll see."

After I made the customary four stops, I wheeled the green Schwinn down an alley to a new address. I knocked on an apartment door. A man yelled for me to come in. Four cats met me in the kitchen, rubbing against my legs and purring. When I walked into the living room, I saw a man was seated in a wheelchair. Well, half a man. He had no legs. He was torso and arms. His grizzled face grinned wide.

"I'm Rudy," he said. "I would have gotten the door, but…" He threw his hands in the air.

"Lee," I said. "Don't worry about it." I pulled his tapes from my bag. "Here you go."

"Thanks so much."

I turned to go.

"Would you like a drink or something to eat?"

He was the first customer who'd said more than three words to me. I wondered if I should back out the door and pedal my ass back to the dorm. But I decided a man in a wheelchair couldn't do much damage.

"Some water would be good," I said.

"Glasses are in the third cupboard on the right. Would you get me a Coke while you're in there?"

I should have anticipated that. I went to the kitchen and returned with two Cokes. I looked at Rudy as he guzzled his.

"You ever meet Tim?"

I shook my head.

"Good kid. He used to do favors for me, since I don't get out much."

One of the cats jumped onto Rudy's lap, what he had of one, and clawed at Rudy's shorts, seating itself. Its pigeon-esque coos grew louder with Rudy's affection. Its lids drooped.

"How old are you?"

"Nineteen."

"You can vote. That's good." He stroked the cat. "But you don't look nineteen. Don't act it."

"How old do I look?"

"Mid-twenties. You've got intelligent eyes. Old for your age. Almost like you've been through the wringer and back."

"The wringer?"

"Seen some things. 'Course, compared to Harry and me, you ain't seen shit. But," he stroked the cat and peered at me, "could be your mind is blank or there's too much in your head."

He must have been high. I was young and dumb and I hadn't been through any wringer. "Are you nuts?"

"Lil' bit. That don't matter though."

"I should be going."

"Okay, kid. See you next week."

Yellow cancelled deliveries the next week. He wouldn't say why. His mysteriousness pestered me. Problem was, I didn't have easy access to a VCR. I could have used the dorm one, but I didn't want to risk the resident attendant stumbling in on some whacked out snuff film. The week away stoked my curiosity. There was extroverted Rudy and the nameless introverted clients and evasive Yellow. I wasn't about to get anything out of the introverts. They only cracked their doors before slamming them shut again. And Rudy, though he liked to yammer, wasn't the type to squawk about secretive matters. My best shot was Yellow.

"Are they smutty?"

"Are what smutty?" He didn't look at me, just kept on reading his newspaper. "You know the kind of films I play."

"Not those. The tapes."

He lowered his newspaper and looked at me over the edge of the world affairs section. "It's on the up-and-up. Nothing any reasonable soul would have much to complain about."

"Are they snuff films?"

"How do you know 'bout stuff like that?"

"A girl hears things."

"It's all safe. You have my word. Now drop it 'fore I drop you." He snapped his newspaper back in front of his face.

Rudy proved loyal. I got the not-for-you-to-know response from him.

"But, so, anyway," I told Kris, "That's when I started having the burn dream. Seeing Rudy in that wheelchair, watching Yellow hobble around, and some of the other people. One had a terrible scar on her face. She was so quiet with these sunken eyes. I think my dream was telling me I could be like them, outcast and alone."

Warm, wet air clung to my skin. Kris' voice and the rock of waves lulled me into a calm that came from placing a cool, wet washcloth on a feverish forehead. The nervy swarm I'd felt faded.

"What was on the tapes?"

"I've been talking too much. You tell me something. Like, if you like the ocean so much, why don't you live on the coast somewhere?"

"The factory takes you in and doesn't let you out," she said, sighing. "Have you ever been to the coast?"

"Only Lake Erie." I set my beer to the side, and picked at my cuticles.

"That doesn't count," she said. "I think I like it so much because I grew up on a farm with miles and miles of fields all around. I can't stand staring at a cornfield or a bean patch anymore. But the ocean, it's like a reverse parallel. I can stare at it all day. That's where I usually vacation. North Carolina, Florida, even Maine once."

"Alone?" I focused her profile against the dark night.

"Provides solace." She shifted her weight, slightly grazing my arm with hers.

"Solace?" I didn't understand.

"Comfort."

"I know what it means." I was confused. "Why do you need it? You're so content. You've got everything here. What would you rather be doing?" I grabbed my beer, grabbing for something to hold me steady.

"Something worthwhile." She stared off at something I couldn't see.

"You're good at what you do."

"What I do isn't much." Her shoulders sagged, almost imperceptibly.

"That's true for a lot of people." I twisted the tab on my beer.

"I don't want to be a lot of people. I'm not a doctor. I never went to college. I don't research cures for diseases. I don't put out fires. I work in a fucking factory." She crushed her can. "I sort of fell into the job one summer and never left."

"You're great around the factory. You're good with Ari and a help to Susie. Paul speaks highly of you and Wayne and Joyce." The tab came loose. I thumbed it into my left pocket.

"I know all that. It feels different inside."

"Some people aren't meant to do great work. Some just drift into jobs and their real work is done elsewhere. I mean, you fix things around the factory. You're good with your hands. But you also remodel people's homes. That's something."

"I guess. But something's missing." She bounced her feet against the wall, against mine once, by accident. I wished it wasn't. I wished she was closer. "Something's off."

"What is it?"

She didn't answer. She was still looking at the thing I couldn't see. After a while she said, "Why don't you go back to school?"

"School doesn't mean much," I said, unsure if I sounded convincing. I stretched, setting my beer down away from me so I wouldn't knock it into the water. I was good at reassuring her but terrible about doing the same for myself. If the fiasco the other night said anything about how my future was going to go, I didn't think I was destined for much. I didn't know what to do or be. It was enough to have a self and a body, let alone live in the world. I hadn't been *called* to anything. It sounded like Kris hadn't either. I hadn't been inspired. Not divinely, not breathed into by anything, and it bothered me, finally, for once. I wanted some sort of purpose. For most people my age, the idea of a vocation was dead. We cruised from tedious job to tedious job or went for the secure one with benefits and bonuses. We couldn't afford to care about the nature of the work or how we felt after a day at the office or the plant or the supermarket. I wondered if Kris wasn't asking the right questions, if any of us was. But you couldn't count on inspiration or vocation, you had to find some kind of bliss and stick with it.

Done talking about herself for the night, she asked, "Are you serious about Kevin?"

"Paul asked the same thing." I finished the last swig of my beer. I didn't want to start talking about him. I wanted it all to be over, to stop feeling like an idiot for hanging out with him. "What does it matter?"

"He caused some trouble last summer," she said. It wasn't an answer I was looking for. "I'm surprised they hired him back," she continued. "Nobody saw what happened. But the girl he was dating got her hand jammed near the wrapper on one of the machines. Second degree steam burns and a few stitches." Kris handed me her empty can. I put it next to mine.

"Did he cause it?"

"The girl denied it. Said it was an accident. They'd stopped seeing each other a week before. I don't know why she was protecting him. We never saw her again, and Kevin never mentioned her. He didn't do anything to you, did he? I mean, in the tent, on the canoe trip? He seemed pretty cold when you guys got in the camper with us."

"No," I said. I felt an odd sense of luck that things hadn't gone anywhere with Kevin. I also felt a little irritated with Kris. "No, he didn't do anything. He was just pissed off that I didn't want to have sex. Why did you take him camping?"

"I invited everyone. Besides, I'm not someone who points fingers or gets in other people's way."

"Are you kidding me?" I was miffed that she was unaffected by this. "When someone's safety is at risk?" There was something more to it, though, knowing this possibility. I was just as lost and drifting as Kevin. I certainly didn't think I had any violence in me, but maybe under certain conditions, I could do anything. I shuddered and dismissed the idea.

"Seemed you two were getting along fine," she said. She put her hand on my arm, and the nervous bees swarmed again. "Just be careful." Part of me wanted to take her hand in mine. Another part wanted to shove her in the water. I sat motionless, my insides a buzzing hive.

21

"What does it mean to flake?" Her mind spinning as much as mine, Kris was roosted on the stepladder. I had just come on shift, and was ripping open a supply bag. I dumped it into the hopper and added the milk.

"I didn't go to class. Played video games. Went to the movies. I told you about the theatre and what came of that. Flaked." At my periphery, I could see Kris twirling her pliers. I checked a pressure gauge. I was glad to have a task to focus on. It kept my body's nervous buzz in the background. I adjusted a knob. I checked the gauge again and started the pump. A runny white substance spurted from the nozzle and slowly thickened.

"This job won't help you out of any sense of being lost in the world."

Her pliers spun to a halt and she twirled them again. I threw a sleeve of cookies on the right arm. The novelty of the Icy Bite cookie machine was losing its stainless sheen.

"I had a good time last night," I said. I couldn't address being lost. I looked at her for a second. She pulled her polka-dotted painter's cap off. Hair fell all over her shoulders. I felt lightheaded.

"Me too," she said. Her voice was dry and rough and didn't fit with her long locks and blue eyes. I liked it, though.

"Might stay here after the season ends," I told her. "Joyce says I'm a shoo-in for the union. Punctual. Hard worker. All that." I thought about running my hands through Kris' hair. I threw a sleeve on the left, missing the edge and sending a few cookies to the floor. I was nervous. I could feel my face flush. I threw the cookies more carefully, keeping my back to her.

"Don't get stuck here," she said.

I imagined being stuck in a car with Courtney or Derrick or, god forbid Missy, for days and days. "Doesn't seem so bad." I couldn't believe I'd said it. I was throwing cookies onto a metal arm eight hours a day, sometimes sixteen. It was a dead-end job in a series of endless dead days. It was bad. I could have been in that car with Courtney, belting out 80s tunes, wind whipping through my hair. I wasn't. I was in a factory. By choice. But Kris, on the ladder, made me lose sight of that.

"Maybe not after two months. Wait till a decade passes. Don't screw yourself like I did. I didn't even consider college." She fingered the brim of her cap. "Sometimes I wish I'd done things differently," she said, more to herself than to me. Stepping near, she adjusted a dial on the sandwich wrap, resumed her place. "Can I tell you something? I haven't told anyone. Not in some years. Seems a lifetime ago, now. I got mixed up with the wrong people. I thought I was invincible. I was in a car one night outside a convenience store when two of my friends were robbing it. They'd been planning it. Poorly, but it was planned. They hadn't told me anything about anything, so there I was, blissed out on hash in the back of the car when Debbie and James come running out, screaming. God, I was terrified. Debbie jumped in the back with me. She dumped all this cash in my lap. She was laughing up a storm. James drove off like a madman. The cops caught up to us. We had a suitcase full of weed and hash and pills in the trunk and the cash from the store and a gun. A fucking gun. I was lucky. I spent only a year in prison. This was the only place I could get a job when I got out."

"From one prison to another," I said, a little stunned. This was not something I was prepared to hear. I never would have guessed anything like it would come from her mouth. I suspected this was on her mind the night before.

"I felt so grateful at the time. I was afraid I'd never get a job. I think fear instilled a lot of immediate loyalty."

"*Prison?*"

"Should I have told you?"

"What was it like?"

"Worse than you can ever imagine. The walls closed in a little more every day. I felt like I couldn't get a deep breath, like I was under water all the time. I still feel it every now and then. And you get the best of the best in that population as you can imagine. Concentrated rage. Women are brutal. You have no idea. Let me put it this way. It's not a place I ever want to go back to. I don't even like thinking about it."

We sat quietly for some time until she asked, breezily, "What was Marietta like?"

"Like prison," I said. "Sorority girls are brutal."

She shook her head.

"Too soon?" I thought of how awful and alone she must have felt day after day. My experience couldn't begin to compare. "Marietta is hilly and old. The fall was great with all the leaves changing. It was gorgeous, and school was fine. Supposedly, it's one of the best in the Midwest, but it was rich kids getting drunk and basketball players getting laid. A lot of bullshit. The teachers were good, I guess. Especially good with students who gave a shit."

"There's a lot of bullshit everywhere. You can't get around that."

I didn't respond and kept at my duties.

"What classes did you take?"

Kris' easy questions and light tone helped me relax and set aside the notion of her as an ex-con. I threw cookies on the V without breaking any.

"I was registered for anatomy and the lab that goes with it, a literature course, philosophy, math, history. All the core classes."

"Seems like a lot."

"Pretty standard for a first semester."

The wrapped cookies marched down the belt into the freezer.

"What happened?" Her forehead wrinkled with disbelief.

"Being away from home, sort of on my own, got to be too much. I had all this free time, and it overwhelmed me. Studying seemed like busywork, pointless in a sense."

"Being away from home's no small thing." She twirled her pliers, looking at me.

"I wish my parents could see it that way. I let them down, big time. You should've seen their faces when I got home. Such utter disappointment. I know I can do fine in school. I just flaked. I don't know how to explain it any better."

She offered her blue eyes and a slight smile as response. The cookies inched toward the spout where the cream came out. I threw two more sleeves on. The machine did its work.

"This one professor wore sandals all the time. Even in winter. Her toenails were always painted pink. And this other one, a long-haired hippie turned burned-out prof, always hit on his students."

"He probably wanted you because you looked young but didn't act it."

"I make stupid nineteen-year-old mistakes like anyone else."

"You're not like the others." She tapped her pliers toward the wall that isolated the sandwich machine from the rest of the factory crew.

"I am like the others."

"You're not as wild. You drink and party, but you don't lose control. Of course, I don't know what goes on when I leave the bar and you're still there." Possibly she was rethinking the image of me she'd constructed, just as I was adjusting and re-adjusting mine of her. She continued, "You've got this presence."

My face flushed. I looked down and watched my hands as I flipped another sleeve onto the machine. I squinted at myself, wondering whether Kris was really seeing me. I didn't have a sense of my place or what I was supposed to do. The blue pliers and V arms beckoned me toward a life that on some level I knew wasn't for me. Maybe Kris wanted me to have a sense of purpose because she was missing one, because she was in a rut, a nine-year rut, and couldn't budge. I didn't want to say as much to her, so I just let the thought roll.

I tossed the cookies and opened another box. It occurred to me that I'd like to be driven, that I did want something internal, pushing me forward. I didn't want to drift anymore. I didn't want to be lost, but I didn't know how not to be. Maybe that was what Kris saw that I didn't. Or maybe I was a younger version of her and she was only seeing regret. I looked at her, sitting on the ladder, spinning her pliers, investigating the spin.

Kris needed a break from the smoke and banter of Pinheads. Rain prevented us from going to the breakwall, so she drove me the short distance home. Dad was up watching late night TV. "That wasn't the Jeep that usually drops you off."

"Kris brought me home."

"The canoe lady?"

"Yep."

"You working or spending all your time drinking with the workers?"

I couldn't tell if he was angry or teasing. I was, after all, actually home early. "Both?"

"Watch it." He flipped the channel. "You carrying my mail for the day doesn't square us, so just watch it."

"Why do you continue to monitor my every move?"

"Someone has to."

22

The end of the summer was nearing, my last days at the factory. I was in the habit of looking for Kris in the break room or in the locker room. I looked for her van in the parking lot. I watched for her perfect teeth grinning at something or someone. Knowing that she was around, that she was asking after someone or fixing something with her blue-handled pliers, or tucking her hair into her polka-dot hat, was comforting. Just a plain, straightforward comfort and ease in knowing someone who knows you.

Then the daydreams took over.

I tried not to pay much attention to my nighttime dreams. They scared me. In them, everything around me was frantic and moving. After a two-year spell of nightmares, I tried to block them out. The terrifying ones were the only ones I ever remembered. Ones in which days and nights in succession went black. Like I was in a tunnel that Yellow talked about and the walls were closing in. My chest constricted. I couldn't get a deep breath. The whites of eyes and fangs gnashed at the dark, gnashed closer, gnashed at me. I ran, but only in circles. Small circles because of the walls.

Or the one with my sister where we were chased through the jungle, vines slapping our faces as we fled something. We didn't know what. We never knew what. Island natives and military men came at us out of the depths, took us captive, and put us on the roof of a building forty stories high. We walked endless circles on the square roof, until I stepped out of the pattern and sprinted diagonally, breaking into the air. I flapped my arms, soaring away. In the dream I needed to get back to my sister, but couldn't help enjoying the flight, the freedom. I was almost sorry Freud was dead.

Or the immolation dream where I survived, but was alone.

What should have been nighttime sheet-soakers drifted into my daytime reveries. I'd finally figured out Ned's trick of silently, intangibly getting through a shift. He was fantasizing. It was that simple. I wanted to compare notes, but he was way over in the other wing of the building. Plus, he might have gotten freaked out or turned on by my daydreams. Like this one:

Large room. Red silk curtains. Red silk for walls. Plush red floor. Heart shaped bed. I'm naked on the bed. A silk blue pillow beneath my head. Someone blindfolds me. Someone's hands at my ankles, slithering up my legs. Smooth, strong hands. Woman's hands. Warm. Squeezing. Up my thighs.

Arousal. Unknowing.

Darkness behind the blindfold. Hands on my belly. One hand pushes up between my breasts. Lips below my navel. Lips on my lips. I want the body against me. Skin against me. I stretch into the kiss. Deep. Penetrating. Then the body retreats. I'm left gasping, thirsty, wanting.

When Kris was called away to fiddle with another matter, I thought about her during the empty hours behind the V of the sandwich machine.

I'd had a week of these particular daydreams. I was thinking about Kris all the time. Having sex with her and setting up house with her. Driving around in her white Chevy. Sitting with her in the cold air of a movie theatre. I feared getting stranded in the factory and leading a life of utter toil but couldn't fathom what else to do. Maybe nine weeks of lying on a couch discussing *What Color Is Your Parachute?* would suffice, but remembering the black-eyed penetrating stares of the counselors at the Community Counseling Center eradicated any thoughts of therapy. I had no desire to pull back my skin, open my skull, and let a stranger's eyes scrutinize my brain. Shrinks and counselors were supposed to help, and they sometimes did. But I was already destabilized, and being subjected to further probing and the expectations of a "mother-figure" or "father-figure" or "mentor" or "sponsor" wasn't going to steady me. That and I'd have to pay for it, which would cause further static with my real folks, who barely justified sending me for help the first time around, being people who think families should keep their issues private. They abandoned their pride and sent me to rehab for three weeks. Considering my level of success since then, they probably regretted giving me the help they did.

I could have called Betty, a very caring fifty-two-year-old, new-age, crystal hugging, pseudo-Zen, AA, OA, NA sponsor who followed me around during my year in post-rehab AA because she was concerned about my welfare for the very same reasons the counselors at the center were – to make themselves feel better about themselves. I was not about to call her. She was a deep, unassuming, but also very dense, flighty Tinkerbell. An hour with her would have been worse than four at the factory. Knowing this, I threw cookies on the machine and I tried to think of what to do with myself, and when my mind came up blank, I stalked Kris. I let the fantasies come and go. I came to own them. They were untroubled and good. I willed them into my daily thoughts. They startled into awareness an urgency that had gone dormant, that I had buried post-Hailey, but that surfaced when I was near the actual, physical Kris.

Just as quickly my mood U-turned. I had become accustomed to the solitude of hiding behind the V, Kris on the ladder next to me, her vanilla-honey scent and muscular runner's frame and the nightly conversations. One day, the sandwich machine down, and I was sent to a room with people I didn't like. I had to bag miniature wooden spoons and ice cream cups. I was not having fun. I hadn't seen Kris all day. She was late getting to work. I was nervous and worried, checking the clock so often only two or three minutes passed between glances. I was trying to settle in and bag the requisite eighteen cups: six strawberry, six chocolate, six vanilla, focusing my energy on the task at hand, when someone snuck up behind me, grabbed my sides, and yelled "BOO!" Cups soared everywhere, and everyone laughed.

"Why are you late?" I asked, ignoring the cups on the floor and maintaining my post at the metal chute.

She watched me botch another bag of cups. "Dentist appointment ran over."

I bagged the cups in broody silence. The other employees chatted around me. I felt the imprint of Kris' hands in my sides. I could still feel the pressure. I wanted her hands on me again. I wanted my hands on her hips. I wondered if her hands lingered or if I was extracting too much from a playful touch. I wondered how she'd react to me sneaking up on her, if she'd turn and embrace me, tackling me onto the ground in a mock brawl. The voices around me didn't offer up any answers and Kris was out of sight.

23

A soft-petaled, purple orchid peeked at me from the crux of the V on the cookie machine. Thirty yards down the wing, a janitor I'd never seen mopped the floor. I set the flower on the stepladder and started work. Kris had taken the day off to finish a side job. I made sandwiches. The floor dried. I made more sandwiches. The shift dragged on.

At home, I put the flower in a vase and presented it to my sister.

"What's this for?" She put her book, a slender green volume called *Praise,* aside.

"For being you."

"Really, who is it for?" She smelled it.

"Someone at work gave it to me."

"No way. Who?" Her curiosity was piqued.

"Don't know."

"You've got a secret admirer?"

"What's so strange about that?" I grabbed her book. "It is pretty strange, isn't it? It was on my machine at work. No one's owned up to it."

"That guy with the bad weed?"

"Jesus, doesn't Derrick keep anything to himself?"

"Not really. Not at all, in fact. Was it him?"

I frowned, trying to imagine it. "It's extremely unlikely."

Kevin was back at the picnic bench. For a second, I thought the orchid could have been from him, an apology, but then I saw his rigid back and bloodshot eyes. I turned to go back inside, but for some unknown reason decided not to. I sat down next to him. He mawed out smoke rings, looking at me, forehead wrinkled. Whatever he had to say pained him. "Listen, about the other night—"

"Don't bother," not sure if I was sparing him or me.

"You wanna come out tonight?" Hope slithered forth.

"Are you crazy? No."

"I was just really high. We have an okay time. We smoke. We drink." His eyes were searching. "We could do other things."

"Go back to Missy," I said, a bit of steel in my voice. I was trying to be civil, but I didn't want to be around him any more. I wasn't willing to risk a bruised face or a broken arm. I wasn't about to offer him my dreams for analysis. I didn't care if he opened up or fried his brain. I couldn't change him, couldn't change his warped expectations and terrible behavior toward women, so I let it go. I let him go because doing so was so very easy to do.

"She's a ho-bag. It's done." He tapped an ash into the grass. "Listen, Ted told me that chick went back to Chicago. So if she's out of the picture, I'm back in, right? I can wait. I can be patient."

I clenched my jaw at the thought of Hailey spending my money all over Chicago. Everything was a game to her.

"Well?" Kevin asked.

"No, Kevin. No."

"What the fuck?"

I turned and walked inside. In the glass just before entering, I saw him angrily flick the cigarette away into the grass.

Back at the sandwich machine, Kris rested dreamily on the ladder. All tension in my body relaxed. Her pliers were at her side. She looked at me from beneath the brim of her hat.

"The thing I don't get," I opened right into it—she was having that effect on me—"is why he keeps coming back. After the tent, after the party, especially after the party. What's in it for him? Can't he see we have nothing in common? The only thing we ever talked about was weed and his numb leg." I took a breath. Kris was looking at me, listening. Her face betrayed amusement. I kept going, revealing things to her I was just beginning to reveal to myself. "It probably sounds like I care about him, doesn't it? But I don't. The thing is I'm embarrassed that I was hanging out with him at all. Embarrassed because I was lonely enough to. I used him. Not because I liked him. It was as if I was avoiding myself."

Having patiently let me ramble on, she said lightly, "So you don't think the flower was from him?"

I offered a weak smile. "No."

"He's not the exciting romantic interest?" She was being coy, toying with me, but my mood hadn't shifted enough to play back. She sensed it. In silence, she watched me work and I listened to the hum of propellers swirling the ice cream.

"I've got a party to go to Sunday. You wanna come?" Kris asked.

"I just admitted I was lonely and now you're asking me to a party?"

"I don't mind being used."

24

Above me was an unfamiliar ceiling. A fan spun slowly around. Dry and cracking paint overhead threatened to fall. Someone's eyes were watching me. My head had become a forty-pound bowling ball. I looked over. Kris with a K.

"I think I had sex with a midget last night. I think it was pretty good sex. He crawled all over me."

She humored me. "What makes you think that?"

"I feel bruised and sore like a small person used me for sport, and the last thing I remember is playing pool with someone half my size."

"Statistically, you didn't have sex with a midget last night. It's one of infinite possibilities."

"What about an amputee?"

"Even more of a long shot."

"You're sure the circus isn't in town?"

"You were too drunk to walk straight. What makes you think you could fuck straight?"

I blushed at her brazen use of the F word, then asked, "How do you know I was that drunk?" I flashed to leaning into Kris, or falling, as we walked from her van to some house. I hadn't intended to drink so much.

"You are in my bed."

The breeze from the ceiling fan rubbed against my cheek. Familiar jeans, socks, and shoes confettied the hardwood floor. Her brazenness freed a little space in me and without thinking, I asked, "Did I have sex with you?"

"No."

"Did you have sex with me?"

"No sex was had by either of us."

Twisted and stabbing and not supporting what it was supposed to, my bra became a too-tight corset. I couldn't get a breath. I lifted slightly and adjusted. "Then why am I in your bed?"

"Fucking can be done anywhere. This bed's for sleeping."

She was wearing a long T-shirt. I wondered if she had underwear on. I was still in mine. Why wouldn't she be in hers?

She brought me a glass of water and an aspirin. "You owe me a car wash."

Still not moving, I held the glass by my side. I tongued my teeth. Furry.

"I puked last night?"

"You held your head out the window like a dog and drooled down the side of my van. You wouldn't let me pull over. It's a big van."

The foggy night began to clear and I realized drooled was putting it mildly. Embarrassment crept though me like a sneaky burglar leaving things a little out of place.

"Would've made me wretch worse," I said to cover.

"The tequila caused that on its own. My stopping or starting would have had little effect."

"Should I apologize for anything in particular?" My body cringed in anticipation of what else she might reveal, but her answer came in the form of a mysterious smirk. "What time is it?"

"Noon."

"Fuck. I have to work in four hours."

"Yes, you do."

Enjoying every moment of my agony, she grinned. I suddenly, desperately, wanted to feel normal and kiss her but the bowling ball engorged itself. I didn't say anything, and I didn't move. I stared at the cracking paint and lay there, pinned. I couldn't imagine her wanting to kiss me after last night's display.

I remembered water.

"Do you have a straw?"

She disappeared again and came back with one.

"It's from fast food three days ago." She slid jogging shorts up her legs.

"Can't be any worse than my mouth."

If she'd known the state of my mouth, she would've been grateful I couldn't kiss her.

"Do you need to call your parents?" She pulled her nightshirt off, exposing two beautiful brown nipples, puckered and waiting. A sports bra went on, covering them. She hid her round shoulders with a T-shirt. I was disappointed. I could stare at her shirtless for hours, just look and not touch. Her belly revealed subtle cuts of muscle. She had a small slope at the lower part of her spine. I wanted to roll my knuckles in that very spot, and would have been content to roll my eyes over it for a little while longer.

"Told them I was sleeping over somewhere."

On the edge of the bed, she slipped socks over her bony feet before stuffing them into running shoes. She yanked the laces tight, crossed them, and made a bow. "You planned to wake up drunk in my bed?"

I tried to grin brightly, flirtatiously, but my whole head hurt too much for my muscles to obey.

She cocked her head, waiting for a response. Lips in a tight smirk.

My stomach surged and I bolted for the bathroom, bowling ball in tow. Drunk would have been nice. This was the horrid opposite of nice.

"I'm not holding your hair back," she yelled.

Sunk deep in the mattress of my own bed, trying to sneak in another hour or two of sleep before work, I imagined myself, sober and healthy, back in Kris' bed, her body near mine. I slid my hand beneath the elastic of my underwear, thinking about Kris. I was fairly certain at that point that I was at least eighty-two percent into girls, but what did that mean, really? What did a lesbian feel like? I was still Lee, a typical nineteen-year-old who couldn't decide what to do with herself. I rolled over, scrutinized the ceiling. Smooth, no paint chipping. The off-white stared down at me. The ceiling didn't threaten to fall anymore. The pale white reminded me of a blank movie screen before the lights went low and the previews crashed toward the audience. On occasion in the theatre in Marietta, I'd entertained seeing myself in the white rectangle, larger than life, strutting my stuff. The ceiling overhead, though, was my screen, blank, and I didn't have to strut or cry or overact and I didn't have to re-master what happened. I just had to go about my business in any manner I wanted. And that simple fact didn't have to be overwhelming. On the ceiling, Kris' naked body, her muscular legs and long brown-blonde hair, came into focus. Her brown nipples and tight stomach. I didn't push her away, but touched myself and imagined touching her.

25

Reticence got the better of me when Kris fell into place on the ladder. My face reddened. I dropped a sleeve of cookies on the floor and couldn't help thinking she thought me an imbecile.

"How are you feeling?" she asked as I threw the floored cookies into the trash and swung a new sleeve onto an arm. "Any better? You looked banged up this morning."

Any confidence or comfort I'd felt earlier in her bed was gone. I was nervous again. I wanted to skip past the anxiety and small chatter and get right to my attraction to her.

"I'm okay. I've drunk my weight in water and then some." It was a lie, but what was I going to say? 'Except for the fact that I fantasized about you half the day, then the other half worried that the feelings weren't mutual. You see, I haven't been in a relationship, a real one, and I don't know how to go at it. This awkwardness is too much. Can we please just skip past my slippery fingers and clumsiness, and concentrate on the longing I feel? Can we go someplace where I can express it?'

"Good, then you'll come out tonight?"

Oh fuck. I nodded. I always did.

Monday. None of the other Pinheads were at Pinheads. They started in with the alcohol on Wednesdays. "I thought you said you were good at this," Kris teased. After a quick game of bowling on the other side of the bar, she was beating me at billiards. Again.

"No, that's darts," I reminded her. "I've got a natural Darter's elbow." I shoved my elbow toward her for inspection. She studied the elbow that had recently been cut and was scabbed over. She touched it gingerly. "Your shot," she said.

Instead of looking for the easy angle on the table, I stole looks at Kris to see if she was looking at me. I was trying to gauge her level of attention, trying to calculate if I was her friend or if she felt something more for me. It made for funny math and indecipherable equations. Problem was, I didn't know what signs to look for. Kevin was obvious about his advances, though I refused to see them at first. And Derrick was direct, which I appreciated. Kris, though, was more cryptic.

"Susie's working a double. I've gotta pick up her kid. You wanna ride along before I take you home?"

I nodded. I wanted to be near her, and if that required nothing more than running a minor errand with her, I was willing.

At twelve-thirty a.m. on a rainy Toledo night, the streets were glistening and I was watching Kris' fingers on the steering wheel. Long. Thin. Smooth. Strong. I jumped when her pliers fell to the floor with a thud.

"You all right?"

"Yeah, why?" I said, though I knew why. I wanted to climb over the console between us and kiss her. I wanted to know something about myself. I thought she was opening a door, being careful in her own way, but I couldn't walk through it just yet. "What's your relationship with Susie?"

"Susie and I," she sighed, "are very close friends. We'd do just about anything for each other."

We pulled into a driveway. A bulb without a shade lit the porch. Kris went into the house, and a second later motioned for me. Inside, the room was dim. Kris held Ari, Susie's four-year-old daughter. Her head of frizzy hair was draped on Kris' shoulder. She was a lanky kid. Kris held on with both arms. "Grab that bag, would ya?" she whispered. "Thanks, Helen," she said softly to the sitter, as I held the door so it wouldn't slam. Kris carefully tucked Ari into the rear seat and buckled her in. I smiled at the idea of our makeshift family as we drove quietly through the damp and glistening streets. I rested my head against the back of the plastic seat and felt all my jagged nerves give one last surge before going dormant.

Kris dropped me off at home where my dad was asleep on the couch with the TV in static mode. I pushed the power button and the screen faded to black and the room darkened. "Dad, Dad," I whispered, touching his shoulder.

"Huh?" He opened his eyes wide, as if awakened by the ghost of someone he'd not seen in years.

"You should go to bed. You have to work early."

He tried to focus. "Your sister's not home yet. Past curfew."

"It's only a little after one. She's not that late."

"Twelve-thirty," he slurred sleepily, closing his eyes again.

"Go to bed, Dad."

"Naw, naw," he shook his head, "I'm fine."

I left him on the couch to wait for his youngest daughter to come in. When she did, I waited greedily for the interrogation to begin, but Dad didn't budge from his coma. The stench of wood-smoke preceded Michelle as she came into our bedroom.

"You reek."

"No worse than you each night," she said, blinding me with the light.

"Where were you?"

"None of your business." She sat down and untied her shoes.

"Turn the fucking light off."

"Deal with it."

I threw the sheet back and got up and turned off the light only to have her turn it back on.

"You're such a cunt," I said, pulling the sheet over my head. "Did you have a hot date with Derrick?"

"Jealous much?"

"Turn the fucking light off already."

"You're the one with the stormy social life," she said.

"I've got to do something to break up the boredom of work," I said. I emerged from beneath the sheet, resigned that the light wasn't going off anytime soon.

"Going to a bar every night. Really exciting," Michelle said, wise beyond her years.

"The company makes it bearable." I couldn't help smiling. My little sister wasn't so little anymore. "What's the stamp on your hand from?"

She licked her thumb and rubbed at the ink. "I can't get it off," she said. She looked hard at me for a second, then gave up. "Derrick got me into a bar downtown to listen to a band, but they weren't very good, so we went to some guy's house and built a bonfire." She slipped out of her jeans, shirt, and bra and into a long nightshirt. "Don't even start," she said, "you of all people."

She was right. Michelle had her head together, which was more than I could say for my own. I stepped out of the protective older sister role, if only slightly. "Did you get stoned?"

She shook her head. "I think he quit."

"Impossible."

"He says it screws up his metabolism. He doesn't get the most effective workout and post-workout oxygen consumption. Plus, he ends up eating too much crap when he gets the munchies. Have you seen the amount of food he can put down?"

I futilely tried to envision a clear-headed Derrick. "Does he talk any less?"

"Nope." She disappeared to the bathroom, came back brushing her teeth. "What's so great about weed anyway? It makes me so mellow that I feel dead. And I can't complete a full thought or think about more than one thing at a time."

"Some people like that feeling."

"Jake stared at a cucumber for an hour the other night. An hour! Then he ate a can of cheese whiz. It was totally gross. He ate it right out of the can. His teeth were coated with goo and his breath was awful and he just sat there grinning. It's asinine."

"It makes the world a little softer," I said.

"It makes you silly and stupid."

"It slows everything down."

"It puts a veil over your brain."

"You read all the time."

"You cannot seriously be comparing getting stoned to reading."

"They're both forms of escape."

"When I finish a book, I return to the world with more information. I've learned something about someone or something or myself. I have a new perspective."

"Potheads would say the same thing."

She rolled her eyes. "Why didn't you stay at school? There's nothing going on here. I mean, at least college meant a new town and Mom and Dad not breathing down your neck."

"It's a trade-off. One cramped room with a sibling for another cramped room with a stranger. Mom and Dad aren't so bad when you consider some of the weirdos you have to contend with at school."

"You've got to be kidding."

"Well, Dad *is* a freak."

She flipped the light switch finally and plunked onto her bed. She spoke into the darkness, "Whether in school or not, you should have stayed in Marietta."

"You just want this room to yourself."

"Least then I wouldn't have to listen to you snore."

"You'd miss it."

"Doubtful," she said and flipped over.

"Use Dad's hand degreaser. For the bar stamp."

Soon her breathing was steady.

Michelle was right about the bar scene. Not only was I getting tired of the near-nightly visits, but I was beginning to imagine my liver going sour. Unfortunately, the other employees expected me at the bar. By succumbing early in the summer, I'd set a dangerous precedent. Someone had threatened to teach me euchre and sign me up for that club. Kris liked to make an appearance, if only to make sure people were calling cabs when they'd had too many drinks. But Wednesday night, Kevin's Jeep was in the Pinheads lot. Kris did a U-turn back onto the road. Appearances evidently weren't always imperatives.

"Wayne fired him today. He failed a drug test."

I smiled. So did she. Then I panicked. Dread filled the space around me. "Am I gonna be tested?"

"Factory never tests unless there's a complaint or issue. Kevin was an issue."

She drove us out to Point Place. The black water rocked into the wall. Side-by-side again. This time I was brave. I needed to know something, and the worst she could do was push me into the water. It was only a four-foot drop and the night was warm.

"You said you and Susie are close friends. How close?"

"We'd do anything for each other."

"Close, like friends-with-benefits close?"

She frowned. "Friends with benefits?"

"You know, more than friends, less than committed. Fuck buddies," I said brazenly. I was masking an unsteady feeling and trying to brace myself for an answer I didn't want to hear.

She didn't push me in the water. "We're not together. Not in any conventional sense. I mean, yes, I was with Susie for awhile."

"So you're gay?"

"I guess. If loving a woman and having sex with one means I am, I am. I don't go to gay bars or marches or any of that stuff. Before Susie, I had a boyfriend for six years. He got a job in Chicago. I didn't want to leave." She stared toward the line where water met sky. "Security's a dangerous thing."

"Do you regret staying?"

"I used to. I visited him a few times, but the distance…"

She didn't have to explain. I knew what distance could do.

"So, bisexual?" I bounced my feet back and forth against the wall.

"I suppose. The labels don't mean very much to me."

"Fifty-fifty, eighty-twenty?"

She smiled at me.

"Seventy-thirty? Susie?"

"Susie doesn't have a care in the world. She's sunny. Her personality is infectious. She can make you smile on the shittiest day. She's a free spirit, in love with life." Kris leaned back on her arm and closer to me.

"She was pretty funny on the canoe trip." I could sense Kris' skin, the heat from it.

"That was nothing. As you get to know her, you'll see how crazy she is. She moved into my place so we could split expenses. Her daughter was two at the time. We messed around for a few months. I took it for more than it was. She had a fling with Paul when we were winding down, then the thing with Paul blew up. His wife found out and Susie didn't know how to tell me. Paul was confiding in me, and I let him. He didn't know anything about Susie and me. I was already attached to Ari, so I let them stay. It was the biggest, hardest clusterfuck for a long time. We're basically housemates now.

Friends and housemates and family. I help her out with the kid. She helps out with rent and chores."

"So, friends with benefits but not sexual benefits?"

Water slapped the stone beneath us.

"It's comfortable now. Mostly. The factory's a soap opera. You don't know what's gonna happen next."

"You're not mad at Paul?"

"Why should I be? He didn't know Susie and I had anything going. We kept it pretty quiet. I was pissed at her for a long time. A *long* time. Paul could do just about anything and I'd forgive him. He's that kind of guy."

"People just don't get over things like that."

"I was angry, but I was also a different person then. I'm a lot more open now to the fact that people move in and out of your life."

"It sounds so messy. Have you been with anyone since?" I asked, suddenly aware that I'd been asking question after question, though Kris didn't indicate at all that she was uncomfortable. I straightened out of my slouch, stretched my arms above my head. Kris yielded her study of the horizon and looked at me. "No," she said. Her eyes softened and her lips opened slightly. I thought there was something in the look, a welcoming, a sort of homecoming. The look went on despite internal misgivings and I couldn't move. I sat, immobile, feeling connected to her on a quantum level. Finally, I had to look away.

26

Kris wasn't on the stepladder the next day. In fact, the stepladder was gone. I made sandwiches in silence most of the night, fearing I'd pushed too far with my questions and we'd frightened each other off, revealing so much. Even Paul didn't have anything for me when I passed him on my way out the labyrinth's door for lunch. I'd learned the string trick. I could come and go at will. The allure of the cookie machine was completely gone. Its challenge, pure boredom. Its shiny stainless steel, tarnishing with use. Its solitude, not for me.

"I'm older than you."

I jumped. Late into hour five, I was lost behind the V, easy in the knowledge that Labor Day and season's end was a week away. An hour earlier I'd stopped expecting Kris to spin her pliers from the stool that was no longer near my machine. I was also pleased I'd made a dent in the money I owed my folks. And since making me lug his mailbag for a day, Dad had even stopped his harangues. In his eyes I'd lived up to something. In mine, I'd broken free of the ceaseless machine.

"Nine years."

She was looking for an out. Though I had no idea what I was getting myself into, I was not prepared to let her off easy.

Blue eyes peered from under a polka-dot hat. "Are you going back to school?"

"I'm not leaving the city, if that's what you mean."

"Staying on here?" she cringed.

"I don't know. There's a regular income here. I still owe my parents. Or maybe I'll try community college or something," I said, not knowing why. Community college had the whiff of failure about it, but then so did the factory. "You could start your own business. Set your own hours, you know."

Wayne sped by. "Kris, you're needed on One."

She went, though I didn't want her to. I wanted her close as I ground out the last two hours, wanted us to continue our talk.

Wayne returned, clipboard in hand. He stepped in front of me and flipped the machine nozzle closed. "Okay, Lee, time to shut this down."

"I've still got two hours."

"We've hit the sandwich quota. Making more would exceed the demand. I've got other work for you to do."

"What about the mix still in the bin? It's a third full."

"Drain it." He started to walk away.

"But that's wasting it."

"Drain it and find me when you're shut down," he said. He didn't appreciate being questioned. He had orders to follow and orders to give. Disputing either of those was not on his clipboard. I pulled the bottom tray from the bin and mix gathered at the floor grate.

Wayne was rewiring the Popsicle box machine on Two when I found him twenty minutes later. Packers shuffled in place, unsure of what to do, but happy for the respite. "You clean out the tank?"

"Yes."

"You put the extra cookies in storage?"

"Yes."

"And the boxes?"

"The boxes and the wrap and the mix. Wayne, I know my job."

He scowled. "You can go home, then. There's nothing else to do."

"Seriously? I can't go home."

"Go help on cups, then."

"I hate cups."

"Go home or go help on cups," he said, ending the discussion.

So I went and I sent cups flying off the metal tray. Accidentally. Missy laughed at me. The cup machine was her machine. She stepped forward and prissily slipped two rows of six cups into a plastic bag and passed it to the cincher. The cup operator handed me a broom. "Why don't you sweep?" she said, not waiting for an answer.

I pushed the broom around on the floor.

"Hey," a custodial specialist said, "don't do it that way."

"What?" He couldn't possibly be serious.

"You have to do it smoother." He took the broom out of my hands. "You can't raise the bristles off the ground. That sends dust into the air, which gets into the product. Watch." He swept the floor with the grace of a ballerina.

I laughed.

"What's funny?" he asked. "This is no joke. You have to do this the right way." He handed me the broom and watched me sweep for the next ten minutes, correcting me twice.

Missy watched our interaction from the other side of the room. Her heckling laugh found its way to my head. I glowered. I'd be the talk of another T-town party tonight.

Then Wayne came through again. "Keep the bristles on the ground."

I'd entered the Twilight Zone. I hadn't been scolded since the first week, and certainly not like this. I wanted to crack someone's head with the handle. I squeezed the stick until the blood drained from my hands. My arm muscles tensed. I had no idea I had such rage in me. But then, I'd never been chastised for improper sweeping.

Kris was leaning against the passenger side of her van when I walked out the factory door, still fuming. "You wipe the dog drool off that?"

I tugged at my shirt, pleased that she was there, but tense just the same.

"You sleep with any more midgets lately?" She smiled wide, and right then I knew I'd get another chance to wake in her bed.

We avoided the bar. Gus didn't want any factory workers around for a while because Kevin cracked some paneling with a bowling ball. We circled through town, Kris' familiar fingers on the wheel.

"Wayne had me dump mix down the drain. It's such a waste."

"Happens all the time," she said, resigned. After nine years at the factory, she'd learned to look the other way.

"Doesn't make it right. The real wringer on the night is that I was taught proper brooming technique."

Kris laughed loudly and let me brood in silence for the rest of the drive. At the breakwall, clouds covered the sky and waves crashed high against the stone. She walked ahead of me and sat down. I straddled the wall, facing her. We watched each other, not sure who should do what first. I braced my hands on the sides of the wall behind me and leaned back. She leaned close.

"I can't start my own business," she said.

I hadn't expected the night to begin there, but I went with it. "You're not happy at the factory. You could make remodeling a full time job. Set your own hours. No time clock to punch."

She ran a hand through her hair. "I don't know."

"You could do it. It'd be a big change, but you could do it. You'd have evenings free."

"Have you ever kissed a woman before?" she asked, out of nowhere.

"Yes." I studied the intricate weave on her shirt. She probably thought I was looking at her breasts. "Three."

"Three?"

"You're surprised?"

She put her lips on mine, closed at first. We slowly opened our mouths to each other. We knocked teeth. She pulled back. I raised my fingers to my gums checking for blood. None.

"Did you kiss them like that?"

"Don't blame that on me. You're the one with buck teeth."

"I have perfect teeth." She ran her tongue over her incisors.

"Yeah, you do."

"Three? Really? Who were they?"

"Courtney, the one who went to Alaska. Hailey, who I knew before Courtney. And Hailey again, years later, though I'm not sure I'd call what we did kissing."

"Technically that's only two."

"Courtney was sleeping over at my place a lot because she couldn't bear to be at home. She was having crazy dreams about her brother who'd killed himself. He was beckoning her, faceless sometimes, and she couldn't do anything. Sleeping at home made the dreams worse. Her parents wouldn't leave her alone. Kept checking on her. She was in my sister's bed, and I was in mine. She was crying. I didn't know what to do, so I got in bed with her and held her. I held her tight and I stroked her hair. And after a couple of minutes, she wiped her eyes and looked up at me. She whispered a thanks and kissed me." Remembering Courtney's pain and that period in my life, imagining her grinning over a fish or staring at mountains, brought tears to my eyes. She was gone and I was not able to talk to her. "It didn't make me want to jump her bones or anything. I guess it let me know how close we were."

Kris rubbed my shoulder and the back of my neck. "Nothing happened after that?"

"No." I wiped my eyes. "We never talked about it either, just had an unbreakable connection. Like twins almost. But it was a fluke. One of those in-the-moment things. I never really could admit it back then, but I wanted it to happen again." I leaned into Kris' embrace.

"And the other, Hailey?"

"The Fat Lip," I said, going red inside thinking of Hailey. "I was such an idiot. The first time around it was like eating without being nourished."

Lake Erie spread for miles toward southern Ontario and western New York. With little light coming from the docks, the water looked black and dangerous.

"And the second time around?"

"A strange, strange night. What happened with you and Susie? I mean, how did it start?"

"I lunged at her. We were watching TV. We'd been drinking a lot and I just did it. She was shocked, but she kissed back. We fell into each other. Well, I fell. She leaned for a bit."

27

With the broom lesson in the past and Kris' kisses to look forward to, I whistled my way to work. Wayne was waiting at the square gray clock. He was sterner than usual. "Punch in, Lee, then follow me."

Binders and data sheets were scattered over desks and file cabinets in Wayne's office. The room was small, the air stale. Two desks crowded the right wall. On one of them a computer screen lit the room. Wayne adjusted his hairnet. "I hate to do this, Lee. You're a good worker and all, but I'm stuck." He held out a sheet of paper to me. "We have to drug test you. You can take this down the street, on the clock, get it done and come back."

The concrete walls of the office moved a foot closer.

"What do you mean?"

"Random tests. It's in the handbook."

My legs were suddenly very weak. I sat down to avoid falling down. "Yeah, but, everyone says the factory never tests."

He pushed the sheet at me. "Sometimes we're forced to."

"I haven't done anything wrong. You said so yourself. I'm a model worker."

He set the sheet on the desk next to me. "Because I like you, I'll level with you. Someone complained. When there's a complaint on file, we have to do something."

"Who?"

"I can't say."

"C'mon, Wayne, this is my job. I deserve to know. You know I won't pass. My parents will find out. Fuck." My dad's clenched jaw and rage formed in my mind. I imagined him finally giving up and kicking me out.

"Kevin and Missy," Wayne offered, dropping his head. "No one can know that I told you."

"Those fucks? Kevin doesn't even work here anymore."

"Calm down. He issued his complaint last week. Missy put hers in yesterday."

A vision of the cup machine and Missy's haunting grin and dark roots swept across my eyes.

"You can't do anything?"

"I shouldn't be telling you any of this." He pushed the sheet at me.

"I won't pass."

"If you refuse the test, we have to fire you."

"So I should quit?"

He nodded once.

"Can't we ride it out? I've only got a week until Labor Day."

"Doesn't matter. Paperwork's in."

"It's Friday. Can I have the weekend?"

"I'm sorry," he said. "You should've been more careful."

"What goes in my file?"

"Nothing. That you quit before I talked to you. I can give you that much. Pick up your last check next Friday. Turn your uniforms in then. Washed first."

"Fucking hell," I muttered and walked out of Wayne's office, past Kris, past Paul and Ned, past Joyce, and out of the crank of machines and the smell of ammonia. I dumped my hairnet in the garbage and didn't bother punching out. I walked into humid air and a sunlit sky. I could go anywhere, do anything. I should have felt free, but I didn't.

With the soda change in my pocket I bought myself passage on a full and stinking bus. I pushed my way to the rear door for the air each time it opened. I stared at nothing and thought about nothing as night came on. The bus wheeled a long route. On narrow streets, branches flailed the windows and dragged their tips the length of the vessel. The bus made its way downtown where offices were closing for the weekend and little was happening. Itinerants looked for shelter or loose change or things they lost years ago. The driver pulled into the main station and kicked me out.

I had the weekend to brood. I avoided my parents. I avoided Kris. I tried to avoid Michelle, but we shared a room.

"What's wrong with you?"

"Everything," I answered.

She left me alone.

My plan was To Act As If.

Monday, I dressed for work and left the house at three-thirty. I found the Friday bus. The driver recognized me. "You can't ride all day," he said, his moist eyes peering into my eyes. "Unless you pay each time round."

I counted the change in my hand. "Where can I go?"

"What about a movie?"

"I've seen everything."

"Library's open 'til nine, and it's free." He pulled the door shut.

"Library it is."

The five floors of the public library made for wide wanderings. The reference desk personnel didn't notice when, bored, aimless, I passed their desks six and seven times. I was glad they didn't ask if I needed help. I needed more than they could give. Eventually, I gave up and sat in the domed, drafty lobby, watching mothers with their squeaking kids, old ladies with armfuls of romance books, old men with newspapers turned to sports or finance, students with bulky backpacks. The Purple Lady passed and disappeared up the stairwell, going to the third floor where she could always be found during evening library hours. Dressed in a long purple robe and carrying a large purple, shepherd's staff, she'd been Toledo's icon for years. She called herself a queen and bathed in fountains, constantly mumbling to herself and shaking the staff. A few years back, a charity organization set her up in an apartment and got her a job. She refused both, preferring the streets. Her turf. She knew the area well, felt most at home there, I guessed. I considered following her up the stairs and sitting down for a one-on-one. Maybe she had a worthwhile nugget to pass along.

I went up to the third floor. Seated on the faded cushions of the window nook, the Purple Lady was looking toward the window. I don't think she was really seeing anything. She looked lost. Gone. I busied myself by half-watching her, half-looking at the books in the aisle nearest her perch. Dewey Decimal 700s. Art books. I haphazardly pulled several from the shelf, sat myself on the floor, and flipped through them. The first was about Cubism. I couldn't find anything in the paintings to focus on. I looked with some interest but didn't understand. I went on to the next one, something about the surrealists. There was a giant drawing of a pipe with some words in French and another picture of melting clocks, like sad time or a time warp. I kept flipping through the pages, trying to find something a sustained distraction.

Some time later, a loud cough startled me. The Purple Lady stood up and came toward me. "The soul," she said, as she stepped over me, "can only move at the pace of an ass on fragile shale."

To Act As If. I intended to keep up the façade at least until payday. Though Mom was asleep and Dad was at work, I put the whites on.

"What's going on?" Kris asked when I answered the phone on my way out.

"Heading to work," I said.

"You got another job already?"

"You could have warned me."

"I didn't know. They kept me out of the loop on this one. Conflict of interest, obviously. Anyway, this shouldn't come between us."

She was right, but I was still mad. I couldn't steer my anger the right way. It sat heavily in my head, spreading inertia all through me. I couldn't do anything.

"Can I see you again?"

With plans in place for Wednesday night, I hung up and continued the subterfuge. Instead of hiding in the backs of buses or following the Purple Lady around, I went to the art museum. A grade school memory of the tombs in the Egyptian Room drew me there. *The Coffin of Ta Mitt* in its decorated wooden case stood in a box of glass.

"Pretty fabulous, isn't it?" Jeremiah. Black Jesus boy.

"It's not how I remember. It's not evoking fear and not helping me savor my bad mood," I told him, though I didn't mean to. I was disappointed and the words just came out.

"What's wrong?" he asked.

He was dressed sharply in khaki shorts and a polo shirt, brown loafers and no socks. He always had a cap on at work and his full head of curly hair surprised me, but the novelty of his appearance wore off, and I wanted him to leave. "I don't want to go into it," I said. "What are you doing here, anyway? You're supposed to be in the freezer."

"Oh, I got moved to first shift about a month ago. It's so nice. I'm studying the portrayals of Jesus throughout art history. That paper I gave you? I have to expand it for a conference this fall."

The paper. Right. The one I hadn't read. And still didn't want to. "Exciting," I said lamely.

He stared at me with unblinking, oil-stained eyes. "You know, Lee, I find it's better to be straight-up with people. You don't do them or yourself any favors by lying. I can see you're not into what I'm into. Jesus is for everybody, but not everybody's for Jesus. That said, you might try opening your heart to other human beings. You'll find it brings us closer to God."

"Fuck God. I don't believe. That whole lack-of-evidence thing gets in the way. I'm sorry I led you to think otherwise. And, you know what? You're a nice guy, but I'd really prefer to be alone right now. Is that straightforward enough?"

"Indeed," he said very calmly. "I'm sorry I didn't get to know you, but good luck with everything." He walked off toward the nearest painted Jesus.

I decided that being a bitch might not be so bad after all. I did feel better, except for a node of guilt growing in my stomach. I could have been more tactful.

Elsewhere in the museum, paintings and portraits stared at me, eyes following everywhere. The security guards were the exception. They only woke when I passed into the next room. I imagined my great grandfather pounding nails into wooden walls one hundred years back. The museum now, with its marble floors and high ceilings, wasn't his anymore. A woman's firm voice found me in a deserted hallway.

"According to Kandinsky, inner need has three mystical elements: something within that calls for expression, the spirit of the age, and helping the cause of art," said a wrinkled old woman from behind a podium. Her voice, loud and assertive, didn't fit her body. "The inner life," she continued, "is life. Kandinsky's agenda was to express emotion and to express the spiritual through form. The form then will evoke the same emotions within the viewer. Feel the inner element being expressed through the repetition of circles and triangles and the contrasts of colors."

The overhead lights dimmed and a projector splayed images onto a white screen. There were squiggly lines and straight lines and shadings and empty spaces, a crucifix with crazy shapes on a yellow background, and another colorful painting with rectangles and small lines. These seemingly random shapes were supposed to be projections of the psyche. The blank spaces were fitting. The woman's words were self-indulgent and ridiculous, but I was intrigued. I loitered, remembering Hailey. She'd said her photographs derived from Kandinsky. She was after the inner essence of objects. I thought of her differently. Four years ago when I knew her she was full of spunk and rebellion. Now it seemed there was something more behind all her frantic energy. Everyone around me seemed to have a lust for life. Old and new Hailey. Dreaded Courtney seeking adventure. Crusty old Yellow was alive in the world, engaging his customers about movies and local politics and providing a special service for his other customers. Even my little sister had her own lust. Yes, Derrick, but more so her knowledge of books and writers and artists. Where was my lust? Why was I being left behind?

28

Indian style on Kris' Tibetan tapestry. There was a sofa and a TV and a VCR. Scratched end tables, some toys in the corner. A bookshelf. I could see myself owning such a house. Kris handed me what looked like a Sea Breeze. I lurched at the thought of the railroad bridge.

"She's in Dayton for a few days," Kris said, referring to Susie, and sat on the floor next to me and leaned against the couch, stretching her legs in front of her, one over the other. She rested a hand on my thigh. "Her parents are there. I'm not cheating on her. You're allowed to be here."

"It still feels strange." I sipped. A fruit juice concoction. Healthy, no liquor.

"Don't let it. What'd you do all day?"

"I solved world hunger, found shelter for the homeless, and neutered a few stray dogs."

She squeezed my leg just above the knee. I pulled away, grabbing at her hand. She wouldn't let go.

"Okay, okay, mercy, uncle! I'm sorry," I said. "I didn't do anything. I wandered around for three hours and sat at the library for four."

"You should just tell your parents. Get it over with."

"I came across all this stuff on psychology. Like, Freud says we're all divided between seeking pleasure and living in reality. And Adler thinks we all feel small inside and that's why we do the things we do. Jung says we're all a blend of extroversion and introversion. But he's got this other thing going about the shadow, which is all the traits in us that most people ignore and suffocate. I think I've been a living shadow. It explains everything."

"Like a split personality?"

"Sort of."

"That's crazy."

"Seriously, I've never really thought about why I do some of the things I do. Not *really* thought about it. I skated the edges in rehab. But how deep can you go at sixteen? Not very. It's all about rebellion and hormones." Or was it? The information was all so heady and fascinating in a way I hadn't felt before. I crawled over to the bookcase and scanned the titles: *Joy Luck Club, Geek Love, Oranges Are Not The Only Fruit.* I pulled a photo album from a shelf. In one of the pictures, a shirtless toddler with brilliant orange hair curled Afro-tight smiled at me from her perch on a red tricycle. Her blue eyes were familiar. "What happened to your ball of fire of a hairdo?"

"Head lice. My dad shaved all my hair. It was never the same after that." She moved near and looked at the photos over my shoulder. "Funny to see ourselves at different ages. I look at that kid and have no idea who she is." Kris kissed my neck and touched my back with her long fingers. "Are you planning to wake up in my bed again?"

We kissed, mouths wide and tongues searching and teeth not clashing. She leaned back. I followed her to the floor. Rug-burning elbows and chafing butts and knees, we wrestled and rolled. She tugged at my ear with her teeth. She barked. Pants off, panties on, her head between my legs, lips on thighs, mouth on mound, she exhaled into my crotch. I twirled her hair between my fingers. She slid a finger beneath the elastic band.

She asked if my ass was still bruised.

I told her she'd have to check.

She said she'd bruise it again if it wasn't.

With my fingers inside her, I searched for something I'd already found. She shifted and turned under me. She pushed against my hand, grabbed my wrist and pulled me into her harder, deeper. I might have been swallowed up. And that would have been okay with me. Staying in her, moving in her, I put my mouth on her clit and tongued it slowly, softly in circles. Wetness merged. She tasted like soap. She tasted like Kris. She shuddered and shuddered again. She pushed my head back. I grinned like a schoolgirl who'd just pulled a prank and gotten away with it.

29

Friday. Payday. I approached the factory with caution. I didn't want to get sucked back in, and I didn't want to have to piss in a cup. I was almost nostalgic. It was the last time I'd have to wait in this particular line. I took the check and ran. Dad's hand wasn't outstretched, waiting just inside the door. Instead, he sat on the couch. The newspaper hid his top half. He hadn't heard me enter. I tiptoed to him, flicked the paper with my finger. He lifted off the sofa, rattling the pages.

"Damn it all! Where you been?"

"Out with Kris."

He folded the paper in his lap, eyeing me as if I was a suspicious stranger.

"The canoe lady."

"A blind guy walks into a bar with a seeing eye dog," he said. "Gropes around for a seat. He tells the bartender his order. Bartender mixes him a tall, cool one, sets it on the counter. Blind guy yanks the dog's leash, picks the dog up, spins him over his head. Bartender jumps back, says, 'What the hell are you doing?' Blind guy says, 'Looking around.'"

"I've got one. A sandwich, an ice cream sandwich, walks into a bar, orders a beer. Bartender says, 'Sorry, we don't serve food here.'"

He didn't blink.

"Heard that one at work."

"Wild bunch *you* work with."

I held out five hundred single dollar bills to him, a peace offering. For once I wanted him to have it. Though I was trying to be funny. He cracked open the newspaper, lost himself behind it again. "Keep it."

Carpet grew over my feet and tied itself in knots and I couldn't move. I'd been out of work for a week, the precise week that he decided to go easy on me. I didn't entertain what his response would have been to my wandering the city the last four days. "How do you do it, Dad?" I asked, still holding my station. Every once in a while questions such as this bothered me.

He peered over the edge of his paper. "How do I do what?"

"Get up in the morning, go to work. Every day. Doing a job you don't particularly care for."

"What do you mean, how? I just do." Sometimes he was as dense as a brick. "Job's not all that bad as far as jobs go. I walk all day. I get exercise. Sometimes nice people give me water or lemonade. It works for me. Most days."

By the looks of his gut and the sorry state of his back, he was delusional about the exercise bit.

"I have three people to provide for. A mortgage. Retirement. You should know why. Responsibility. You've had it all summer."

My mouth went dry. Guilt clamped its shackles on my throat. I wouldn't be able to hide my joblessness much longer. I needed to tell him that responsibility hadn't motivated me. I worked because I had no other real options. To get him off my back. To earn back his respect. To stop feeling so guilty. I'd started the factory job because I had to, and I continued it because I had to. "You know it's not the same."

He was looking at me. "I do it so you and Michelle won't have to."

"How do you figure that? We'll have to work."

"Every parent, the good ones at least, want better things for their kids than they ever had. They don't want to see them struggle too much. A little, sure. But not a lot. You get some education and maybe you get a job that pays a little more and you like a little bit."

As he talked, I knew. I'd known all along that this was behind his insistence on my going to school and getting a job, that it was behind his and Mom's working extra hours, not going out for dinner or buying much for themselves. They were saving their pennies for our educations and futures. They probably didn't know exactly what those futures looked like—bigger houses, better clothes and cars, careers that meant something or did some greater good, or even just delivered greater contentment—but they wanted more for us. They'd been giving themselves up for that.

Hazy light lay across a corner of the room. Sprawled languidly, Kris took up most of the bed. Through the window screen came the warm, sun-caressed air of a lazy afternoon. I'd stayed four nights in a row. Susie smirked at us but genuinely didn't seem to mind, even made jokes about hedonism and robbing the cradle and getting knocked up by magic hands. Ari impressed me with slides onto an imaginary home plate on the carpet. And Kris impressed me with her acumen. I even helped her wallpaper a house one morning. Though I was enjoying myself, I knew I was avoiding the inevitable. I slid out of bed and headed to my parents' house where my dad was on the floor, his feet propped on the couch.

"What are you doing on the floor?" I asked, putting off the inevitable as long as I could.

"Back hurts."

I braced myself to tell him about the factory fiasco. Ready for another lecture, a heft returning to my shoulders. His brow wrinkled. He kneaded his forehead with his hand.

"Where've you been?"

"I called. Said I wouldn't be home."

"Where the hell've you been?"

"Kris'."

"Kris'."

"Yes."

"Doing what?" He rocked himself into a sitting position.

"Hanging out. Girl stuff."

"Girl stuff."

"Yep."

"How old is she?"

He was pushing us someplace I wasn't ready to go. Not after all that had happened. Not after it had happened so fast.

"Twenty-eight."

"Girl stuff, huh?"

It occurred to me that he thought about my life. He thought about it while he walked eight miles a day, house to house, winding through neighborhoods, tramping groomed lawns or cracking concrete sidewalks. He probably had lots he wanted to tell me but couldn't. The issue of the canoe lady wasn't something he could leave in someone's box.

He continued, hand still squeezing his forehead. "You're spending a lot of time over there."

Not a lecture. Not about work.

Blood drained from my face. My hands moistened. I lost my breath. I didn't want to disappoint him any more than I already had. I'd dodged his expectations again, in a way that was bigger than money.

"I think we're dating," I said.

"You *think*?"

"We're dating," I said.

"You're a lezzie?"

I was not at all prepared for that question coming from him. He'd asked, painfully. I didn't have to make an announcement, not that there was much to announce. Kris and I had a naturalness between us, though that didn't help when it came to explaining my sense of the relationship to my dad. A month back, the LPGA was in Toledo at Inverness. Jamie Farr had returned home for ceremonial pomp. Reading the paper one day, my dad paused at a photo on the sports page, "Hey, the dykes in spikes are in town again." He'd said worse things. Brought worse jokes home from the post office. Mostly though, he kept them from Michelle and me and my mom because he thought them inappropriate for women's ears. Though he still held old-school male values such as never cooking or doing laundry and barely interacting with his family, since the day I walked his route and delivered his mail, he'd been easing toward me, letting me do my own thing in my own time. So I quietly hoped anyway.

"Are you?"

The term was like a too-tight shirt or a stray hair on my tongue. *Off*, somehow. My hair was long. I didn't listen to the Indigo Girls. I didn't play golf or hate men, but I *was* having sex with a woman, and it wasn't the first time. "I guess you could say that."

"Why?" He folded his arms and peered at me.

"I don't know, Dad. It could be genetic or environmental or something else. I haven't studied it. I like being with her. Seems like that's enough." I wrung my hands. I had no idea what to say. We'd never talked so intimately. I longed for one of his jokes.

"You've been with boys, right?"

I nodded. I didn't know what else to do. I couldn't believe he was continuing the conversation. "Yeah, I've been with boys, but I'm with a woman now and I like it. I like it a lot. There's really no comparing the two."

"The hell there isn't." His hands were on his head again. "It goes against God."

"You don't believe in God."

"Don't tell me what I believe," he snapped.

"But you don't. You never went to church when mom used to take us."

"This ain't about what I believe. It's about this phase of yours and your need to constantly push my buttons."

"I'm pretty sure it's not a phase, and I can definitely say it's not about pushing your buttons. It's not about you at all. It's about me. And Kris. What don't you get? There's a woman. We like each other a lot. There's not much more to it than that. You don't have to understand it." He just had to accept, or at least tolerate it. He was capable of that, having tolerated much more: drug use and dropping out, daughters who weren't pink-wearing, pretty princesses, or athletes, his job, his marriage, his failing back. Name it. He'd adjust. That's what Henry does. That's what humans do.

He took a breath. "It gets better, you know. The sex. Boys don't have any idea what they're doing at your age. Give it time, work at it some and then, it's better. One day, it's a lot better."

He'd just summed up twenty years of life with my mom.

"It's not about that," I said.

"It's not right." He got up, winced, and paced back and forth. "Why are you doing this to me?" A sucker-punch. It hurt. A lot.

"Doing this to *you*?" Talking to him was aggravating. He was taking it all so personally. "It's not the easiest thing for me. Do you think I like seeing your face, or Mom's face, all creased with disappointment?"

"Then stop disappointing us!"

I sat on the edge of the chair, watching his feet wear down the carpet.

"We're not demanding, Lee. We let you and Michelle be. What am I supposed to tell the fellas at work?"

"You don't own the bragging rights to my life. I don't care what you tell them. It's not their business."

He frowned. "People ask."

"Who cares? It doesn't matter what the fuck you tell them. It doesn't matter at all." I tried to look him in the face, but he kept marching from the living room to the dining room.

"It does matter. People don't like it. They're cruel."

"I don't care what people like."

"That include me and your mother?"

"Yes. No. No, I care what you think, but it won't change my feelings for Kris."

"Feelings for Kris? Christ, Lee. She's ten years older than you. She's manipulating you, got you all screwed up."

"It's not like that. It's not like that at all."

He marched and I watched him, waiting.

"You're a fucking piece of work. I'd slap some sense into you if I thought I could."

"You can't. You know you can't. It's my life. I'll fuck whoever I want."

He shook his head, muscles tense in his body.

"Look," I said, "you're all over the place. What's your real objection?"

He didn't say. He dropped his arms to his sides, mad, defeated. He was my father and I wasn't living up to his expectations: go off to school, land a good job, a good guy, like a dentist or a pediatrician, have some kids, pay off a thirty-year mortgage in ten, vacation regularly somewhere warm. That wasn't me and life was hard enough, regardless of sexuality and doing typical things. I stared at him. I didn't know what to feel. Angry? Relieved that that part was over? Happy that he was not throwing things? My insides were muddled like a bad cocktail. He didn't say more, and his non-answer led me to believe he didn't know just what he objected to. I was also left in limbo. I didn't know where I stood with him, so I left.

At the 7-ELEVEN I bought a Slurpee I didn't drink. On the bus bench down the block, I sat in the stirred silence of cars passing on the street. My head made enough noise to keep any narcoleptic awake. I felt like someone had stun-gunned my temporal lobe. I wished I were bopping my head along to whatever beat Courtney heard, the one that shoved her out onto the open road. I wanted to be anywhere but where I was.

I called Kris and she picked me up.

"You did what?"

"I kicked myself out. Sort of."

"Why?" she asked, keeping her eyes on the road.

"I don't know. It was weird. We were going along fine. Reasonable, even. But then something gave. I just couldn't continue the conversation. Got frustrated or something. All of my hatred and love came out. He was shaking, like he was about to cry. I've seen him get like that before with my mom. He once told me that he works things out by walking, walking his route. Sometimes he takes short ones in the evening after a fight with my mom. I guess it's not a bad way to deal with things. But sometimes he never brings up the topic again. I was sure he found out I'd quit my job. He didn't mention work at all, though. I suppose I bluff with the best of them. Can I stay with you? I don't really know what else to do."

She pulled us into her driveway. "Of course," she said. "For a night or two." We went into an empty house. I was glad not to have to confront Susie's airy energy or her daughter's need to be the center of attention. Kris cooked a small bowl of pasta that we shared.

"We read these myths in my philosophy class," I said. "One says that before we were born we were these round things. We had four hands, four legs, two faces. Basically two people in one. Just completely joined. Somehow we pissed off the gods and were ripped apart. Since being cut in two, we long for the other half. So we spend our lives searching for that other half to make us whole. What do you think about that?"

"I think wholeness is a myth."

I did the dishes and didn't mind it.

"There's this other one that says the soul chooses its path before birth. Chooses its parents, its troubles."

"That one sounds ridiculous."

"What about the end of the world, then? There's this guy on Family Radio, Harold Camping, who reads the Bible like a calendar. He says the world's going to end in May 2011 and all the righteous will fly up to heaven."

"Now *that* I believe. That makes perfect sense."

We fell into bed. I was naked and next to Kris. She was wearing a long shirt, but no underwear. I rolled my hand across her hip, under her shirt, to her belly and breasts. Right where I needed to be.

"I like the easy explanation of the myths. Like we're all fated."

"We're not fated," she said. "We make choices every day." She lay on her back, and then turned toward me. "Do you want to stop this?"

For a split second, I worried about how I was touching her. I kept my hand at rest on her belly. "Because of the trouble with my dad?"

"I've got nine years on you. You're just getting started. It's an exciting time and you have some things to figure out."

"Is that what you want?"

She twirled my hair with her fingers. My stomach turned and I was aware of my naked body.

"You'll probably be going back to school, meeting people your age, doing the college thing. I don't want to be in the way."

"You won't be in the way."

"You can't know that."

"You can't promise your feelings won't change. And if that's the case, why bother, anyway? Why get close to anyone?"

"You know why."

"Do I? This is a first for me. If anything, you're the one who should be wary because I don't know what the fuck I'm doing." All of a sudden, I felt silly lying next to her. "You've been where I'm at. Loved and lost and all that."

"That's not fair. That doesn't make me any less scared about it this time. If anything, I'm more scared."

"You've got Susie and Ari and a stable job. All these things in place." Her room was in place. Clothes in the drawers. Plates in the kitchen cupboard. Companionship in the next room. She didn't need me.

"That comes with growing up. You'll see."

"Don't patronize me. That's the last thing I need. I don't know. Maybe you're right, maybe this can't work." I sat up and pulled my jeans on. What was I doing? How *would* it work? I'd been so caught up in the novelty that I hadn't stopped to think about anything.

"I just want us to be aware of everything. Where are you going? We're just talking."

"First my dad, now you. I thought this was good, that we were on the same page. Kick me while I'm down, why don't you?"

"That's not what I'm doing, and you know it."

"I don't know it. I don't know what I'm doing. This is crazy."

"So it's crazy. No crazier than us being carried to the heavens in 2011."

Kris followed me to the porch, but no further. I was the one dodging. I was the adult who wasn't going to be chased after and pacified. I knew all of these things, but I kept walking. That was my dad in me. I walked it out, whatever it was. Or maybe I just walked away, avoiding, hiding.

FACTORY

Late into the Toledo night, alone and homeless, I walked to Courtney's house and sat on the opposite curb and stared at the many windows. The house was dark. The street was quiet except for the occasional cricket's chirp. There was no movement anywhere. Not even the wind. I imagined Courtney gazing down on me from her bedroom window. I expected us to maintain our friendship, but her leaving, I was beginning to understand, rendered our friendship short-lived.

After a while, I left the curb and headed west. There was little traffic on the freeway when I hopped the guardrail and climbed the fence to the back section of Wildwood. I found the spot where Courtney and I tossed matches at each other, where the thrill of escaping fire remained. I lay in the field we burned. The grass had grown back. It was softer than I remembered. It occurred to me that maybe it was that simple: Courtney needed a change and made one. A big one. One day you wake up and you're done doing whatever it was you'd been doing and you want to try something else. I always knew I was different. Courtney buffered me. She made me forget. Kris did that as well. With her, it wasn't about avoiding myself. It was about discovery and watching her amused curled lip catch on her perfect teeth.

I lay in the field with its new growth, thinking I'd do it. I'd buckle down. Sit through enough classes to finally figure out what interested me. I'd go to the library or borrow Michelle's books. It would be better than pushing a broom or tossing cups in the factory for the next four decades. That sort of life, you don't choose, not if another choice is available, one that offers possibility and meaning. Not that Paul's and Kris' and Joyce's and Susie's lives weren't meaningful, but they'd already answered something for themselves. I still had to find the right questions.

I slept dreamlessly. In the morning, light played with me from behind the tangled branches of the trees. Later, with the sun full above the tree line and the morning traffic tapered, I made my way back to Kris'. Susie was leaving with Ari. "She was sitting on the porch, waiting for you all night," Susie said with hardness. "She was worried. You could've called. It wouldn't have mattered how late."

"I know."

"Get whatever it is figured out before you do any real damage."

I sat on the edge of the bed and touched Kris' hip. She opened her eyes to me. "There's grass in your hair."

"Remember those tapes I told you about? The ones I delivered? Yellow never told me what was on them, but I found out." I kicked off my shoes and leaned against the headboard with my feet crossed. I told Kris the rest of the story:

I handed the tape into the human pincers and started to leave, but then I rode around to the back of the house and dumped my bike in some bushes near an old garage. The lock on it was completely rusted. There was an old car in it half covered with a tarp. The backyard was a mess of grass, overrun with weeds and ivy, some trash. Some animal must have been living back there somewhere, it smelled so foul. I stayed low and skulked like a proper Peeping Tom. A tall wooden fence ran along the left side of the house. I propped myself on the top beam, walked carefully down it, my hands on the house. The first window I came to was the kitchen one. Inside, the trash bin was filled with empty aluminum cans. Otherwise, the kitchen looked old and empty. It had those porcelain countertops and a really thick refrigerator like from the 60s. There were no lights on. Not anywhere and most of the curtains were drawn. I kept edging my way along the fence until I came to a TV room. Seven or eight wooden chairs were lined up in front of the TV, as if for an audience. But in the chairs were dolls, the ones with large, round eyes that stare at you wherever you are. Then the woman came into the room. She was rail-thin and veiny. Her eyes were sunken deep in their sockets. Made worse by mascara and pencil lines for eyebrows. Her dress, a sleeveless silky one that clung to her body, was stained and the hem was loose. She looked over her audience, speaking to them. I couldn't hear the words. She slipped the cassette into the VCR. The screen opened into the black and white credits of a movie called *The Girl Who Had Everything*, starring Elizabeth Taylor. The woman stood stiffly in front of the audience. Then she moved, mimicking Taylor, whose face looked odd. It was all wrong. Her dark, almond-shaped eyes and those high cheekbones that angled into a tiny chin were missing. Her soft, pampered features, gone. In their place were the recessed eyes and emaciated jaw of the woman who had taken the tape from me. Who was now trying to mimic Taylor's every move, pretending to be the character in the movie. I watched this for some time before noticing a clock on the wall. The hands were stopped. I was leaning in more, trying to see the time, when the fence beam broke loose and I fell. I crawled off under a shrub. The woman came to the window, panic in her eyes. She was holding one of the dolls. I could have sworn all four eyes were staring at me.

I got on the Schwinn. I peddled over the bumpy brick streets, back through downtown Marietta, past the old castle on Fourth Street. Its octagonal tower, attic windows, and stone-capped spires leant easily to the surreal aura around me. The world had gone watery. Buildings fluttered like large tapestries. The air was thick enough to swallow. I couldn't figure out why anyone would want to see themselves super-imposed on someone else's body. At a funhouse for a quick picture, sure, but a whole movie? Fucking with the art of it like that? I had to get the images out of my head, so I rented the real version and watched bratty, beautiful Jean Latimer fall in love with her father's mobster client.

But that was the least of it. The woman haunted me all week. The chairs before the TV, the cans in the kitchen, an old car covered with dust. She was like a character out of a book. But she was real. She must have been so lonely. The front of her house didn't look so bad, a little rundown. But the things going on inside, no one would have any idea about. The lifeless dolls and the woman's stiff gestures were with me when I went to see Rudy the next week. I was trying to block her out, but holding Rudy's tapes made my hands shake. I liked Rudy, but it scared me to think what he might be doing when I wasn't there. I handed him his tape and tried to leave.

"Not staying for a soda this time?"

"Can't. I have a class."

"It's a little late, isn't it? What's going on with you, kid? You seen a ghost or something?"

I spilled it. I shouldn't have, but I told him every last detail of what I saw. "It was freakish, Rudy. Horrifying."

"Who the fuck are you to judge? None of that's your goddamn business. Did she see you?"

"I don't think so."

"You don't think so?"

"No! Yes! I have no idea. And even if she saw me, what did she really see? What's on your tapes, Rudy? Elvis? Do you jailhouse rock?"

"Don't fuck with me like this. Don't fuck with anyone like this. It's no good for them or you. It'll come back at you, I guarantee." He was angry, fuming, and trapped in that chair. He couldn't do anything. "Playing games, it's not worth it." He looked down at the space where his legs should be. "Not fucking worth it."

"What's on your tapes?"

"Lot's of things, kid. Things you wouldn't know a good goddamn about." He stroked at a stump of thigh.

"What? Like old footage from when you were younger?"

"No," he shook his head. "Digitally re-mastered movies. Sometimes I'm the good guy. Sometimes I'm the villain. Sometimes I get the girl." The anger dissipating, he crossed his arms, almost hugging himself. "Don't ever sign up for the army, kid. You gotta have rough skin to get through this life. You play it straight though, it'll go a lot better that way." One of Rudy's cats jumped onto his chair, cuddling into him. He pushed it off.

"What do you do?"

"Do you think I get up and act out scenes? Do you think I flail around on the floor, trying to? No! I sit in this goddamned chair and feel sorry for myself."

"Rudy—"

"Don't even. People don't want you to know about them. That's why they take the trouble to hide themselves. You know what? Don't come back. Stay the fuck away from me."

The next day I walked into the theatre with the green Schwinn. Yellow stood behind the counter. He was icy. "I thought you had something. I thought you were all right. Leave the bike and don't come back."

I looked at Kris, who was lying at my side, gazing up at the ceiling, listening. "I don't ever want to end up a shut-in and daydreaming about who I could be. I don't want to regret not acting when I should have. I get it. Choices, actions, consequences. I'm going to go to school, one class at a time, I guess. I want that, some sense of purpose or a better job, and this. *This is* what I want, whatever comes of it. You, us."

Still, I didn't go home right away, though I knew I had to at some point. I stalled. I stayed with Kris a couple more nights, and by default, with Susie and Ari. It was comfortable, playful, like being at summer camp.

At first.

I helped Kris with some remodeling projects, fumbling with paint and hammers and screws and drills, mostly fetching things for her, more an assistant than a worker. In the afternoons I played games with Ari. There was no limit to how many rounds of Chutes-N-Ladders she could roll through. And at night I played different games with Kris. When Susie and Kris went to work I sat on the couch and watched hours of TV, from *Santa Barbara* to *Phil Donahue* to that weird new show *The Seinfeld Chronicles*. I read *Beloved* and attempted *Geek Love*. I left the house sporadically to sneak into double features. Not doing the right thing, I saw *Do the Right Thing*. I wasted away. I sat on Susie and Kris' couch and watched my life drift by. Again.

I was blending into the fibers one night. Kris had decided to work a double and Susie came home. Having picked Ari up from the babysitter's house, Susie put her in bed, opened a wine cooler, and collapsed in the chair near the couch.

"Turn on Arsenio Hall. MC Hammer's on again," she said.

"Ew. Arsenio has the longest fingers in the world and he's not funny."

"You think Pat Sajak's funny?"

"He's dorky funny."

"Seriously. Change the channel."

"Seriously, that guy is not funny. And MC Hammer's a tool."

"I don't care."

It had been tense around the house, particularly between Susie and me since I'd finished almost all of Ari's Fruity Pebbles and the last of Susie's favorite lotion, since I'd been yelled at by her twice to get out of the bathroom because she needed in, since I was there, always there, in her space.

"Seriously?" Susie said.

"What?"

"You're really going to sit on my couch, watch whatever the hell you want, eat my daughter's food, use my things, and fuck your brains out four nights a week?"

"I'm sure it's more than four."

"You bratty little cunt. You cannot stay here any longer." She got up from the chair and ripped the remote from my hand and changed the channel to Arsenio's long, long fingers.

"I don't think that's up to you."

"The hell it isn't. Kris and I have known each other for years. We've been through a lot. If you seriously think she'd jeopardize our friendship, you have no idea who she is. I've been biting my tongue for days now, days, but I can't anymore. This is too fucking much, seriously. You are too much. You have to go."

"Can you use 'seriously' one more time?"

"Get the fuck out."

I did. I had to stop waffling, sliding between contemplation and preparation, and take action. I needed that extra nudge to get me moving, to get me home.

30

Mom pounded tenderizer into a few small slabs of meat. She stopped for a second to turn the broiler on. "How do you know this is what you want?"

"I suppose the same way you knew Dad was right for you."

She wanted an explanation, in detail. But I didn't have one ready for her. I didn't feel the need to make sense of it, to make profound announcements. When thinking about my relationship with Kris, trying to explain it, I kept comparing it to relationships with men. I couldn't help that. It was what I knew, what I was taught, what I saw around me. Focusing on Kris and only Kris, what I liked was that she knew her body and took care of it, and she knew my body, and when she didn't know, she asked.

Mom was easier to talk to than Dad, though just as disbelieving. She put the meat under the broiler and set napkins and forks on the table. Almost as an afterthought, she grabbed a candle from the pantry. "I'm sure I'll like her, but that doesn't mean I like the idea of you two together."

The front door slammed and I heard Dad's heavy steps in the hallway. "Damn muffler finally fell off today," he said, coming into the kitchen. "What are you doing here?"

"Tell her you were worried and that it's good to see her."

"Yeah, that too," he said. "Now what are you doing here?"

"I'm back," I said. "I have a plan."

He grunted.

"I'm not going anywhere. Kris isn't either."

"I'd like us all to have dinner so you can see she's nice and not corrupting me."

"She's too old for you."

"Age is irrelevant in matters of the heart."

"You pull that load of bull off a bumper sticker?"

Michelle froze when she saw our parents and me in the kitchen. Her lip wrinkled and she slipped into a seat. "You pregnant?"

"Worse. I'm dating a woman."

"An old woman," Dad said.

"A woman? Does this mean you'll be listening to Ferron all the time?"

The doorbell rang. "Hello?" Derrick.

"And how old are you?" Dad scanned Derrick's eyes and face, then studied his muscled physique appreciatively.

"Old, sir." Derrick handed over a six-pack of Miller Lite. Michelle must have clued him in to Dad's go-to beer. They shook hands and the slightest wince jabbed Dad's cheek as he dropped his right shoulder into the shake.

"Call her," Mom said. She collected the everyday plates from the table and set out the good porcelain. I sunk inside a little. The group dinner came much sooner than I'd planned.

We sat around the kitchen table prettified with a new tablecloth and the good China. It was a special occasion, after all. The Bauers had guests.

"You work at the factory, Kris?" Mom asked.

"Yes. I'm a shift manager."

"That's not all she does. She also remodels people's homes."

Dad got up and stood staring into the refrigerator.

Michelle watched each of us with keen interest, her head swiveling back and forth.

"Did you grow up here?"

"Not too far away. My parents have a farm in Michigan."

"A farm. That's nice. Oh, but how has all the heat treated them?"

"Not good. It's their worst year in decades."

"The meal's great, Mrs. Bauer," Derrick said. "Just the right portions of carbs and proteins and fats. Thanks. Hey, Mr. B., I heard you like jokes. Where does carbon-60 go to dance?" Derrick paused, waiting for one of us to answer. "A Buckyball."

"I like jokes I get," Dad said. He came to the table with a beer in hand. "How long you been skipping work?"

"Henry, it can wait."

"No, no. I don't think it can. It's time to cut the crap. Kris, it's nice to meet you and all, but we have some things to hash out. Sorry you have to be here for this." He dropped down into a chair, clunking his beer on the Formica table. He jerked his laces untied and kicked off his boots. Then he rolled his socks off and scratched the bottoms of his feet on the rung of the chair.

Kris smiled weakly.

"Actually, I'm not sorry. Not at all," he said. "It's good you're here. You'll get to see sides you haven't seen."

I doubted that. She'd seen more sides of me and done more to me than he could possibly know.

"How long, Lee?"

"Almost two weeks," I said.

"Christ." He leaned back into his chair. "Why?"

"I quit."

His eyebrows joined his hairline. "You quit?"

"That wasn't our agreement," Mom said, trying to be stern.

"Why the hell would you do that?" he said over her. "You were in good, right?" He looked at Kris. "She was in good, right? They liked you. Job wasn't too demanding. Pay was fine. You could have moved up. She could have moved up, right?"

Kris, my unbelievable Judas, nodded.

"I was packing ice cream bars."

Kris sat back in her chair. "Do you mind if I get one of those beers?"

"I'm sorry, honey. Yes, help yourself."

"Get me one," said Michelle.

Kris handed a beer to Derrick, who was uncharacteristically quiet.

"Your mother pours coffee and I carry mail. You don't hear us complaining."

"I didn't mean it like that."

"You're a Bauer. Like my dad and brothers. Working class. You had your chance at school and blew it."

Michelle sat quietly, watchfully, eating her meal, taking notes about things to avoid.

"You lied to us."

"I just didn't tell you," I said, unhelpfully. Sins are sins, whether of omission or commission. Attempting to thwart further disappointment, I omitted something else. "The janitor told me how to push a broom. I couldn't take it anymore."

"Huh," Dad half-laughed. "What are you going to do? What the hell are you going to do? You only get so many chances. This is *your* life. Do you realize that? You can't keep this up. You can't keep going at things half-assed. Doesn't work that way. If some guy wants to tell you how to push a broom, you let him. At the end of the day, a paycheck is a paycheck."

"At the end of the day, I still need my sanity."

"If you're not gonna go all out, then check your mind at the door, kid. That's the only way to survive."

"Seriously?" Michelle said. "You can't mean that."

"For you, no. For her, yes."

We all six of us sat in awkward, awkward silence. The only sounds were of mashing food and swallowing.

"And I don't like this funny business with you staying out all night." He wasn't finished after all. "It's not right."

Mom said, "You can't keep lying to us. We always find out."

"They do." Michelle nodded her head. "It's true. You can't escape." She smiled, making trouble.

Dad shot her a hard look. He yanked his beer from the table, spilling it slightly. He was tight-lipped, about to sip when he said, "It's your life, Lee, but it's my house."

"Our house," Mom corrected.

Dad sawed away, scraping his knife through the meat and against the plate. He was not looking at anyone as he shoveled forkfuls of food into his mouth.

"It's okay, Mom. Look, Dad, I know I've screwed up."

"That's putting it mildly."

"Would you just listen to me? You spend all your time barking orders at me—'Do it this way, study hard at school, get in good at work'—it's no wonder I resisted. I can't suck it up and push the broom how everyone else wants. I'm done fighting you and mom. I'm not playing those games anymore. I'm going to school."

He nearly spit the food back on the plate. "We've been down that road."

"It's real this time."

A stiff silence blanketed him. I watched him eat.

We all six of us sat in silence, awkward, awkward silence, once more. I looked at Kris, who was concentrating on her plate. Her shoulders were at her ears. She was braced for anything. Derrick chewed the steak and sipped at his beer.

Since no one was talking, I asked Michelle, "Who's Ferron, anyway?"

"Sings that dykey song Harmless Love. No offense."

Kris stared at her quizzically.

"She's Canadian," Derrick said. "Did you know that? And influenced by Dusty Springfield?"

"Since when are you the trivia master?"

"Since always."

"What are you studying Derrick? You're in school, right?"

"Biochemistry."

"Where's that lead?"

"Lab research. Healthcare. Pharmaceuticals. It's a wide-open field once you have a higher degree and some good experience."

Dad nodded approval.

"Exactly *how* old are you Derrick?" I asked. "Ohio's age of consent is sixteen. Michelle's on a precarious cusp. *You're* on a precarious cusp."

"C'mon, Lee. I've always been on your side."

He had, and I was sorry I'd said it because Dad now looked at him with newfound suspicion.

"Seriously, Michelle and I are just friends," Derrick said.

"Do you know who Kandinsky is?" I asked, quickly trying to change the subject.

"The Unabomber," Michelle replied, pushing the steak around on her plate. "I want to let you know, Mom, you don't have to fix me any more meat. I'm a vegetarian now."

"I'll eat it," Derrick said, just as Dad knifed her steak and flopped it onto his plate.

"No, not the unabomber," I said. "Kandinsky, an artist. A Russian painter."

"Some would call the Unabomber an artist," Michelle said. "He was all about human freedom, after all."

"Didn't his brother turn him in?" I asked.

"What are you trying to say?"

"I know where you keep your diary."

"It's not a diary."

"I know where you keep it. Anyway, I'm being serious here."

"Wassily K. Yes, I know about him. What do you care? You never care about this stuff."

"Humor me."

"Whatever. He lived in the early half of the 1900s. He was set to be a lawyer, then found art. He lived in Germany before the war then moved to Paris. He was an Abstract Expressionist, but that simplifies his work and it's not really accurate." She sounded like a textbook. "Abstract Expressionism has do with emotional intensity and the feeling of spontaneity in a work but there was usually lots of careful planning that went into it. It's supposed to be characterized by rebelliousness and anti-figurative works."

There was a lot I didn't know. It overwhelmed me if I let it.

"How do you know so much? Never mind. Don't answer that." I knew the answer. Michelle read. She paid attention in school. She researched things outside of school. She had conversations with other smart people about smart things. All the things I didn't do, but needed to start doing.

"He was about revealing the essence of objects. And revealing the inner life—emotions, states of being."

Sounds of metal on china and saliva coating food hurt my ears.

"I want to keep living here," I said. "The women's shelter is pretty nasty from what I hear, and I don't think a box under the Maumee Bridge suits me. Just until I get enough money for a deposit on an apartment."

"Where the hell are you going to get that?"

"Let me worry about that. You worry about getting the muffler repaired and taking days off work so you don't lose your vacation time or your mind."

"Where *have* you been staying the last three nights?" Michelle asked.

"With Kris."

"Shacking up not going so well? Trouble in gay paradise already?" Michelle smirked.

"She lives with her friend Susie and Susie's daughter. It's a little crowded. Besides, Susie and I don't get along."

"Her friend?" Mom asked.

"Yes, mom. Friend. Literally."

"It's way too soon to be living with a boyfriend, or girlfriend, anyway. I mean, really, you two just met."

Kris nodded assent.

Mom looked at her family. Sadness streaked across her face. She knew she couldn't do anything to pull us closer.

Dad pointed his fork back and forth at Michelle and Derrick. "Don't think I'm going to let this funny business between you two slide."

"Sir, I've got the best intentions here."

"I give two shits about intentions. Action is what counts." He finished off his beer. "How much do you press, anyway?"

"Two-thirty."

"Christ." He got up and cracked another beer. "You've had many chances with us," he said to me. "Why should this one be any different?"

"It is different. I signed up for an art class and a required writing one for the fall term."

"How are you paying for that?"

"With a loan."

"You're such a cliché," Michelle said. "Right out of any book. You have a little existential crisis and take an obvious escape. Art. Love. Take your pick. Boring. Art mimics life which mimics art which takes us around in circles."

"What are you talking about now?" Dad asked. "Last week it was something about pleasure being the root of evil."

"No, pleasure being the root of all critical appraisal, even sports commentary. Find the pleasure first then all else follows," Michelle said, finishing the sentiment.

"Sounds like something you would say," I said to Derrick.

Michelle blushed, caught taking credit for quoting someone else.

"You know what those books never show," Mom said, "is the ever-after. The crisis never goes away. We just find things to cushion the way."

I thought about telling them about Hailey's photograph and how it awakened something in me. Something vague, yes, but unsettling just enough for me to do something. I thought better of such revelation. Derrick would tell me 'right on' and slap me on the back, Michelle would laugh, and my parents, well, they would stare as usual at their alien daughter.

31

It's long after Labor Day and into the new year. I didn't get the end-of-season bonus, but I made it through. I got out. Of myself. Of the factory. Into something else. I'm not sure it will last with Kris, her being nine years older and pretty fond of Susie and her daughter. But it's been eight months now and it's all right, more than all right. We're not going to marry or have a ceremony or go on a talk show. Neither of us is much into pomp and formality. She told me never, ever to buy her flowers, though I probably will and she'll smile her shy, pleased smile and put them in water. We're still in a blissful stage where everything is birdsong, where elation propels you into and past anything, and it has. Something will give eventually. Always does. Crisis, as Mom says, never disappears completely, but I'm content to wait awhile before I hear the snap, before any new mess comes around. Though maybe I was raised just well enough to trust myself and to know that any real or perceived threat, internal or external, in the end will turn into a lesson or transform into a story to tell to a stranger.

I'm about finished with this assignment, sitting here in this too small room I share with my sister, making final changes to the story before turning it in. I contend it's still a strange form, memoir at twenty. If your life's that interesting, won't someone else write it for you? I understand, though. You have to know your story before you can enter anyone else's. I finished two night classes last quarter, which I actually attended and liked. Most days anyway. Now I've got this Narrative Psych class, Adolescent Psychology, and two others and mounting loan debt already. I'm wondering about school and Hailey and Courtney, all of the others who've marked me, and if this is to be my life or if some other novelty will come along and knock me around. I'm wondering, hoping, I think, that I'll latch on to something decent and helpful to others and that my life won't be a waste. This isn't a story where love comes swooping into the struggling protagonist's life and everything, suddenly, is glorious and happy ever after. Love arrived, yes, but the rest remains ahead and unknown, and I have things to do. Lots of other things.